## "I was just thinking about a woman who came by the office."

David's father smiled at him and said, "What did she want?"

David wondered whether he should say. Maybe a discussion was what he needed to put everything in order.

"She wanted me to find some guy she had a one-night stand with. Seems she's carrying his kid."

"Not exactly an everyday request," Charles said, "but I don't see the problem."

"She made me drag every detail out of her like I was a prosecuting attorney. Even when I explained that she had to be totally honest, she held back crucial information."

"What was that?"

"She was wearing a wedding band, yet she said nothing about being married. And I gave her plenty of opportunity to spit it out."

Charles shrugged. "So she was embarrassed or ashamed or both. I'm not saying that dealing with a cheating spouse is pleasant, just part of the job. And there's nothing that says we have to like a client."

"But this one didn't look like someone who should be lying."

Charles let out a long sigh of understanding. "Ah, so that's the problem. You *do* like her."

Dear Reader,

I love to read about heroines and heroes.

In this world of cranky kids and kitty litter, unbalanced
checkbooks and bad-tempered bosses, sagging skin and
stretch marks, it's great to be able to open a Harlequin
Superromance novel and find a gal who handles life's petty
concerns with such panache that she inspires you to think
your best thoughts, do your noblest deeds and be your
finest self.

That's what I call a heroine.

The guys who win the hearts of these gals have to be
special—and they are. Tough, tender and downright
tempting, they can melt the polish right off your toenails.
I'd like to introduce you to four such men. The Knight
brothers are a talented team of investigators whose
modern-day armor consists of quick minds, steel bodies
and strong integrity. Their motto is When You Need Help,
Call On A White Knight. These men are ready to put
themselves on the line for what's right and for the women
they love.

That's what I call a hero.

David Knight's story is the first in the WHITE KNIGHT
INVESTIGATIONS series. David has earned his share of
battle scars and is convinced he's prepared for anything—
until he meets Susan, the lovely nature photographer who
desperately needs his help in finding the father of her
unborn child.

I hope you enjoy David and Susan's tale. And may love
always find the heroine in your heart.

Warmest wishes,

M.J. Rodgers

# Baby by Chance

## M.J. Rodgers

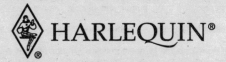

## HARLEQUIN®

TORONTO • NEW YORK • LONDON
AMSTERDAM • PARIS • SYDNEY • HAMBURG
STOCKHOLM • ATHENS • TOKYO • MILAN • MADRID
PRAGUE • WARSAW • BUDAPEST • AUCKLAND

ISBN 0-373-71116-6

BABY BY CHANCE

Visit us at www.eHarlequin.com

**Printed in U.S.A.**

# Baby by Chance

# CHAPTER ONE

SUSAN HAD A HARD TIME believing it had come to this. If someone had told her a week ago that she would be seriously considering hiring a private investigator, she would have laughed.

People came to her for help. She was the sensible, self-reliant one who always handled whatever problem came her way. At least, she had been.

She drove past the White Knight Investigations' offices every day on her way to work. When You Need Help, Call On A White Knight, the sign said. The promise implicit in that motto never failed to conjure up the romantic image of a tall, stalwart warrior in silver armor charging on his sturdy steed to help some hapless heroine.

A nice fantasy. But the key word here was *fantasy*.

Even if the King Arthur legends could be believed and men with high ideals had rescued damsels in distress in the sixth century, she knew perfectly well that damsels unlucky or foolish enough to get themselves into distressful situations in the twenty-first century had better be ready to rescue themselves.

Yet knowing all that didn't stop her from slowing as she approached the White Knight offices this morning. She wanted to believe, because she was in a mess. And she gladly would have traded all the idealistic heroes in history on white horses for the help of one fat, balding modern-day cynic driving a VW Bug—as long as he was a competent and intelligent investigator.

Their number was on the sign. Maybe she'd call for an appointment. Then again, maybe not. She'd gotten herself into a situation that was as embarrassing as hell for herself to accept, much less explain to someone else.

An unexpected light in the office window had Susan turning the steering wheel of her SUV. The offices were always dark at this hour. That light beamed down on her like a special invitation, a message that someone waited for her up there, someone who would listen and would be willing to help.

She maneuvered her vehicle into the parking lot and switched off the engine. She sat behind the wheel for a moment as the drizzle smeared her windshield, uncomfortably aware that levelheaded women didn't lead their lives by attributing the guiding hand of fate to an unexpected office light. Still, as long as she was here, it probably wouldn't hurt to go up.

The front door to the office-building complex was open, a bakery shop on the first floor already filling the foyer with the warm aromas of yeast and rising dough. Normally such smells would have been welcome. But today she couldn't get away from them quickly enough. She dashed for the elevator and punched the button for the top floor where the White Knight offices were located.

The elevator made its journey with an efficient *swoosh* of gears. When the doors opened, she stepped out on a lovely curved landing. A floor-to-ceiling picture window overlooked the small city of Silver Valley, jewel-like in the early morning light.

As tempted as she was to linger over the dazzling scene, she knew that if she didn't continue with this sudden impulse, her common sense was going to kick in and have her retreating back to her vehicle.

The light she had seen from the street was spilling out from the reception area of the White Knight offices. Her footsteps made no sound on the thick carpet as she made her way toward it.

She halted in the shadows just outside the open door and peered inside. Her eyes swept over the oak desk, the thick gold carpet, the tasteful assortment of art hanging on the pastel walls, the impressive expanse of windows.

But it was the man facing those windows who claimed her real attention.

He was at least six-three, with shoulders and arms like a logger's. His full bark-brown hair was cleanly cut at the nape of his neck. A dark green sweater stretched over his muscled back. Tailored black slacks hugged his long legs. One of his huge hands hung casually by his side. The other was holding something in front of him that she couldn't see.

The solid strength of his body and the calm, innate confidence in his stance put Susan immediately in mind of the sturdy cedar that had stood outside her bedroom window when she was a child. That cedar had borne the weight of her treehouse, weathered the worst of winter's storms and soaked up the tears shed by her young self.

Her heart filled with sudden hope. Maybe, just maybe, the impulse that had brought her here wouldn't prove to be so crazy, after all.

DAVID SAVORED HIS COFFEE as he watched the traffic beneath his window. Mornings were always his favorite part of the day; he enjoyed watching the world wake up and get busy, especially in this part of the world.

Western Washington wouldn't push open its coffin lid of clouds to let in any real sun until summer. He didn't mind enduring the months of overcast skies ahead. The rain was a familiar companion, and he had learned that there was comfort in the familiar. A man could handle anything when he knew what to expect.

A long, difficult case now hinged on an interview he would conduct with his client's runaway daughter in a few hours. Getting the girl's trust was key. He was counting on what he had to show her to help him. But his approach also had to be right. He had come in early so as to plan what he would say to her.

He checked his watch. Barely eight. He had another full hour before the office officially opened and anyone else arrived. Plenty of time to—

"Excuse me."

David spun around so sharply at the sound of the unexpected voice behind him that coffee splashed out of his cup. He found himself suddenly face-to-face with large, luminous eyes the color of summer clover.

She stood in the doorway, a slim silhouette in a dark business suit with matching, low-heeled pumps. Across her forehead was a curve of shiny, golden-brown bangs. The rest of her hair fell in one long, thick braid to the gentle swell of her right breast. Her cosmetic-free face reflected the pink, creamy glow of youth. She didn't look a day over twenty-one.

"I'm sorry I startled you," she said.

Her surprisingly deep and resonant voice vibrated through David like the melody of a forgotten song.

She took a tentative step into the room. "If you have some paper towels, I can try to soak up that stain on the carpet."

"No," he said in a tone that was far too abrupt and gruff and had nothing whatsoever to do with her offer to help and everything to do with the unwelcome surprise of her. His thoughts must have shown on his face, because her open, expectant expression quickly faded.

"I've obviously come at a bad time," she said, and turned to leave.

"No," he heard himself barking again in that same uncivil tone. He took a deep breath. This was foolish. He was a professional. She was a client.

"Come in," he said, carefully modulating both his manner and tone. "The clerk will see to the carpet when he arrives. I'm David Knight."

He set his coffee cup on the desk and walked over to extend his hand. He was determined that this woman would see him as he really was—a cool, cordial investigator, in control of himself.

She did not immediately take his hand but instead studied his face. There was a question in her eyes. But whatever she wanted to know, she seemed hesitant to ask. When she finally stepped forward and slipped her hand into his, he was taken aback by the warmth and strength of her clasp.

"I'm Susan Carter."

Her name didn't ring a bell. Not that all of the firm's clients were known to him. But he was surprised that no one had mentioned her over the dinner table the night before. His brothers seldom passed up an opportunity to talk about an attractive woman.

Could she be a special client taken on by his mom or dad?

"Is something wrong, Mr. Knight?"

David realized that while silently asking himself these questions, he'd been unconsciously gripping her hand. He released his hold and retraced his steps to the desk, where he grabbed the telephone.

Didn't matter whose client she was. What mattered was that he arrange for her to be taken care of so he could get on with what he had to do.

"Who's handling your case, Ms. Carter? I'll call and let them know you're here."

"There's no one to call. This is my first visit."

He dropped the telephone receiver onto the base. So,

she had walked in off the street. Did she really think that private investigators had nothing to do but sit in their offices waiting for prospective clients?

"We're not officially open for business until nine," he said, maintaining an amicable tone.

"Could someone see me then?"

She'd missed the important point of his message. He tried again. "The clerk will be available to check the schedule when he arrives. But I doubt there'll be an opening this week."

Her disappointed response came out in a rush. "Of course. You're as busy as everyone else. I saw your light while I was driving by and thought—"

Her deep voice ceased abruptly. She had no intention of sharing what she'd thought. He had the sudden conviction that she rarely did. She swallowed hard, squeezing the strap of her shoulder bag in what appeared to be an involuntary movement. "Stupid mistake on my part."

Her self-effacing tone told him she did not like making mistakes. The firm set to her mouth also said that she was harder on herself than anyone else could be.

"Please, forgive the interruption." She looked him straight in the eye when she said those words. Hers was a sincere apology, not a polite one.

He saw then what he had missed earlier. There were dark circles beneath her eyes. She was in trouble. She had clearly acted on impulse coming here. If he insisted she make an appointment, she'd probably talk herself out of keeping it. She was turning to go.

"I have a few moments, if you want to tell me how we can help," David heard someone say in a familiar voice that he tardily recognized as his own.

She halted in mid-stride and turned back. "You'll see me now?" Her question sounded full of surprise and hope.

In answer, he started toward the door adjacent to the

reception room, wondering all the while what the hell he was doing.

"My office is through here. What do you take in your coffee, Ms. Carter?"

SUSAN CRADLED THE WARM cup in her cold hands. She could smell the freshly ground beans, the rich cream, the sweetness of the sugar.

David had prepared her coffee just as she had asked, but she had yet to take a sip. As she tried to get comfortable on the guest chair in his office, she willed her jumpy stomach to settle.

At his request, she'd filled out a card with her address and telephone number. He held that card now as he sat across from her, an immaculate, black marble desk between them. He wore a polite expression of openness and patience. And the way he leaned back in his black leather chair, the thick steam rising from his refilled cup, spoke of a man at ease.

But every nerve in Susan's body told her he was not.

She found his face more rugged than handsome—bold forehead, bold cheekbones, bold chin. His skin had been weathered by time spent in outdoor pursuits. From the lines across his forehead and around his mouth, she estimated him to be somewhere in his middle thirties.

But his eyes—as chilly a gray as the overcast spring day—his eyes were older, wiser and wary. Every time she looked into them, she had the oddest sensation that it was she who made him most wary.

She could have convinced herself that she was imagining things if she hadn't seen the unguarded expression on his face when he'd spilled his coffee. David Knight hadn't just been surprised to see her. He'd been disturbed in some personal way.

Susan normally wasn't reticent about asking questions,

but there was a quality to this man that didn't invite probing. Even his office was intimidating—heavy, dark furniture, ponderous drapes, a carpet the color of granite, and not a personal photograph anywhere. In a corner display case, a massive Ironman trophy stood solemnly erect on a sturdy glass shelf.

A man who had won one of those grueling competitions was the kind who went all out and pulled no punches.

"Perhaps you'd like to start by telling me about yourself," he said. Even now, beneath his artfully projected calm and courtesy, she sensed the controlled tension in the man.

"Your business suit implies that you are employed outside the home," he said.

"I'm a nature photographer," she replied, relieved to start on a less sensitive subject.

"Freelance?"

"I'm on staff at *True Nature* magazine."

One of his thick eyebrows raised ever so slightly. "That's a top-notch publication."

His surprise that she worked for such a prestigious magazine did not sit well with Susan. "Thank you. I think so, too," she said with a politeness that she frequently used to insulate sparks of irritation.

"How long have you been with them?"

"Nine years."

"That long? I wouldn't have guessed you had that much experience. May I ask how old you are?"

She deliberately straightened in her chair before answering, the better to emphasize every inch of her five-foot five-inch frame. "I'm thirty-two. As of the eighth of last month."

"You say that as though daring me to disagree."

"I realize that most women would be happy to be taken

for younger than they are, Mr. Knight. I am not like most women.''

''What are you like?''

His tone carried no inflection, but she felt the subtle, unspoken challenge that lay beneath his words. She could not have explained how he'd conveyed that challenge, but it was as real to her as her own breath.

''I was graduated at the top of my class with a Bachelor of Fine Arts in Photography and a B.S. in Wildlife Science,'' she said. Try as she might to remain unemotional, she still heard the defensiveness in her voice. ''I started out as a copy and caption editor. Each time an opening for photographer came up, I applied. But each time I was turned down while others with less education and experience got the jobs.''

''And why do you think that was?''

She set her untouched coffee down on the table beside her chair. ''I don't *think,* Mr. Knight, I know. People attribute less competence to a person who looks deceptively young, despite their actual chronological age and abilities. I have had to fight to be taken seriously.''

''So you went to a voice trainer.''

She was silent for a moment, able to do no more than blink. ''And just how did you know that?''

''Few women under fifty have a voice as deep as yours.''

He was so calm and reasonable that she was immediately annoyed with herself for having become defensive, and just a mite suspicious that he had pinpointed her sensitive spot and deliberately irritated her so he could see how she'd respond.

''If your youthful looks bother you so much, why don't you use makeup?''

''I have very uncooperative skin. Makeup just sits on my face like curdled milk. Since the alternative is to look like I'm past my expiration date, I'm stuck with what nature provided.''

''I doubt *stuck* is the word most people would use,'' he said.

She didn't know whether he was trying to be polite or trying to minimize her concern over her youthful appearance. She suspected the latter. Not surprising. What could a man who looked as formidable as this one know about the difficulties of looking too fragile?

He took a sip of his coffee as he regarded her once again. ''So, you finally became a photographer after you completed the voice lessons and got a new boss.''

''Four years ago,'' she said, feeling once again oddly off balance by his assessment. ''Just how much of that was a guess?''

''I'm not in the habit of guessing, Ms. Carter. First impressions are hard to reverse.''

''Meaning?''

''Even with your new voice, an old boss could still not get past your youthful appearance. It would take a new boss to really *see* the new you.''

''You appear to have an understanding of human nature.''

He set down his cup and leaned forward in his chair. ''I understand that whatever is bothering you is of recent origin and is keeping you from sleeping at night. You would prefer to keep the matter to yourself. You are a very private person, despite the facade of openness you project. You pride yourself on handling things. Coming here to ask for help is out of character for you. You still wish there was some way you could have avoided doing so.''

She stared at him as the dead-on accuracy of everything he'd said sent the nerves of her back quivering. She wasn't used to someone being able to read her so well.

He casually settled back in his chair. "Don't let my skills upset you. They're the reason you've come to me."

"I'm not upset," she said, and she wasn't. But she was uneasy.

"The point is, we're both observers," he said. "Your expertise is tuned to the sounds and sights of wildlife. Mine is human behavior. Were we out in the wilds, you could probably tell me all about the feeding, mating and migrating rituals of a bird in a tree merely by hearing its call or noting the shape of its wing. Isn't that true?"

"For most species," she admitted.

"And I would be duly impressed since I have no such skills. We are both professionals with special talents. Now, tell me how my talents can be put to use in helping you."

He was right. Instead of being uncomfortable, she should be rejoicing that she had found someone possessing the skills that he had so competently displayed. He had not only eased her into talking, but had also maneuvered her into revealing things about herself and surmised the rest with impressive insight. The time had come for her to put her problem in his hands.

"I need you to find a man."

David retrieved a pad of paper and a pen from his desk drawer. "His name?"

"Todd."

"Last name?"

"I don't know."

"Address?"

"I don't know."

He looked up. "What *do* you know about Todd?"

"He's several inches taller than me, about five-ten would be my guess. Light hair, eyes. Slender. Maybe thirty."

David jotted down a few notes before continuing.

"Why do you want me to find him?"

"I want to learn everything I can about him. We met in a seminar at the local community center six weeks ago as of last Friday, and we didn't have much time to get acquainted."

"What kind of seminar?"

She paused before answering. "Self-improvement."

"What were you trying to improve?"

"Is that really important?"

"I have no preconceived idea of who you are or what you should be, Ms. Carter. I'll be in and out of your life in as brief a time as possible. This is to your advantage. With me, you don't have to pretend."

"I'm not pretending anything. I just don't think that my reason for going to the seminar has any bearing on why I've come to you. Look, this is simple. I should have gotten Todd's address and telephone number before we parted. I didn't."

"You haven't seen Todd again since the night of the seminar?"

"No."

"What did you and Todd do together that night?"

"We…talked."

"And after you talked?"

"He walked me to my vehicle."

David let a moment pass, silently watched her. She knew he was waiting for her to continue. She didn't.

"A woman doesn't hire a private investigator to find someone who merely spoke with her and walked her to her vehicle," he said finally. "Tell me everything that happened."

She considered his words. Of course he was right. A woman wouldn't just want to find a man after such a brief interaction. She was going to have to tell him. Although there was something in this man's quiet self-confidence that made her suspect he already knew what she was going to say.

"We slept together," she said.

His calm expression didn't change. She was certain now that he'd already known, maybe from the moment she'd mentioned Todd.

"Todd didn't offer you his last name."

"No."

"Did you offer him yours?"

"No."

"Do you think that Todd might be trying to find you?"

"No."

"Does that…distress you?"

"No."

"And you haven't tried to find Todd in the intervening six weeks since you met?"

"Last Friday I went back to the community center and asked if they had a list of attendees from the seminar six weeks before. They told me the seminar was open to the public and did not require advanced enrollment, so they had no such list."

"Did that answer seem reasonable to you?"

"Yes. I just walked in myself."

He regarded her quietly before asking his next question. "Why do you want me to find Todd for you?"

"Like I said, I want to know more about him."

"Like what?"

"Anything and everything you can learn."

"And why is that?"

His questions were focused, like he was following a road map with a definite destination in mind. She had no idea what that destination was and that made her even more nervous.

"I just want to know about him," she said. "Isn't it

natural to want to know about someone you've been intimate with?''

"Ms. Carter, I'm going to need a more direct answer."

She forced herself to meet his eyes. A woman had to make her presence felt in order to be taken seriously. She had learned that maintaining eye contact was an important defense against being summarily dismissed.

"I don't understand what you want me to say."

"I want you to say the truth—the whole truth. What exactly do you intend to do with the information that I give to you about Todd?"

"Try to use it to understand what kind of man he is."

"You'll forgive me for saying so, but isn't that something a woman normally does *before* she sleeps with a man?"

She'd been feeling anything but chipper since the beginning of this conversation. But that last comment made her stomach churn.

"No, Mr. Knight, I won't forgive you for saying that. I'm not asking for your approval of my actions. I'm asking for your help in finding out about Todd."

Where there had been only an open expression on David's face before, suddenly there was a sharp, focused intensity. "And if you like what I find out about Todd, are you going to tell him you're pregnant with his child?"

She swallowed hard. "That's a pretty wild assumption."

"On the contrary," David said calmly as he leaned back. "It's the only logical conclusion. You slept with a stranger whose last name you never asked. You haven't made an attempt to locate him in the intervening six weeks. Now, all of a sudden, you're willing to hire a private investigator to find out about him. If you'd discovered he'd given you a sexually transmitted disease, you'd want *him* found so he could be notified. But you only want to find out about him. You're pregnant. And you believe Todd is the father.''

She sucked in a shaky breath, fighting desperately to quell a rising sense of panic and burgeoning nausea. This private investigator was good, all right—too damn good.

''You'd best understand the ground rules,'' he said. ''I have a license to consider and, just as importantly, a conscience to answer to. I cannot take on a case without complete honesty from a client.''

''I haven't lied to you.''

''Omissions are substantially the same thing. You weren't planning to tell me about the pregnancy. Do you plan to tell Todd?''

''I don't know.''

''So, it will depend on what I find out about him?''

''I have a lot of decisions to make. Before I make any about him, I have to have more information.''

''When did you discover you were pregnant?''

''Last Friday.''

''You had no suspicion before that?''

''I thought I had the flu.''

''No missed period?''

''I've always been irregular.''

''Why do you think Todd is the father?''

''He's the only one who could be.''

''Ms. Carter, if there are any other pertinent facts regarding this case that you're keeping from me, I need to know them now. Am I being clear?''

''Yes.''

''Is there anything you want to tell me?''

''I have nothing to add.''

''Who else could be the father?''

''No one.''

''Who else knows you're pregnant?''

''Just the doctor.''

"You've told no one else?"

"That's correct."

"Is there anyone else who has a right to know?"

"A *right* to know?" she repeated, wondering at the oddness of that question. "With the possible exception of Todd—and I haven't decided one way or another about him—no one has a *right* to know."

David's silent scrutiny did nothing but add to the queasiness in her stomach.

"I'm sorry, Ms. Carter. I won't be able to take your case."

"Excuse me?"

He rose. "You will not be charged for this morning's consultation."

Despite the deceptiveness of his calm expression and tone, there was an undercurrent of disturbance displayed in his blunt movements. Before she could take another breath, he had marched to his office door and swung it open.

He stood expectantly beside it. "Have a pleasant day."

She felt her face go white with shock. She'd just revealed the most intimate details of her life to this stranger and—what was just as hard—had asked for his help. And he was throwing her out.

Her icy hands gripped the arms of the chair as she rose shakily to her feet. Somehow she got to the door. She didn't look at him as she slid past. The rush of air as the door closed swiftly behind her was like a blow.

She shut her eyes tightly and fought desperately against the churning, sickening waves. It was no use. She started to run. She barely made it to the bathroom down the hall before she vomited.

As she lay with her cheek pressed against the cold tile floor, she didn't know what was worse—the morning sickness or the moment of temporary insanity that had led her to the White Knight Investigations' offices.

But something she did know for certain now. She had gotten herself into this mess, and she was going to have to get herself out of it. There were no white knights on sturdy steeds coming to her rescue.

She had only herself to rely on. And just as she had throughout her life, she would have to find the strength to face whatever came and do whatever had to be done. Alone.

## CHAPTER TWO

"OUR CLIENT IS VERY pleased, David," Charles Knight told his son as he waved a check. "Getting a runaway to voluntarily return to her parents isn't something we see often. How'd you pull it off?"

Charles sat on the edge of his son's desk. He was David's height and still powerfully built at sixty-four, with the finely chiseled features of the men who swung tennis rackets and rode polo ponies in slick magazine ads.

"Her boyfriend convinced our runaway to bail on her family," David told his dad. "She imagined herself in love and was ready to give up anything for the guy, until I showed her some live-action video of the slimeball getting it on with another girl."

"Where did that video come from?"

"The guy taped it himself. He gets his kicks filming his conquests of underage girls."

Charles shook his head. "What are you going to do about him?"

"He's twenty-one. Jared has all the evidence he needs to make an arrest. I just wanted to be sure our client's daughter was home safe and out of the fray before the law got involved."

"Smart of you to bring your brother in on this, David. As always, you have thoroughly thought out every aspect of this case. So, why are you frowning?"

David took the file in front of him and shoved it into his open desk drawer. "Didn't realize I was."

"Something on your mind?"

David closed the drawer and looked up at his dad. Those steel-blue eyes had him in their sights. Charles might have the look of a country club man, but David knew his dad had the keen instincts and cunning of a cougar.

"I was just thinking about this woman who came by yesterday morning before the offices were open."

"You caught a cat burglar?" Charles asked with a smile.

"Probably would have been better if she'd turned out to be one."

The teasing smile faded from Charles's lips as he studied his son's solemn face. "So, what's this woman's name?"

"It's not important."

"Something about her is. You going to tell me?"

David wondered whether he should. Maybe a discussion was what he needed to help put all the churning images and emotions into a semblance of order.

"She wanted me to find some guy she had a one-night stand with. Seems she's carrying his kid."

"Not exactly an everyday request," Charles said, "but I don't see the problem."

"She made me drag every detail out of her like I was some prosecuting attorney grilling a hostile witness. Even when I explained that she had to open up and be totally honest if I was going to help her, she still held back crucial information."

"What crucial information?"

"She was wearing a wedding band, yet she said nothing about being married. And, believe me, I gave her plenty of opportunity to spit it out."

Charles shrugged. "So she was embarrassed or ashamed or both. I'm not saying that dealing with a cheating spouse is pleasant, just part of the job. And there's nothing in the private eye book of rules that says we have to like a client.''

"But this one didn't look like someone who should be lying through her straight, white teeth.''

Charles let out a long breath. "Ah, so that's the problem. You *do* like her.''

David knew there was no point in arguing. He was attracted to Susan, had been from the first moment he saw her. Not even her evasions or the fact that she was married changed that.

He shot up from his chair, feeling suddenly confined and inexplicably cornered. He stomped over to the window and stared out at the gray day.

"For two solid years attractive women have entered and left this office on a regular basis and my heart hasn't skipped a beat.''

"Something about this woman has changed that. Don't beat yourself up, David. Had to happen sometime. Your body's just telling you the time has come to get back in the game.''

"The timing's lousy. Makes no sense at all that I'd be attracted to her.''

"Hell, son, I've yet to hear a logical explanation as to what happens to a man's normal good sense when he gets around a certain woman. But if you feel that uncomfortable around this one, maybe your brother Richard better take her case.''

"The case isn't ours.''

"She changed her mind?''

"I turned her down,'' he said as he twisted to gaze at the now empty chair where Susan had sat.

"That's not like you, son.''

David knew that. Only too well.

He turned back to the window, where miles of slick, silver streets and gray forest spread out before him. On the distant horizon the majestic snow-capped peaks of the Olympic Mountains gathered what was left of the day's fading light. But all he saw was the stricken look on Susan's face when he had all but thrown her out of his office.

"Maybe she didn't tell me about her husband because he's some big, mean bastard who beats her," David said. "Or maybe he's having sexual problems and can't perform, and she didn't want to reveal his weakness."

"What do you want to do?"

"I want to make this right."

Charles walked over to his son and rested his hand briefly on his shoulder. "If that's what you want, then that's what you'll do."

"I'm glad one of us is confident."

"I know you, David. When you have a destination in mind, nothing gets in your way. You meticulously map out the steps you need to take, and you doggedly follow them until you get there."

David glanced at his dad. "That used to make you groan when it was my turn to pick the route for a family vacation."

"Only because your old man is the adventurous sort who likes to set off and see what's around the bend," Charles said with his usual hearty flare and no hint of apology. "You have to admit, we came upon a lot of amazing sights when we winged it. Things no amount of planning could have uncovered. Something your mother has never fully appreciated, I might add."

"You always got us lost," David said with a growing grin.

"And you always got us there. Using the shortest route. Within the scheduled time frame. Or earlier. Damn showoff."

David took the punch of pride his father delivered,

knowing the spirit in which it was thrown, despite the rocking force of the blow against his upper arm.

Charles checked his watch. "Speaking of time, I'd better get going. Have to swing by Jack's office to see if he's completed a background check I asked him to do before I pick up my car at the shop. Got the brakes adjusted today."

"Need a lift?"

"Thanks, but Jack's already agreed to drop me off. See you tomorrow."

After his father left, David resumed his staring out the window.

Might be a good idea to do a background check on Susan Carter and her husband. If he understood their relationship, maybe he'd understand why she had slept with another man.

He really wanted to understand. Susan didn't seem like the kind of woman who would cheat on a husband.

Still, when it came to attractive women, David knew perfectly well that he had shown himself to be just as blind as the next fool.

SUSAN TRUDGED through the front door of her small town house. The morning sickness was bad enough, but this draining fatigue was something that had begun to plague her all day.

"Hi, Honey, I'm home," she called out as she kicked the door closed behind her.

There was no response from the quiet house. She figured he must be out in the back. She weaved her way through the jungle of houseplants that were threatening to take over her foyer. She dropped her keys into the smiling jaws of a life-size, brown bear made of wood and slung the strap of her shoulder bag over its head. She turned around to step on the foot of a large, ceramic frog wastebasket.

"Honey?" she called again before she separated the only important piece of mail from the bevy of advertisements in her hands. Sticking the envelope between her teeth, she dropped the junk mail into the frog's open mouth.

When she released the foot lever, the frog gulped down the junk-mail dinner, a happy *rivet* emerging from its voice box.

She absently patted the frog's ceramic head with one hand as she removed the mail from her teeth with the other, slitting open the envelope as she strolled into the living room. The local newspaper had sent her a confirming copy of the ad she had placed in the next edition. She read the wording critically, trying to imagine him picking up the paper and seeing the ad for the first time.

> Todd. Susan would like to talk to you about that
> night you met six weeks ago. Extremely Important!
> Please write to her at Ad 54.

Short. Attention grabbing. Direct. If Todd read the newspaper, she felt confident that he'd know the ad was for him. She'd much prefer knowing more about Todd before seeing him. But she needed answers, and talking to him seemed to be the only way she was going to get them.

"Honey, where are you?" she called as she stuck the ad copy into her pocket and looked around.

In response, a West Highland White Terrier with one floppy, honey-colored ear came dashing down the stairs.

Susan dropped to a squat and opened her arms. The little terrier hopped off the final step and trotted toward her, dragging a boot in his mouth and wagging his tail with enthusiasm. When he reached her, she gave him a quick rub of welcome.

"How did you get into my closet?" she asked, as she

tried to wrestle the boot from his jaws. After a playful tug-of-war, Honey reluctantly relinquished the boot.

As Susan rose, she looked closely at the large size and encrusted mud on the boot's sole. Not one of hers.

She looked around, noticing what she had missed earlier because of her preoccupation with the ad. Out of place in the tidy room was an empty wineglass. The wine bottle was nowhere in sight.

Uh-oh. Not a good sign.

Her eyes traveled up the spiral staircase, where she spied the boot's mate on the top step.

She trudged up the stairs with Honey trotting along beside her. She entered the bedroom and spied the empty bottle of wine lying on top of the nightstand.

Honey jumped on the bed and headed for the dented pillow where he had obviously been sleeping when she'd come home. On the other pillow rested a head covered with long, curly black hair.

She circled the bed and plopped down on the edge. She gave the bare foot poking out from the covers a gentle shake.

''Ellie?'' she called.

The woman asleep in the bed snored.

''So, what's the trouble with Ellie?'' Susan asked her terrier.

Honey twisted around on his short legs to look at the sleeping woman. He gave his fury round body a mighty shake.

''Don't know either, huh?'' she said. ''Guess we better get the coffee on and try to find out.''

ELLIE TREMONT SLUMPED over Susan's kitchen table, her hands circling a cup of black coffee, tears streaming down her rosy cheeks. Susan's best friend had the face of a cherub, the body of a Victoria's Secret model, and the unerring bad judgment of a Las Vegas gambler when it came to picking men.

"She's a gourmet cook and knows the season's statistics of every Seahawks player," Ellie lamented before punctuating her words with a sob. "How do I compete with a woman like that?"

Susan rested her hand briefly on her friend's arm. "Love isn't a competitive sport, El."

"I got so filthy on the Port Townsend shoot that I had to drop by the apartment to change before going back to the office," Ellie said. "And what did I find? *That woman* in the kitchen, wearing nothing but a smirk."

"*That woman* did you a favor, El. Always better to find these things out sooner rather than later."

"Why wasn't I good enough for Martin?" Ellie said, and let out another moan.

"You were always too good for him," Susan said. "Remember, this is the guy who thinks a romantic evening is *your* picking up the pizza and beer and serving him while he sprawls on the couch watching sports on the TV."

Susan watched Ellie straighten. A good sign. Her friend was listening.

"I'd also lay odds that he's a lousy lover," Susan said. "Men who cheat are too self-absorbed to really care about a partner."

"I should have suspected something when she became his boss," Ellie said. "Being underneath a woman doing all the work has always been his favorite position."

Ellie grabbed a tissue, dabbed at her eyes. "I should be glad to be rid of him," she continued. "He's nothing but a lazy, cheating, lousy lover!"

"That's the spirit."

Ellie smiled. "You're a good friend."

"Takes one to know one," she said, returning the smile.

"Yeah, but you never dump on me the way I'm always

dumping on you. Last thing you'd ever do is hook up with the wrong guy. Not that you've hooked up with any guy since Paul died. Why would you want to? Paul can never be replaced. He was perfect.''

While Ellie sipped her coffee, Susan stared at the gold band on her finger and all it represented. The courageous, steadfast widow honoring her wonderful, dead husband.

She wondered what Ellie would say if she told her about that insane night with Todd. And the pregnancy. The staid, straight Susan Carter gone mad. Would Ellie even believe her? Probably not. Susan still barely believed that night had happened.

Honey grumbled loudly from beside her chair. When Susan looked down at him he was sitting on his backside, food bowl in his teeth, front paws slicing frantically through the air.

''Oops, sorry, Honey. I forgot the time.''

She slipped out of her chair and headed for the refrigerator. She pulled out a small piece of cooked steak, removed the plastic wrap and dropped the meat into Honey's waiting bowl. Honey set his bowl down with an audible sigh of doggie relief.

''You did the right thing choosing a dog over a man,'' Ellie said, watching Honey happily gnaw on his dinner. ''They are a hell of a lot more loyal.''

''Sometimes,'' Susan said as she slipped back onto her chair. ''And sometimes you come home to find them in bed with your best friend.''

Ellie smiled. ''You want to know the truth? Honey's a better snuggler than Martin ever was. I should get a dog. At least if they stray, you can have them neutered.''

Honey's head swung toward Ellie, his ears straight up as he made a noise of considerable doggie alarm. He grabbed his steak and ran for the doggie door leading out to the backyard.

"He sure doesn't miss much," Ellie said, laughing, as she watched him hop through. "Which reminds me. Did I miss anything at work this afternoon?"

"Nothing that won't keep until tomorrow."

"You covered for me," Ellie guessed.

"Just like you would have covered for me."

"Except you'll never need me to."

"You never know, El."

"Oh, I know. Even when we were teenagers and my dingbat of a dad and your ditzy mom were screaming mad and taking their frustrations out on both of us, you never let either of them get to you."

"I'd had a lot of practice dodging insults by then."

"That's what I mean, Suz. You know how to tough this stuff out. And you'd sure as hell never move in with the wrong guy and let him treat you like dirt."

Susan put her hand on her friend's arm. "Neither would you. That's why you came here when you found out about Martin's cheating. You had too much respect for yourself to stay there another minute."

Ellie sighed. "I get soused on a bottle of wine and somehow you manage to make me feel proud."

"You should be proud. When you give your word you keep it—not like those bozos you've been all too ready to believe. One day you're going to realize how great you are. When you do, I bet you find a guy who really appreciates you."

"I'd like to, Suz. I really would. But there are just so few men out there who want to make a commitment and settle down. You were so lucky to find Paul."

She released Ellie's arm, realizing her friend had missed the message she had been trying to send. But that was Ellie. She heard the things she wanted to and ignored the rest. Susan suspected she probably did the same thing.

"So, what's on for you tomorrow?" Ellie asked.

"I'm driving over to the other side of the Sound. One of the staff at Camp Long called to say he saw a red fox bring food to a vixen at a den site. He thinks she might have a new litter. Some good pictures of the pups would make a cute spread in next month's issue."

"I suppose you'll be leaving at the crack of dawn?" Ellie asked.

"Oh, long before it cracks. Red foxes hunt at night. If I'm in position at first light, I might get lucky and catch the male returning to the den with a late meal."

"I was afraid of that."

"Why afraid?" Susan asked.

"I don't want to go back and move my stuff out of Martin's apartment tonight. I was hoping I could stay here with you guys."

"Not a problem if you don't mind Honey jumping on the couch with you when I leave tomorrow morning. He hates being alone when I go out on an early shoot."

"I never object to sharing my bed with a warm male," Ellie said smiling.

"Then, that's settled. There's leftover chicken casserole in the refrigerator, twenty-three of our favorite romantic comedies on tape, and Ben & Jerry's Chocolate Chip Cookie Dough ice cream in the freezer."

Ellie laughed. "I keep getting my heart broken and you keep pulling the right medicine out of the Susan Carter doctor bag. Tell me, why am I always falling for the wrong guys?"

Susan knew Ellie didn't really want to hear the honest answer to that question. The only time Susan had ever given her one, her candor had nearly cost her their friendship. Sometimes the most important part of being a friend was knowing when to keep your mouth shut.

"A gal can only choose from what comes swimming by," Susan said as vaguely as she could.

"Which has to mean I've been fishing in a piranha pool," Ellie said, with a sad shake of her head.

Actually, she wasn't far off.

"At least I didn't let go of my apartment this time," Ellie said.

Yes, that was a good thing. Maybe Ellie was getting a little smarter. "You ready for me to heat up that casserole?"

"You can have the casserole," Ellie said. "Just bring me the ice cream and a spoon."

THE EARLY MORNING BREEZE was brisk and wet with mist. David hadn't been able to feel his feet for the past half hour. But as he continued to watch Susan through his binoculars, she remained dead still, lying on her stomach within the photographer's blind, high in the tree, her telephoto camera lens trained steadfastly on the fox hole on the other side of the clearing.

How she could lie so still he didn't know.

They had told him up at the lodge that she'd been at the site since before dawn. She wore thick, black sweatpants, a black parka and black hiking boots. But there were no gloves on her hands and no hat to cover her ears. She had to be freezing, and her still position had to be wreaking havoc on her circulation.

"A dedicated professional," Greg Hall, her editor, had described her, when David had called, identifying himself as a fan of the magazine. In truth, the magazine had been a favorite of David's for some time. But to make his call credible, he had spent time the day before carefully looking through the local library's copies of back issues.

Weaving a believable yarn when he needed to was part of a good investigator's tools. But David soon found he had no reason to stretch the truth. The wildlife photographs packing the greatest punch had Susan's name prominently displayed in the photo credits.

He'd discovered quite a bit more about her over the past few days from his other sources. Everything he'd learned had been unexpected.

David prided himself on being ready for anything, but since the moment he'd met this woman, she had been giving him one uncomfortable surprise after another. He prided himself on not judging his clients, but he'd sat in judgment on her and had let his unwanted reactions get in the way of his work. He prided himself on not jumping to conclusions, but he'd jumped to a conclusion about her—the wrong one.

David tried to tell himself that he'd made an honest mistake. Young widows whose husbands had been dead nearly three years didn't normally still wear their wedding rings. But the reality was that he hadn't acted like the professional he knew himself to be. His behavior reflected badly on him and on his family's highly regarded firm.

He had thought about leaving a message on Susan's answering machine at home. He had considered calling her at work. He had ultimately decided against both.

He was not a man for whom apologies came easily, but he did know that the only decent way to deliver an apology was in person. Of course, taking her case wouldn't be appropriate, even if she still wanted to employ him—which he seriously doubted.

But his brother Richard would be available soon. And he would give her Richard's card so she could call him.

David would see that she got the help she needed. He knew that was what he had to do to make this right.

But he had to wonder how long she could lie on that flat board, wet and chilled to the bone.

Finally, after what he figured had to be nearly three motionless hours, she started to move. He watched her progress through his binoculars. She first placed her camera in a protective case, then put the case in her backpack. Using a thick rope slung around the tree branch, she slowly lowered the backpack to the ground. Once the backpack was safely there, she began to snake backward toward the sturdy trunk of the tree.

He watched as she wrapped her body around the trunk. He was glad to see there were steel stakes in the bark for hand- and footholds. Still, he found himself tensing as she wobbled from side-to-side during her shaky descent.

She moved slowly. The circulation obviously hadn't returned to her arms and legs after her long hours of immobility. She was a fool to be coming down before massaging her limbs. She could hurt herself—

His worst fears suddenly took shape before his eyes as her foot missed the final metal stake, her hand slipped off another and she fell to the forest floor.

He dropped the binoculars and took off at a run. The branches whipped against his arms and legs and stung his face. He paid them no heed as he hurried through the thick underbrush. He wasn't that many yards away but the vegetation slowed his movements.

He was breathing hard when he crashed into the clearing where he'd seen her fall. She was lying on her back, her eyes were closed, her face white. He dropped to his knee beside her, probing for the artery in her neck.

His own blood pounded. He had to concentrate hard to feel her pulse. Finally, a slow rhythmic beat registered against his fingertips. Relief spread through his chest. He watched her eyelashes flutter, then open. A line of puzzlement drew her eyebrows together as she focused on his face.

"Where did you come from?" she asked.

He was happy to note the strength in her voice, but

ignored her question as he ran his hands up and down her arms, checking for broken bones.

"What do you think you're doing?" she demanded, flinching beneath his touch.

Once again he ignored her. But when he moved to grasp her right thigh, intending to check her legs, she suddenly sat up and swatted his hands away.

"Watch it, buster."

David sat back on his heels as he inspected the color flowing into her cheeks. He held back a smile.

"You appear to be all right," he said, managing to keep all emotion out of his voice.

She rolled onto her side and began to pull herself toward the tree she had so recently dropped from. "Why wouldn't I be all right?"

"Just a wild guess, but maybe because you fell out of a tree?"

"I didn't fall. I deliberately let go. It was only a couple of feet, and I knew the soft moss between the Osmanthus would provide a soft landing."

David didn't know what Osmanthus was, although he suspected them to be the evergreen shrubs on either side of the mound they were on.

"Why did you let go?"

"Because I wanted to." She latched onto the tree trunk and struggled to pull herself upright. Her wobbly extremities weren't cooperating.

"Why didn't you wait until you had some circulation back in your arms and legs before trying to get down?" he asked.

"Why is any of this your business?"

He was getting uncomfortable watching her determined but unsuccessful attempts to get to her feet. "If you rub your legs, you'll be able to stand a lot sooner."

"I know how to take care of myself, thank you. What are you even doing out here?"

"I'm an Eagle Scout trying to earn my merit badge," he said in frustration. Hell, he was only trying to help.

She looked him straight in the eye in that arresting way of hers. "What, no little old ladies around to help across the street?"

"Only Boy Scouts get merit badges for helping little old ladies across streets. We Eagle Scouts have to contend with cantankerous photographers who insist on dropping out of trees."

He hadn't tried to keep the irritation out of his tone this time. He squatted beside her, grasped her legs, and proceeded to give her muscles a brisk massage, no longer caring whether she objected.

She didn't bat his hands away this time. He could feel her eyes searching his averted face.

"When are you going to tell me what you're doing here?" she asked.

"When are you going to tell me why you didn't prepare yourself properly to descend that tree?"

When she didn't answer, he looked up to find that she was glaring at him. The flash of spirit looked good on her. He switched his attention back to her legs. They weren't bad either, strong and supple beneath his hands. Rubbing them was something less than a chore. Still, he kept his mind strictly on the business of getting the circulation back into them. Well, almost strictly.

"That's enough," she said after a moment.

He released her legs and stood. But when he held out his hand to help her up, she ignored the offer and instead grabbed hold of the tree trunk. With what seemed like more will than strength, she pulled herself to her feet. But she wobbled and leaned heavily against the tree for support.

"You're dizzy," he said, suddenly understanding.

Her face had lost color, and she rested her head against the trunk. But she delivered her next words with strong, sweet sarcasm. "Such amazing insight."

"You didn't eat breakfast, did you," he demanded more than asked. "I thought you were a professional. You should know better than to begin a long assignment without any food in your stomach."

"First a private investigator, then an Eagle Scout, and now a mother hen," she said. "Such versatility."

"You're probably dehydrated, as well," he said, knowing there was no probably about it.

"Don't you have a wife you could be annoying?"

Despite her continuing attempt to be tough, she looked absolutely terrible. "If I did have a wife, and she pulled some stupid stunt like this, I'd—"

He stopped his tirade as he watched her sink back to the forest floor. Closing the distance between them, he swept her collapsing body into his arms. Her head rolled onto his shoulder as a soft sigh escaped her lips. She had fainted.

Her face was as white as the delicate flowers spraying the front of her jacket. Her bangs were wet with morning mist, and a silky strand of golden-brown hair from her braid tickled his neck.

A full minute passed before David's heart stopped skipping beats.

What a fool she was. And what a fool he was for giving a damn.

He twisted around and grabbed her backpack. The thing weighed a ton. How did this woman lug around such heavy stuff? He slung the backpack over his shoulder and started down the trail.

SUSAN SLOWLY OPENED her eyes to find herself lying beneath a spectacular blue spruce. The hazy mist of the overcast morning curled through the heavy branches. She didn't recognize the beautiful tree. She felt a soft, wool fabric beneath her fingertips. She didn't recognize that, either.

"Don't try to get up," David's voice commanded from behind her.

His voice she *did* recognize. Her memory came back with a bang. She'd gotten dizzy while descending from the blind. She'd let go of the steel stakes to drop onto the soft mound of moss beneath the tree. While lying there, trying to get her equilibrium back, David Knight had suddenly appeared to pester her.

Pushing herself to a sitting position, she fought the immediate dizziness brought on by her abrupt movement. When the earth and sky finally resumed their correct positions, she discovered that the red plaid blanket beneath her was next to a brown dirt road.

"I told you not to get up," David said, scowling at her. He stood a few feet away, beside a silver Ford truck with an F250 logo on the side. He was pouring steaming, dark liquid from a thermos into a cup.

She glanced around her. This certainly wasn't the clearing with the fox den. This place didn't look familiar at all, and neither did that silver truck.

"How did I get here?" she asked.

He put the thermos down on the truckbed and walked toward her, carrying the cup. "You fainted."

Had she? Odd. She'd never fainted before in her life. But maybe not so surprising. She had certainly been dizzy enough.

"You carried me here?"

He reached her, dropped to a squat and held out the cup. "Drink this."

One whiff told her that he was offering her hot chocolate. She shook her head and leaned back. "No, thanks."

He scowled at her. "If you don't get something in your stomach soon, you'll faint again."

She scowled back. "The last thing I need is something in my stomach."

He held out the cup again. "Trust me. You'll feel better."

"Trust me. I'll puke."

He pulled back the cup and regarded her closely. For a moment she could have sworn she saw something like discomfort flash across his face. But then his frown was back and she figured she was imagining things.

"Morning sickness?" he asked.

She nodded. "Nothing passes these lips until noon, and sometimes even then it has a round-trip ticket."

He plopped down on the blanket beside her. "So that's why you haven't eaten."

"And I had begun to think you'd lost all your detective skills."

He sent her another scowl before turning his head away to stare at the line of trees along the dirt road. He was good at that scowling thing. Must have had a lot of practice.

As he sipped the hot chocolate he'd poured for her, she tested out her limbs and found them to be a little tender but otherwise okay. She looked around once again, trying to get her bearings. Where was east, west? Would have been a lot easier to determine if the sun were out. But then, it so rarely was.

"How far are we from where I was shooting?" she asked.

"About a mile and a half. If you're worried about your camera, I put your backpack in the truck."

A mile and a half. That was a long way to carry a one-hundred fifteen pound woman and forty pounds of her camera equipment. Looked as though his muscles weren't just for show.

His concern for her welfare actually seemed genuine. He'd even been thoughtful enough to bring along her equipment. Maybe there was a heart hidden somewhere inside that hard chest, after all.

She studied the bold lines of his profile. Nice, straight, well-shaped nose. Full, well-defined lips. Not bad, actually. Maybe not a handsome face, but definitely not quite as forbidding as her first impression.

He turned his head and his eyes met hers.

"Feeling any better?"

"Some," she admitted. "Thanks for being concerned about me."

He looked quickly away. "Forget it."

He was uncomfortable with her thanking him. What had she done to rub this man the wrong way?

"Time you answered my question," she said, happy to hear herself sounding calm, reasonable. "What are you doing here?"

# CHAPTER THREE

THERE WERE A LOT of things David knew he should say to Susan. Number one was the apology he owed her. But admitting he'd been wrong suddenly did not seem like such a good idea, not with her sitting so close to him, looking directly into his eyes in that bold way of hers.

This was not the time for him to be admitting to any kind of weakness.

"I came to talk to you," he said simply. He stared at the bushes that lined the road, although he couldn't have described them if he tried.

"How did you know I'd be here?"

"I'm a private investigator, remember?"

She was quiet for a moment, but he could feel her studying his face. He wondered what she saw, then reminded himself not knowing was a lot safer.

"What did you want to talk to me about?" she asked.

He dug into his pocket. But he didn't retrieve his brother's business card. Instead he pulled out the ad from the personal column he'd clipped out of the paper. "This isn't going to flush out Todd."

She gave the clipping of the ad he handed her a brief glance before stuffing it in the pocket of her parka and getting to her feet.

"What I do or don't do to contact Todd is my business, Mr. Knight. Now that we've closed that subject, what direction do I take to get to the lodge from here?"

He squinted up at her. She had delivered those last two

sentences with enough frost to freeze a man, and she still had the guts to look him directly in the eye. She had a backbone.

He pointed. "The lodge is a mile that way." He raised his other hand and pointed in the opposite direction. "Your SUV is a mile that way. Makes more sense to head for your SUV."

"Aren't you just full of helpful suggestions this morning."

Her sarcasm was delivered so sweetly he almost smiled. "I thought you were a sensible woman," he said with a shrug. "My mistake."

She stared down at him. "Do you know what a nature photographer's most valuable asset is?"

He didn't see the connection to his comment but he gave the answer a try. "A good eye?"

"An obliging bladder."

He blinked at her in surprise.

"Unfortunately, there's something about being pregnant that can transform the most obliging bladder into a most unobliging one," she said.

He knew his flippant comment about her being a sensible woman had goaded her into explaining. She smiled down on him with ill-concealed satisfaction, confident that her explanation was going to make him feel sheepish.

She wasn't wrong.

He gulped down the last of the hot chocolate. "I'll drive you over."

THE CAMP LONG LODGE had a rustic, airy feel with its high ceilings, tall windows, a stone fireplace and hardwood floors.

As David waited for Susan, he stood on the outskirts of a large group gathered around a naturalist who was pointing to a map that showed the route they would take on their upcoming hike.

The naturalist was a knockout—a big, bosomy brunette who was making several of the men in the crowd openly drool. The effect was calculated. She had on thick eye makeup and painted lips the same deep red that adorned her long nails. She wore blue jeans and a red sweater, both a size too small.

David took the scene in like the clinician he had been once and the man of indifference he had become.

Then he saw Susan emerge from the lodge's rest room. No painted lips and no painted nails. She carried her parka over her arm. The turtleneck she had worn underneath was faded cotton, quite loose, and in a pale shade of natural pink.

He watched her approach. There was a sweet grace to the sway of her shoulders and hips, as though she walked to music she alone could hear. The mid-morning light fell through the tall windows, turning her long, braided hair into a rainbow of shimmering browns and gold.

There was nothing calculated about her. Just a natural sensuality that took his breath away.

Still, only an idiot in his position would do anything about an attraction to a woman in her position. He was no idiot.

She stopped in front of him. "You didn't have to wait."

The naturalist was raising her voice to get the attention of the group. David took Susan's arm to move them out of earshot. The worn cotton of her top proved to be soft and yielding.

But there was a muscled arm beneath, which quickly pulled away. She did not like to be touched. At least, not by him.

"Thought you might like a ride to your SUV," he offered.

"The walk will do me good."

He shrugged, careful to convey nothing but nonchalance. "Suit yourself. But if you faint again, you could break an arm. Might even land on your camera."

The way she had so carefully tended to her camera before attempting to descend from the tree told him that hurting her camera would rank right up there with hurting an arm. Her quick change of mind didn't surprise him.

"On second thought, Mr. Knight, I would appreciate that ride."

They stepped out of the lodge to find the mist had lifted. The air was still chilly. When she swung the parka around her shoulders, he grabbed the sleeves to help her put her arms through. But he was careful to touch only her jacket this time.

They didn't talk on the drive. Once they reached her vehicle, he circled around his truck to open the door for her. He held out his hand. She didn't take it or attempt to get out.

"You didn't come here just to tell me my personal ad wasn't going to work, did you?" she asked.

"No," he admitted, dropping his hand.

She held onto the door frame as she slipped off the seat. She stood before him and raised her eyes to his expectantly.

David knew the time had come to apologize for rejecting her case without explanation and to hand her his brother's business card. But he also knew that he wasn't going to do either of those things.

"I'll find out about Todd for you."

He turned around and headed toward her dark-green SUV. He opened the passenger door, slipped her backpack off his shoulders and laid it on the seat. By the time he'd closed the passenger door, she'd walked to the driver's side.

But the question still hadn't left her eyes. "Why?"

"You do want me to find out about him, don't you?"

"Yes, but I meant why did you change your mind?"

"I have a case to finish up today, but after that, my schedule will be free. What time will you be home tonight?"

"Around six, I guess, but—"

"I'll be by at seven."

He whirled away from her then and quickly closed the distance to his truck. He purposely did not give her a chance to respond. He slipped behind the wheel and drove off, not once looking back.

On the long drive around Puget Sound to Silver Valley, David congratulated himself on the solid logic behind his decision. Handing Susan's case off to Richard made no sense.

Today he and his brother, Jared, a detective in the Sheriff's Department, would see that the bastard who seduced, videotaped and then dumped his underage teenage victims was arrested.

But after he wrapped up that last loose end, he had a clear schedule. Richard would still be tied up on his current case for another week. David already had knowledge of Susan and her request.

Handling Susan's case was the professional thing for David to do.

Besides, his dad was right. His attraction to Susan was simply a sign that he was ready to get off his self-imposed celibacy bench and back into the game. Of course, playing any games with her still remained out of the question.

She was a vulnerable, pregnant woman in need of his help. He would never take advantage of a woman in such a situation. Besides, now she was his client. The number one rule for a private investigator was never to get personally involved with a client.

David was a man who knew how to follow the rules.

SUSAN WAS RELIEVED that David had agreed to find Todd for her. He was obviously a very good investigator. But she also couldn't help feeling annoyed.

David was coming to her home tonight. She did not invite men to her home, and she had not invited him. He had invited himself.

This was a business arrangement she had entered into with him. She didn't want him invading her private space. But her subsequent call to his office that day had not been successful in changing the arrangement.

A male clerk had informed her—in cordial if clipped tones—that David was not in, was not expected to come in and could not be reached.

Her mood hadn't improved when she'd discovered that she'd only gotten two marginally good shots out of the long morning shoot. On top of that, heavy traffic caused her to be late getting home. She was irritated and frustrated when she pulled her car into the garage just after six-thirty.

She stomped out of the garage and sprinted up the few steps to the entrance to her town house. She worked long hours and looked forward to unwinding in the evenings.

Only tonight, David was coming by at seven, less than half an hour away. That was the time when she and Honey were normally having their dinner. Surely, David didn't expect her to fix him something? He might. There was no telling with that man. He was so damn hard to figure out. She opened the door and stepped inside.

"Hi, Honey, I'm home."

He barked happily, his white fur a whirl of moving light in the dark entry. He flew into her outstretched arms with all the unbridled love that only a cherished pet could put into a homecoming. All Susan's irritation fled the instant she hugged his exuberant little body, and he washed her cheeks with his warm tongue.

Without Honey, these past few years would have been unbearably bleak. She would always be grateful for that day he came into her life, and her heart.

As she stood and switched on the light, she saw with sudden dismay that Honey's paws and nose were thick with mud. He was up to his old tricks, digging holes in the backyard. He'd gotten the mud all over her, as well. A thick glob was hanging from her bangs.

She sighed. That was love for you. So damn messy. And what was this affinity males had for mud?

She dropped her shoulder bag and keys onto the brown bear figurine and picked up the squirming terrier. ''Shower time for us both, little guy,'' she said as she carried him up the stairs.

She would be lucky if she even had Honey dried by seven, much less herself. She hated being late, even if she wasn't the one who'd set the schedule. Of course, men were seldom on time. David might not even show up until eight.

But whenever he did show, one thing was for sure. If he came around expecting food from her tonight, she'd hand him a bag of dog kibble.

DAVID RANG SUSAN'S doorbell at exactly seven. He knew she was home. He'd already glanced through the window of her garage and had seen her green SUV inside. Lights shone through the glass panels above the front door of her town house. A dog barked from somewhere within.

David let a minute go by before pressing the doorbell again.

Almost immediately the door flew open and a small, white terrier charged out. Since David had two dogs of his own, he was well versed in the proper etiquette when entering their territory. He stood still and let himself be sniffed. The dog efficiently circled his legs, wagged his tail happily and let out a welcoming bark. David leaned down to give him a pat.

The dog was a cute little guy and openly affectionate, if a little damp. He rubbed his head against David's hand, obviously expecting a lot more than just a passing pat. David indulged him, rubbing his ears and back and getting a blissful little moan in response.

"You're making a mistake," Susan said. "He's not going to let you alone for a minute now."

David turned his head. The first thing he saw from his crouched position was her bare feet. Slowly his gaze followed the lovely curved bone of her ankles, long shins and cute knees. But when he got to the middle of the firm flesh on her slim thighs, the edge of a white terry-cloth robe suddenly intruded to spoil the rest of the view.

The robe was securely fastened around her waist and drawn closely over her chest. A white towel covered her hair. She was not happy he was here. The firm set to her mouth made that very clear. But as her eyes followed his hand still stroking her dog, there was a softness in her expression that he had not seen before.

She stepped back for him to enter. "Honey will have to entertain you while I get dressed."

David stepped through the jungle of her entryway, the dog trotting happily at his heels. He noted the shiny hardwood floors, the large bear that held her shoulder bag and keys, the whimsical frog wastebasket.

When she stepped past him to close the door, he caught a whiff of her freshly washed skin and hair. He reminded himself that the sudden tightening of his stomach muscles was normal, natural, nothing to be concerned about.

"The living room is that way," she said with a casual wave of her hand. "I'll join you in a moment."

She padded across the bare wood floor and easily sprinted up the spiral staircase to the second floor. She was lithe and agile and displayed none of the physical clumsiness that had plagued her that morning. He felt reassured. He didn't want to worry about her, but he had.

He'd decided to meet with her at her home because he wanted to get a deeper sense of who she was. Understanding a client was important. A woman's home often reflected her more strongly than any other aspect of her life. Especially a woman who lived alone.

He already knew of her struggle to be taken as a serious professional, her hard-held independence, her deep need for privacy. Still, he had a feeling there was a lot more to know.

David thought he'd prepared himself for whatever he'd find, but when he entered her living room, he hadn't expected to be walking into a shrine. From floor to ceiling, the walls were covered in dramatic, larger-than-life photographs of wildlife, giving him the impression that he'd been transported into the wilderness.

A majestic eagle soared over a diamond-blue waterfall. An elk herd fed on dewy grass in the dawn light. Furry bobcats ran across snow-covered forests. White-tailed deer glided through golden meadows. A brown bear lunged at pink-bellied salmon leaping up an emerald stream. The room vibrated with movement, with wild beauty, with life.

He barely noticed the furnishings. A nondescript couch and chair, a coffee table and several throw rugs—all in muted greens, grays and umber. Nothing distracted the eye from the dramatic scenes on the walls.

And that was when he knew. This was the living room of a woman with a deep respect, reverence and love for nature. Those beautiful pictures were not an extension of her work. Her work was an extension of herself.

SUSAN SHOULD HAVE KNOWN that David would be one of those rare men who actually showed up when he said he would. She rubbed her wet hair with the towel, well aware the effort was futile. An hour under the blow dryer would be required to dry the long strands in the humid air. She didn't have that kind of time.

She settled for rubbing the moisture out of her bangs, and swept the rest into a golden scarf, tied turban-style around her head. She pulled a pair of clean black sweats out of her closet and hurriedly put them on.

Just because he was in dark-blue slacks and the collar and cuffs of a dress shirt peeked out of his blue sweater, there was no reason for her to dress up.

Damn, he did look good, though.

Still, this was her home. She had a right to be comfortable. She was not going to change anything just because he had the bad manners to invite himself over. But instead of reaching for her comfy, beat-up slippers as she normally would have, she opted instead for a pair of socks and her new walking shoes.

When she came down the stairs a couple of minutes later, she found David sitting on the couch with Honey beside him. His face was turned toward the dog, so she couldn't read his expression. But there was a relaxed set to his shoulders and his long legs were comfortably stretched out in front of him. He was stroking Honey.

She stood at the edge of the living room silently watching them. She wanted to be put out with David, but she found that difficult. He was being so nice and attentive to Honey. A man who liked her beloved pet couldn't be all bad.

"Is he a good watchdog?" David asked, obviously aware she was standing there although he hadn't taken his eyes off Honey.

She stepped into the room. "I doubt he'd do anything to a burglar except beg for attention."

He glanced up at her, the look on his face almost friendly. The edge of his lip twitched. Was that the beginning of a smile?

She waited expectantly, suddenly very curious to see what a smile would do to his face. But none was forthcoming.

"He's munching on my fingers," David said. "I think he's hungry."

"We eat at this time," she said, happy for the opportunity to bring up the subject.

"Then, you'd best eat," he said, not a hint of apology in his voice.

"Come on, Honey," she called, shaking her head. "Go get your dinner bowl."

Honey didn't have to be told a second time. He barked his excitement as he flew off the couch. She followed the dog into the kitchen. She heard David enter a moment later as she was taking Honey's meal out of the refrigerator. She unwrapped the steak and placed it in the bowl Honey held in his mouth. Honey expertly lowered the bowl to the kitchen floor and dug in.

"Steak for dinner," David said. "Honey's a lucky dog."

"He's a loved one," Susan said, staring down at the ball of fur.

"That's what I meant," he said. "Get your coat. You can take your pick of Italian, Chinese or a steakhouse. They're all within a twenty-minute drive."

"I'm not dressed to go out," she said, looking up in surprise.

His impressive height and massive shoulders dwarfed her small kitchen. The overhead light played through the thick, rich brown of his hair.

"You look fine to me."

There was absolutely no readable expression on his calm face, but his voice told her he meant those words.

She knew then that he had intended to take her out to dinner all along. Damn. She wished he had said something. She would have dried her hair and worn something suitable. How thoroughly annoying this man could be.

She looked away from him and turned toward a cupboard.

"I was going to have some soup and a salad," she said. "There's enough for two if you're hungry."

She fiddled with the dishes and waited through the stretching silence, slightly appalled at the sudden impulse that had her inviting him to share a dinner with her here.

"I'll make the salad," he said.

He hadn't offered. He'd told her. She did not appreciate the caveman approach. A spark of annoyance skittered across nerve endings she recognized were already taut. A small, reasonable voice inside her tried to suggest that he might have offered to make the salad as a way of being helpful. But she didn't really want to listen to that voice at the moment.

She felt him move behind her to the refrigerator. Felt the cool air as he opened the door. Felt the impressive breadth of him that blocked a lot of that cool air. He was crowding her, and she didn't like to be crowded.

But what Susan really didn't like was her sudden suspicion that David might actually be a considerate man. She hadn't been prepared for that. The possibility threw her off balance in a most unexpected and disconcerting way.

SOUP AND SALAD, she'd said. Sounded simple enough to David. But as he was fast discovering, nothing about Susan was simple.

She'd added sliced apples, pears, grapes and then finely

chopped almonds, walnuts and pecans to the assortment of greens he'd put into salad bowls. Instead of salad dressing, she topped off the blend with sharp, shredded cheddar. The combination turned out to be both unusual and quite delicious.

She'd put chicken broth to simmer on the stove. Then she'd chopped an assortment of springtime vegetables into the broth—asparagus tips, onions, garlic, snow peas, spinach—and added tender juicy chunks of freshly cooked chicken seasoned with ginger and ground pepper. The flavors blended well and tasted great with the warm corn bread she served right out of the oven.

David had planned from the beginning to take her out to dinner. He hadn't dreamed she'd offer to make him a meal. But he was glad she had. And not just because the meal had turned out to be superior to what they could have gotten at a restaurant.

Watching her prepare the food, he'd discovered her penchant for neatness and for organization. Every inch of her small kitchen served a specific and useful function. He'd discovered some of her preferences, as well. Fresh fruits and vegetables were clearly major players in her diet. She was concerned about what she put in her body. He'd discovered her attention to detail in the way she sifted and measured and made sure quantities were correct. She was not a careless woman.

They had eaten at her country-style, cloth-covered kitchen table. Her town house had a small formal dining room, but he was certain she rarely ate there, because few photographs adorned the walls. Every inch of the kitchen was covered with them.

The photographs in the living room had told him a lot about her. These told him more. They were all of baby animals—a doe nursing her new speckled fawn, a mother bear playing with her twin cubs, a tiny hummingbird flittering protectively over her hatchlings. And whereas the living room scenes had been full of the bold vibrancy of wildlife, these were filled with the warm, cherished charm of new life.

When they finished eating, David helped her clear the table and put the dishes in the dishwasher. "I have a few things I'd like to go over," he said.

"All right," she agreed as she led the way back into the living room. She took a seat on the chair. He sat across from her on the couch. Honey hopped up beside him and nudged his hand, clearly communicating his desire for more petting.

David gave in to the demands of the little terrier, unable to resist. But even as he looked at the dog snuggling against him, the woman sitting so silently across from him claimed his thoughts. He was more confused than ever by her and by the reason she had come to him.

She was not the kind of woman to casually have a fling with a stranger. Everything about her told him that. And yet, she had. He had to know why.

Susan watched Honey stretch out beside David, legs in the air, total trust shining out of his big brown eyes. David's large hand gently rubbed the terrier's tummy. The little dog sighed with delight. The expression on David's face as he looked at Honey was that of a man fast becoming wrapped around the charming paws of a pooch.

She decided she could forgive David a lot when she saw that look. Maybe even forgive him for his intrusion into her home tonight.

"Your husband died two years and ten months ago," he said, breaking the silence. "You went to the community center six weeks ago to attend a bereavement seminar, not one on self-improvement."

So, he had checked up on her. Seemed odd he had done so after having turned down her case, and odder still that he was now willing to help her. There was so much about this man that was confusing.

But his voice had been surprisingly gentle when he made that statement. And so was his hand on Honey's tummy.

"Being able to deal effectively with grief is a form of self-improvement," she said, trying not to sound defensive.

His immediate response told her she had failed. "I'm not trying to corner you. I'm trying to understand. I'm well aware that losing a loved one can be devastating. Did attending the seminar help?"

She looked down at the gold band on her finger. "No."

"Tell me how he died."

"How will that help?"

"I'm not sure that it will. But I'd like you to tell me."

There was a sincerity in his tone that caught her off guard. He really did sound as though he wanted to know. Yet when she looked up, she found his attention still focused on the dog, his hand stroking Honey's tummy in a soft, circular motion that was almost hypnotic.

"Paul was a fireman," she began. "He was a courageous man, dedicated to saving lives. He worked long hours. When he came home that day, he was very tired. But there was a game on TV he wanted to watch, so he decided to stay up for a while."

The images from the past were clear. She saw Paul as he'd plopped on the couch in his striped boxer shorts, a beer in his hand. He had grinned at her over his bare shoulder, and she'd seen the familiar light stubble on his chin, his blond hair—as always—in need of a trim.

"I put some wash in the dryer, kissed him goodbye and went off to do the grocery shopping," she continued. "When I got home, I found the block surrounded by fire engines and the house...Paul...everything was gone."

She didn't remember much of that part. Probably better that she didn't.

"How did the fire start?" David asked.

"I'm not sure. Paul had fallen asleep on the couch. They found...him there."

What was left of him. They had spared her the details—something for which she would always be grateful. She stared down at her walking shoes, concentrated on the gold and white stripes on the sides.

"I didn't mean to bring it all back," David said.

She looked up to find him watching her. His face was full of understanding. Strange she had thought his eyes cold. They were looking at her with the same warmth that was in his voice.

"Did you get grief counseling after his death?" he asked.

"I've never been one to go to other people for help. I was certain I could handle the grief, and I did. I accepted Paul's death. I got on with my life. Everything was going well. But, then, a few months ago, the dreams started."

"What kind of dreams?"

"Vivid," she said. "I know people are supposed to dream every night. I suppose I must. But I've never remembered my dreams before."

"What happens in these dreams?"

"Paul and I do everyday things together. I bring lemonade out to him while he's digging the trench for our sprinkler system, and he suddenly tackles me, and we're rolling in the mud laughing. Or we're on a scary roller coaster together, and I'm holding on tightly and screaming my head off. Or we're building sand castles on the beach just like we did on our honeymoon. I see him so clearly that when I wake up, I expect him to be beside me."

"But he's not," David said after a moment of silence.

She stared at one of her favorite photographs—the one of the eagle soaring over the waterfall, powerful wings shimmering with sunlight, proud head rising above all the cares of the world.

"I faced the pain. I faced the grief. I put them both

behind me. Only now the dreams have come, and I don't know why."

"What did they suggest you do at the seminar?" David asked.

"We were supposed to write a goodbye letter."

"How far did you get?"

*Dearest Paul— Why am I dreaming about you?*

"Not very far," she admitted. "I was staring at those empty white pages while everyone around me was scribbling away. I knew I was getting nowhere. I got up to leave and collided with Todd."

"He was sitting beside you?"

She shook her head. "He was on the end of the row in the back. I was hurrying up the aisle toward the exit. I didn't see him getting up to leave, and I ran into him. Literally."

"And you two left together."

"He suggested we walk to this bar that was a couple of blocks away, to get a drink. Sounded like a good idea at the time."

"Do you remember the name of the bar?"

"No, most of the letters on the neon sign were burned out. All I remember clearly is that the waitress was sweet and the music was sad."

"So you had a drink," he said in that same soothing voice that had become so easy to respond to.

"I don't even like alcohol," she said, sighing in remembrance. "I hate the taste and the stuff kills brain cells. I've always figured I needed every one of mine. The last drink I had before that night was a sip of champagne at my wedding."

"But that night you drank more than a sip."

"Oh yeah. After four Screwdrivers, I was feeling no pain. Of course, that was the whole idea. I told Todd about losing Paul. He told me about losing his mother. She had died a couple of months before, in a plane crash. They'd been very close. He hadn't been able to write the goodbye letter to her, either. Hearing that made me feel a lot less like a failure. I really liked him for telling me.''

"Enough to become intimate with him?''

"Hardly. Sex was the last thing on my mind. That only happened because…''

Dear heavens, how could she explain to David what she still didn't understand herself? Why did she want to? She normally didn't care what men thought of her. But for some reason, she was beginning to care what David thought.

"Whatever you can tell me will help,'' he said.

"He walked me back to the community center sometime after eleven,'' she said, doubting any of what she had to say would really help. "The lot was deserted except for my vehicle. Todd told me he'd arrived late for the seminar and had parked on a side street somewhere. Neither of us was in any condition to drive home. He offered to use his cell phone to call me a cab. But I couldn't leave my vehicle parked there overnight. All my camera equipment was inside. I couldn't risk someone breaking in and stealing something.''

"So you spent the night in your SUV?''

She nodded. "I always carry a sleeping bag. Part of a nature photographer's essential equipment. Todd helped me to unroll the bag, and I was out like the proverbial light as soon as I lay my head down. Next thing I knew I was having one of those vivid dreams of Paul. I could feel him beside me. He was snoring away.''

She paused, clasped the wedding band on her finger, stared at it in the room's soft lamplight.

"You can tell me what happened,'' he said.

There was something so soothing and accepting in his voice that she suddenly believed she could.

"When Paul snored, I would kiss his cheek so he'd wake up, roll onto his side and go back to sleep. But when I kissed him that night, he woke up and kissed me back. Then he started to make love to me.''

"But it wasn't Paul," David said quietly. "When did you know?"

She wanted to say *afterward*. She *wished* she could say *afterward*. But she had done something for which she was ashamed, and she wasn't going to make herself feel even more ashamed by lying.

"I was still pretty smashed. But at one point I sensed something was different, opened my eyes and saw Todd's face. I realized then that he must have passed out beside me. When I kissed him, he must have awakened and thought..."

"That you wanted him," David supplied when her voice faded.

She gave a long exhale. "Todd kept whispering my name over and over. I closed my eyes and let it happen."

"And in the morning?"

"When I awoke, Todd was gone, much to my relief. I don't think I could have faced him. Because the truth is, I don't know why I slept with him."

"Hard to know why we do things sometimes."

She looked up to see he was watching her, that calm acceptance still on his face. He was telling her that he wasn't judging her. She appreciated that, more than she could say. But she was judging herself.

"I've always known why I've done things," she said. "I may not always have been thrilled with the reason, but at least I've known. Now, not knowing...not knowing is very unsettling. I can't tell you how unsettling."

"You don't have to even try," he said, getting to his feet. "I've been there. Thank you for dinner and for your honesty."

"You're leaving?" she said, surprised.

He nodded. "I know what I asked of you tonight wasn't easy to give. But what you've told me has been important, and will help me to find out about Todd. I hope that will be worth the pain you went through. I'll call you tomorrow."

He headed toward the front door. She followed. When he paused to lean down and give Honey one last head pat, she smiled. David was turning out to be quite nice and not nearly as unapproachable as she'd imagined.

Maybe now was the time to ask the question that had plagued her since she first saw him in the White Knight offices.

"What bothers you about me?"

David straightened. "What do you mean?"

"When we first met," she said, "I could tell you didn't like me."

He stared down at her. They were barely a foot apart. She was suddenly very aware of him.

"There is nothing about you that I don't like," he said in a soft whisper. "Good night."

He pulled open the door, stepped out into the dark night and shut the door behind him.

The breath whooshed out of Susan's lungs as she stood facing that closed door, stunned to her toes. She could barely believe what her senses were telling her. David had just said there was nothing about her he didn't like. She'd seen the truth of his words in his eyes, heard that truth in his voice.

He was attracted to her.

She felt a sharp quickening of her pulse and an undeniable response deep inside her—a response she hadn't felt in a very, very long time.

# CHAPTER FOUR

DAVID LAY IN BED that night thinking over what Susan had told him. When he'd checked into her background and discovered her husband had died, he'd visited the fire station where Paul Carter had worked. A memorial picture of him hung on the wall. Paul was blond, five-ten, slender, with light eyes. That was exactly how Susan had described Todd.

She'd gone to the seminar seeking closure to some unresolved issue that had her dreaming of her dead husband. Instead of a resolution, she had found herself under the lethal influences of a terrible sense of failure and a potent dose of alcohol. And there was Todd, a sympathetic, fellow sufferer, looking enough like Paul to pull all the right heartstrings.

David could understand why Susan had let him make love to her. But what he still wasn't clear about was Todd's motives. Was he really grieving? Or was he an opportunist who had seen her pain, plied her with alcohol, and, then, when she was most vulnerable, taken advantage of her?

A man who took advantage of a vulnerable woman was scum. If he found out that Todd had done that to Susan—

David punched his pillow and turned onto his other side. No. No matter what he found out, he wasn't going to get physical with the guy. This was just a case like any other. She was just a client. And David was a civilized, educated man in full control of his impulses. *All* his impulses.

When she had asked him what he didn't like about her, he'd been very tempted to show her how much he liked everything about her. But he'd held back and left without laying so much as a finger on her.

Even if he had stood too close to her and gazed into her eyes a little too long.

David punched his pillow again and turned to his other side. That had been a mistake. He wished he *just* liked the way she looked. The way she sounded. The way she moved. The way she smelled.

But he also liked the way she spoke her mind and refused to back down when she believed she was right. The way she took such pride in her work. The way she took such loving care of her pet and her home.

David threw the pillow to the bottom of the bed, let out a frustrated breath, rolled onto his back and stared at the ceiling. No matter what he liked about her, pursuing Susan was simply not an option.

Time to take his brother, Jack, up on one of his double-date offers. Jack's sojourn into show biz had left him rubbing shoulders, as well as more interesting body parts, with some of the most beautiful women on the TV screen. As David's dad had so accurately pointed out to him a couple of days before, his body was telling him to get back in the game. With one of Jack's women, a man didn't have to worry about holding back.

Tomorrow morning David would concentrate on getting a lead on Todd. Thanks to Susan's openness and honesty, he had some clues to follow.

Tomorrow night he'd let Jack introduce him to someone who wasn't a client, who wasn't still mourning her dead husband, and who wasn't going to want to see his face over the breakfast table the next morning.

He might be ready to get back in the dating game, but the rules were definitely going to be different. This time around, he wasn't going to look for emotional entanglements of any kind.

"COME ON, SUSAN," Paul said, dragging her toward the roller coaster. "It'll be fun!"

Susan looked up at the big, bright neon sign in front of them that said Death Ride. Nope, this didn't sound like a whole lot of fun.

"Paul, a roller-coaster ride isn't my idea of a good time. I have this inner-ear problem. I get car sick on a bumpy road."

"Suz, you've got to come with me," he coaxed. "This ride is the absolute best. A real adrenaline rush."

She planted her feet. "My adrenaline is rushing at the right speed, thank you."

"Is it?" he said as he wrapped his arm around her waist and drew her to him. "Maybe I'd better do a quick check." He bent down to nuzzle her neck. She closed her eyes and leaned into him.

The next thing she knew, he had scooped her into his arms, planted her on the seat and hopped in beside her. The safety harness swooped down to lock them in place.

"That was pretty damn sneaky, Paul Carter," she complained as she looked over at the satisfied grin on his face.

He laughed. "You're a sucker for that neck-nuzzling trick."

The loaded cars had begun to creep up the track toward the top. Susan's stomach gave a nervous twitch. There was no getting out now. Not that she had a particular problem with this part. But she had seen roller coasters operate. She knew there was a downside.

A *real* downside. Their car reached the top. Within seconds they were barreling toward the earth at sixty miles per hour, taking hairpin turns that rattled her eye sockets and careening around neck-yanking loops that had Susan clutching the safety harness in pure terror. Her head was pounding, and her stomach was churning, ready to erupt.

But when she looked over at Paul, he was grinning, his face flushed, so happy and so full of life.

Susan awoke and instinctively reached for Paul. But her hand rested on a ball of fur. Then she remembered.

Paul was gone.

Why was this happening to her? She had faced the loss of the wonderful man she had married. She had allowed herself to feel the pain of his passing. She had accepted the need to get on with her life. She *had* gotten on with her life. Why was she having these vivid dreams of Paul?

SUSAN WAS AT HER light table carefully looking through the negatives of her morning shoot, when Barry Eckhouse interrupted her concentration.

"I picked up your prints from the darkroom while I was getting mine," he said.

She sent him a look of gratitude as she took the prints from his outstretched hand. "Finally. I've been waiting for these. Thanks, Barry. I'll hug you later."

"That makes three hundred and seventy-two hugs you owe me."

She knew Barry wasn't really keeping score, nor did he expect to collect. They had been promising each other hugs for years.

He was a good-looking guy who wore the "I'm so bored I'm cool" expression that only he and the guys on the cover of *GQ* seemed able to pull off.

He was also one of her favorite people. Because of his strong urging and recommendation three months before, Greg had promoted Susan to one of the three coveted senior photographer slots. Barry had never said a word about having stood up for her, which was one of the things she liked most about him.

She took a moment to glance at the prints he'd handed to her. "I requested these two days ago. Why is the darkroom always so backed up?"

"Their turnover is worse than a Burger King," he said. "They got another new trainee today. Can't wait to see how long before this one disappears. Speaking of disappearing, have you seen Ellie? I stopped by her cubicle to deliver her prints, but she wasn't there. Matter of fact, I haven't seen her all day."

"She's probably in the coffee room making an espresso."

"Which can only mean she's broken up with her latest loser," Barry said, shaking his head.

Susan concentrated on shifting through the prints, saying nothing.

"Relax, you didn't give anything away. I know that Ellie always hogs the espresso machine for days after one of her lovers screws her over."

She should have known Barry would figure that out. He was smart and observant. When she had first seen Barry looking at Ellie, she'd thought he had a thing for her friend. But however attractive Barry thought Ellie, he was always so negative when he spoke about her that Susan had given up hoping for a romance between them.

"Be nice to Ellie," she told him. "She's going through a rough time."

"She's always going through a rough time," he said, the disgust thick in his voice, "because she always asks for it."

"Of course, you've never made a mistake in the romance department," she said with light sarcasm, knowing perfectly well just how bad a mistake he'd made in the selection of his ex-wife, who everyone at the office called "the psycho."

Not that he wasn't absolutely right about Ellie, of course. But Susan was loyal to a lovelorn friend.

"Not fair," Barry protested. "I was barely twenty-five when the psycho did her number on me. Did I tell you she violated the restraining order her third ex-husband got on her?"

"That the one in Texas?"

"No, Florida. Her second husband filed the restraining order on her in Texas. Anyway, she picked the lock on her third husband's house after he'd gone to work and spray painted everything black. She's a genius at lock-picking. Her old man is still doing time for a decade of breaking-and-entering raps."

"Now, remind me again what awful thing her third ex-husband did to deserve this?" Susan asked.

"He married her, against all my warnings, I might add, just like husband number two. Not that I totally blame them. The psycho's got legs that go on forever and these big blue eyes and full lips—"

"So what you're telling me," she interrupted, not caring to hear any more about his ex-wife's physical attributes, "is that a man doesn't really care if a woman is psychotic as long as she's sexy."

He shrugged. "No one said we were the smarter sex. But I have learned from my mistake, unlike Ellie."

Barry quickly looked around, then leaned closer. "You're her best friend, Susan," he whispered. "I know *you* can spot these losers she keeps getting involved with. Why aren't you setting her straight?"

"Only time I ever tried to set Ellie *straight,* as you call it," she whispered back, "I ended up hurting her feelings, and she didn't talk to me for two months."

"You tried to warn her about that married guy she was mixed up with a few years back, didn't you?" he asked, his face alight with the revelation.

Susan didn't answer. She'd already said more than she should have.

He straightened and resumed his normal tone. "So that's why things were so strained between you two then. And all the time I thought you were fighting over me."

"Don't you wish," she said, smiling. "I'm glad you're concerned about Ellie. Why don't you ask her out?"

"Hell, no," he said with feeling. "I told you. I've learned my lesson."

"Ellie's no psycho."

"Yeah, but she's got another serious problem. Incredibly bad taste in men." With that Barry waved and left.

She knew he was right. Put Ellie in a pitching boat in heavy seas and she could not only instantly determine the precise knots that two dolphins were swimming and how many feet away they were, but also the exact F-stop, shutter speed and fill-in flash required to perfectly capture them on film.

But put Ellie in a room full of eligible men, and her brain would inevitably malfunction and she'd pair up with the worst possible choice.

Susan's thoughts were interrupted when her telephone rang. She picked it up and answered distractedly. "Susan Carter."

"David Knight."

She sat straight up in her chair, every cell in her body vibrating to attention.

"I…uh…" *Oh, that was erudite, Susan. Could you sound any more brain dead?*

"Can you talk?" David asked.

"Apparently not," she said with a small chuckle.

"That wasn't a jab at your verbal skills, Ms. Carter. I was attempting to ascertain if you were in a private place that would enable you to discuss personal matters freely."

He was cordial, but clearly all business. The gentle

warmth that had imbued his voice the night before was nowhere in evidence.

She had thought a lot about David after he left her home, and those thoughts had been disturbing. Her preoccupation with them seemed kind of foolish now, in light of his formal manner. Maybe she'd been so tired after her long day that she'd imagined what she'd seen in his eyes. Maybe she had imagined her response, as well.

"Ms. Carter, did you hear my question?"

"Sorry. My mind was on something else. Just a minute."

The four-foot partitions around her cubicle did nothing to mask conversations. She rose from her chair and stretched so as to camouflage her real reason for getting up, which was to see who was sitting on the other sides. As she had suspected, all around her cubicle were fellow employees frantically clicking their computer keys, getting articles and captions ready for the next issue.

"The answer to your question is, not really," she said into the phone as she sat back down and scooted her chair closer to her desk.

"Probably just as well we meet. I'd like to show you something. Can you be outside the front of your building in five minutes?"

She checked her watch. Four-thirty already? She needed the rest of her contact sheets from the guys in the darkroom. She also needed to select and crop the photos that would have to be printed. "Will this be a quick meeting?"

"Should be. I'll drive by and pick you up. Bring your coat and umbrella. The rain is coming down cold and hard."

Before she could respond, the dial tone blared in her ear. She shook her head as she hung up the phone. David was back to his all-business self, all right.

She was relieved. This was not the time to be getting sidetracked by a man.

Grabbing her shoulder bag, coat and umbrella, she made a dash for the rest room before heading down to the lobby. Exactly five minutes later, his silver truck slid alongside the curb in the front of the building. She used her umbrella as a shield as she dashed for the truck.

He had the passenger door open by the time she got there. She hopped in sideways and pulled the umbrella closed, dropping it to the floor once she was settled on the seat. The moment she'd closed the passenger door and buckled up, the truck was rolling.

"Are you always so punctual?" she asked as she looked over at him.

He wore a brown leather jacket over a silver-blue dress shirt, brown dress slacks, and leather boots polished so brightly she could see the chrome beneath the brake pedal reflected in them.

His eyes remained on the road when he answered. "Promptness is simply a part of keeping one's word."

"What do you say to all the people who accuse you of being too rigid because you live your life by the clock?"

"Probably the same thing you say to such people."

She wasn't surprised that David had surmised she also was a "promptness freak," as so many of her friends liked to call her. Not after all the other things he'd been able to deduce about her.

"Okay, Mr. Detective, tell me what I say to those people."

"You say you'll be somewhere at a particular time, and you are there at that time, because you care about them and wouldn't think of wasting their valuable time by making them wait for you."

She chuckled. "Well, I may not have said that before,

but I'm certainly going to say it from now on. Where are we going?''

''Someplace private where you can look at a picture and answer a few questions.''

The private place proved to be a parking facility located next to a nearby park. The heavy rain had driven away the park's occupants, leaving the garage empty. David selected a space on the upper level with a view of the gray landscape but far enough within the structure's overlapping roof that the rain wouldn't pound on the truck.

As soon as he'd switched off the truck's engine, he reached into the back seat for a manila folder. He opened the folder and drew out the contents.

When he leaned toward Susan to hand her an eight-by-ten inch photograph, she caught the tangy scent of fresh orange coming off his hands.

''Recognize it?'' he asked.

She studied the rows of people facing forward in the photo. Her first impression was that she was looking at a picture of a classroom. Then she noticed some familiar posters on the back wall.

''This is the lecture hall at the community center,'' she said.

He pointed at a face in the third row center. ''That's you.''

He was right. Not exactly a flattering shot, but then, she'd never seen a flattering picture of herself. They always looked too much like her. ''I didn't know they were taking pictures.''

''You're looking at a still frame from the security video.''

''Since when do they have a security camera at the community center?''

''Since some controversial guest speakers drew anonymous death threats a few years back. Do you see Todd?''

She focused her eyes on the far row and pointed. "I'm pretty sure that's the top of his head there. He's the only man with blond hair. The faces that far back are hardly more than shadows, though."

She returned the picture to David. "Will that photo help?"

He replaced the photo in the manila envelope. "Don't know yet. There was a U.S. commercial jet crash about four months ago, but none of the surviving family members had the name of Todd. When he spoke about losing his mother, did he say anything to you that indicated the crash might have happened overseas?"

She shook her head. "He just said a plane crash. Although he did mention something about the bad feelings that followed because of the crash or something to do with the crash."

"What bad feelings?"

"I'd had a few too many Screwdrivers by then to remember his comments clearly. Just something about how unsavory the circumstances surrounding his mother's death had become, and how she didn't deserve to be remembered that way. He was very upset."

"Sounds like her death generated some sort of a scandal. If he was telling the truth."

"What do you mean, 'if he was telling the truth?'"

David looked at her. His facial expression revealed nothing but that relaxed professional calm he wore so well.

"There are men who frequent seminars such as you attended, looking for vulnerable women."

"You think Todd made up the story about his mother so he could win my sympathy and take advantage of me?"

"He was the one who suggested you go for a drink."

"Even so, I can't agree," she said with conviction. "He wasn't like that."

"Men who prey on the weakness of women can be very deceptive."

"Don't let this young-looking face of mine fool you. I'm not an easy mark."

"You were under a great deal of...stress that night."

She stared out the windshield at the park trees being mercilessly battered by the strong wind. "I've been under worse...stress. Right after Paul died, there were a lot of men who made the mistake of thinking that I'd succumb to their sympathetic ministrations, and several of them were Paul's friends. They didn't take me in then. No one takes me in now. I know all the lines. I know all the moves."

"There are new lines and moves cropping up all the time."

"If Todd knew any lines, he didn't use them on me. He barely even spoke until after I did. He made no physical move on me until I kissed him by mistake. I opened my eyes to look at him because I knew from his inexperience that he couldn't be Paul."

"Inexperience?"

"Todd was shy and...clumsy."

"Or maybe just drunk."

"No," she said, shaking her head. "A drunk man may be ineffective because his body won't cooperate. But a shy man's body is fully cooperative. He's just not a very good lover because he lacks confidence and experience with a woman. Todd definitely fell into the second category."

"Don't you think—"

David didn't finish his question. Instead he deliberately looked away from her and out the windshield. She had a strong feeling he still wanted to ask her something. A nerve was twitching at the side of his jaw.

"You said last night that Todd had arrived at the seminar late and had parked his car on a side street because the community center lot was full," he said after a moment.

"That's right," she confirmed.

"Did you get a look at his car when you walked to the bar, or later when you returned to your vehicle?"

"We could have walked right past his car, and I wouldn't have known. He didn't mention what kind of vehicle he drove."

"I'll swing by there after I drop you off and take a closer look," David said as he turned the ignition key and started the truck. "If I remember right, those side streets have restricted parking."

"Does this mean all the questions are over?"

"For now."

He backed the truck out of the space and started out of the parking structure.

"You began to ask me something before and stopped," she said.

"Wasn't anything important."

Despite his denial, she had a strong feeling that he did consider whatever he had failed to ask to be important. Still, if the reason he hadn't asked was because the subject was too sensitive, maybe she shouldn't press.

"I tried to reach you at your office earlier," he said. "They told me you were out on a shoot. You don't carry a cell phone?"

She shook her head. "I understand they become addictive. I don't want to have to go through a twelve-step-program someday."

His lip twitched. "I might need to get ahold of you on short notice. I could use a schedule and location of your shoots."

"Changes all the time. Give me your e-mail, and I'll add you to my computer's address list. That way every time I update, you'll receive the revised schedule."

He slipped a card out of his pocket and handed it to her.

His business card was classy and subtle—very much like him—embossed with the firm's name, his name, address, telephone and e-mail. Up in the corner was the White Knight Investigations' logo—a white chess piece.

She brought the card up to her nose for a closer sniff. Warm from the heat of his body and wonderfully tangy.

"You always sniff business cards?" he asked as he flashed a look in her direction.

"Your hands smell like fresh oranges."

"Things got busy today. Lunch was fresh fruit. Sorry."

"No, I like oranges," she said, turning her head to smile at him. "You smell nice."

Her remark had been casual. His response was not. She stared as the hard lines of his face melted into a smile.

Susan had once wondered what his smile would look like. Now she was sorry she had ever been curious. Whatever had made her think this guy wasn't handsome?

She stuck his business card in her coat pocket and gazed out the window for the rest of the ride, as though the heavy slanting rain had suddenly become fascinating.

A few minutes later, David pulled up in front of the building that housed *True Nature* magazine.

"I'll be in touch," he said.

"Good," she responded as she undid her seat belt. Before she could get out, she felt his hand clasp her forearm. He had touched her before, but each time her irritation with him had insulated her from the effect. She wasn't insulated anymore.

"Don't forget your umbrella," he said.

She nodded her understanding, neither speaking nor looking at him. She didn't trust herself to do either. The instant he released her arm, she grabbed her umbrella and slipped off the seat.

She didn't try to open the umbrella in the driving wind.

She shoved the door closed and made a run for the building. The rain slammed against her face, and she welcomed the cold sting against her warm cheeks.

When she got inside, she shook the rain out of her hair and off her coat, and gave herself a mental shake, as well.

She found David attractive. So what? Probably every female within range of the guy found him attractive. She'd just been slow to realize how handsome he was. Now that she had, well, she could admit she didn't mind feeling like a woman again. Because that's all this reaction was—a reminder that she was still female.

Susan listened hard to that inner voice of wisdom, the one that had prevented her from making so many stupid mistakes in the past. Then she calmly headed toward the elevators to return to work.

JACK KNIGHT SHOOK his head at David's frowning face. "Something about Gabrielle you don't like?"

They were in one of Jack's favorite restaurants. Their dates had just gone to the powder room together, leaving the brothers alone with their after-dinner drinks.

David glanced over at his brother. Jack and his twin, Jared, had inherited their father's blue eyes, their mother's dark hair and a sense of rollicking fun that never seemed to falter from their Uncle Reginald.

David enjoyed spending time with Jack precisely because of his lighthearted approach to life and love. Jack knew how to have a good time. But tonight his brother's high spirits were making David feel at least a decade older, despite the fact that they were separated by only two years.

"Gabrielle's fine," he said.

"You're describing a six-foot blond beauty queen as *fine?*" Jack said, a rising note of disbelief in his voice.

"Okay. She's terrific."

"No, she's perfect," Jack corrected. "She's gorgeous,

not interested in commitment, and she's been hanging all over you. Do you have any idea how envious every guy in this room is of you?''

David leaned back in his chair and stopped fiddling with the drink he hadn't touched. If there had been any envious looks cast his way, he hadn't caught them. That wasn't like him. He normally was very tuned in to what was going on around him. He had trained himself to be. But three simple words had been running through his head all evening, separating him from his surroundings and all the fun he could be having.

*You smell nice.*

Susan hadn't been hanging all over him when she'd said those words. But she had been smiling, and she had meant them.

Even if she had turned away afterward and ignored him for the rest of the drive. Even if she hadn't bothered even to look at him before getting out of the truck or heading back into the building.

She showed absolutely no interest in him. David told himself he was damn glad she didn't.

Gabrielle, on the other hand, was just the kind of woman he wanted to have show interest in him. She'd laughed at his jokes, touched his arm, and brushed her thigh against his as they sat next to each other.

Yet, hearing those three simple words from Susan and seeing her smile when she said them had been more exciting for David than anything Gabrielle had said or done all evening.

He let out a heavy breath. ''I screwed up, Jack. I thought I was ready for this.''

''You are ready for this. I'm not letting you screw it up.''

''I appreciate everything you've done tonight, but—''

''Is it Theresa?'' Jack asked.

"No."

Jack took a swig of his drink. "Well, that's a relief, at least. So what in the hell is getting in the way?"

"I'm... A case I'm working on is getting complicated."

"Work?" Jack shook his head. "And to think I once admired you. I still remember all those babes that were calling you at fourteen, while Jared and I were still searching the bathroom mirror for our first whiskers to come in."

"A lot of years have passed since I was fourteen."

"The last two of your years wouldn't even rate a PG-13."

"Funny, I don't remember talking to you about my sex life," David said a bit stiffly.

"You don't need to talk about it. If you were getting any, I'd see a *real* smile on your face. Hell, I can't remember the last time you smiled. Oh, wait a minute. Yes, I can. Mom and Dad's Christmas party two years ago. Theresa had finally said yes and you two announced you were getting married on the following Valentine's Day."

A startled look came onto Jack's face as he suddenly stiffened in his seat. "Don't tell me it's been *that* long?"

"When I was a practicing psychologist," David said in his deepest and most deprecating tone, "we had a name for guys like you who were always fixated on sex."

"Happy?" Jack said.

David contained his grin. There was no stopping Jack.

Jack leaned across the table toward him. "Now look here. We Knight brothers have a reputation to uphold. As much as it pains me to point this out, you have not been keeping up your end."

"Ah, I see," David said. Of course, what he really saw was Jack's concern and affection for him.

So Susan had smiled at him when she told him he smelled nice. She only meant she liked the fragrance of fresh oranges. He was foolish to be so affected by a passing comment from a client. In view of her situation and his, a client is all she ever could be.

"All right, what the hell," David said, lifting his glass in a salute to his brother. "The last thing I'd ever want to do is tarnish the good name of the Knight brothers."

Jack's smile spread ear to ear as he lifted his glass to David's. "Now you're talking. Here's to all the White Knights. May we forever ride to the rescue of those damsels in need of some serious loving."

Jack and David clinked glasses just as their dates returned.

SUSAN HAD REMOVED the damaged pipes underneath her kitchen sink. She had cleaned off the rust and debris. She had greased the washers. She had slipped the new pipes that she had bought at the hardware store into position and fastened them securely.

And the damn sink was still leaking. She was covered in grease, and she had absolutely nothing to show for the past two hours of labor but a bruised thumb and a sopping wet kitchen floor.

She got up off her knees and threw the do-it-yourself manual in a drawer. She wiped her hands on a paper towel and sank onto a kitchen chair in defeat.

She'd watched Paul repair things dozens of times. She'd carefully read the manual. She should be able to do this. Why couldn't she do this?

*You're so stupid, Susan.*

She flinched as the remembered put-down repeated in her mind. A lot of years had passed before she'd finally stopped believing she was stupid. Even now, in times of stress and weariness, her mother's hurtful words would come back and she would have to remind herself that they were untrue.

She grabbed for the telephone book, found the number

for a local plumber and placed the call. The man promised to be around in an hour.

As she hung up, another one of her mother's favorite mantras replayed in her mind. *A woman's got to have a man around.*

Susan exhaled, deep and hard. Her childhood had been a front-row seat to her mother's die-hard addiction to men. Memories of the incredible assortment of losers her mother had allowed to move in with them still made her shudder.

But she had survived. And even if she couldn't repair a leaking kitchen sink, she could pay for the repairman who would. She didn't *have* to have a man around. She wasn't her mother.

Her thoughts went to the tiny life growing within her womb.

She had promised herself that a child she brought into the world would have two intelligent, loving parents committed to it and each other. That no child of hers would ever be put down, or go through life dreading who would be coming to live with them next, or have to wonder who her father was.

She rested her hand on her tummy. *Well, Sweetie, looks like I already blew the promise of two loving parents right out of the water. But I swear to you, I'm going to make good on the others.*

*You will never be called stupid.*

*You will never have to worry about who lives with us.*

*And you are going to know everything there is to know about your father.*

There was a lot she was unsure of, but of that she was certain. *I'll find out about Todd for you,* David had said. She knew he would do what he promised.

But what would he find? Who was Todd? Would he be the kind of man she could tell about the baby? The kind who would want to play a role in their child's life? The kind *she'd* want to play a role in her child's life?

Susan's eyes rose to her kitchen walls. The doe and her speckled fawn. The bear and her cubs. The hummingbird and her hatchlings. All the female of the species taking care of the young. Alone. No males around.

If those mothers could give their offspring such good care alone, so could she. For if she couldn't provide her baby with a loving, caring, committed father, then she knew her baby would be better off with none at all.

# CHAPTER FIVE

DAVID SAT IN FRONT of the laptop computer on his desk and logged onto the Internet, looking for any news stories on private plane crashes that had occurred in the United States four months before. He found two. One was a downed Aero Commander in Texas. The second was a lost Cessna in Washington State. He figured the local one was a better bet and clicked on it.

The reference was from a small community newspaper. The news brief was without a byline and simply said that a Cessna Skyhawk had been reported missing near the Olympic Mountains the day before. A search team had been dispatched.

He looked for the follow-up story. Curiously, there was none. The National Transportation Safety Board often took months to investigate a crash before handing down a ruling as to the cause. But finding no further information on the plane that had gone down, who had been on board, and if there had been any survivors seemed a bit unusual.

He picked up the phone and dialed the news desk of the local newspaper.

*"Silver Valley Sun,"* the gravelly voice answered on the first ring.

"Any newspaper in western Washington that's loony enough to put *Sun* in its title better figure on lining a cuckoo clock cage," David said, immediately recognizing Lew Sargentich's voice.

"Yeah, and any private investigation firm that has the

balls to call itself White Knight better be packing a good sense of humor as well as some seriously loaded guns,'' Lew countered.

David had known Lew since they were sophomores in high school. David had been Lew's best man and was godfather to his three kids. After the two longtime friends had finished several more rounds of their insults, David got down to business.

"I've come across something that's puzzling me, Lew. There was a report of a private plane being lost near the Olympics about four months ago. Couldn't find a followup. Ring any bells?''

"Not even a tinkle. How'd you hear about it?''

"Small community newspaper south of us ran a news brief. Said a search party was dispatched.''

"No paper would have run even a news brief without some kind of confirmation on the source.''

"Am I right that the county's Sheriff's Department would have been the ones to organize a search on the western side of the Hood Canal?''

"That would be protocol,'' Lew confirmed. "When a sheriff's rescue team gets dispatched, the reporter on the beat generally goes along. Doesn't seem logical for him not to have done a follow-up. Plane crashes always make the national news because the NTSB has to get involved. Wire services should've picked the story up, as well.''

"Some reason why they wouldn't?''

"Not a one I can think of. This *is* a puzzle. Let me make a few calls. I'll get back to you.''

David had just thanked his friend and hung up the phone when the intercom buzzed. He depressed the key. "Yes, Harry?''

"Sir, a messenger from the community center's security team has just dropped off those still photographs from the surveillance tapes you requested. Shall I bring them in?''

"Please do."

A moment later a perfunctory knock sounded on David's office door. Harry Gorman opened the door and entered the room holding a thick green envelope.

Harry was pushing sixty and had a hard wiry body, a broad, blunt face and bright black eyes. His once dark hair hadn't just retreated; it had surrendered. He marched up to David's desk and presented the folder of information as though he had just returned from a reconnaissance mission and was handing over the confidential report to his superior officer.

Actually, Harry had been a career army enlisted man before joining White Knight Investigations five years before. But the only duty he'd ever seen was from behind a clerk's desk. Harry took care of the firm's bookkeeping, kept appointments straight and answered the busy phones with the precision of a military strategist.

David took the envelope he held out. Harry snapped his heels and maintained his at-attention stance, eyes forward, waiting for the next command.

When David had joined his parents' investigation firm, he'd tried to loosen Harry up. He'd failed. Harry's formal bearing proved to be his comfort zone. Now David knew enough to just let the man call him "sir" and stand at attention to his heart's content.

The envelope was hefty. David thanked the clerk and dismissed him. Harry pivoted one-hundred-and-eighty degrees on left toe and right heel and marched out of the office, closing the door behind him.

Before opening the envelope and looking over the contents, David took a moment to compose an e-mail to the newspaper in the small Texas town where the other private plane crash had been reported. He asked the reporter on record for some specific details.

As he hit the send button, he wondered how his mother

and father had run their investigation firm all those years without the Internet. He could just imagine the days spent in the library poring over newspapers, not to mention the long-distance phone bills and worn-out tread on both shoes and vehicles. That wasn't a time he would have wanted to be a private investigator.

Of course, there was a lot of the grunt work still left. Especially since David's specialty was missing persons. But he knew how to ease that load.

The personality profile he developed on the missing person in each one of his cases usually cleared the path to finding them. Once he knew about the individual he was looking for, knowing where to look became a far simpler task.

Trouble was, he still didn't know what kind of person Todd was. He could be a slick opportunist preying on women's vulnerabilities. Or he could be the shy, clumsy fellow griever that Susan had described.

David was still inclined to go with the former. What Susan wanted to interpret as clumsy could just as easily have been the guy's uncontrolled excitement at having her in his arms.

He'd come close to suggesting that possibility. He'd stopped because he'd realized that would have been the wrong thing to say.

Susan wanted to believe this Todd was some shy, sympathetic stranger. She was a smart, careful woman who still had a hard time accepting her uncharacteristic actions on that night. Choosing to see Todd the way she did was probably an important part of her ability to cope. David didn't want to make her feel any worse than she already did.

No one liked falling for a fantasy and finding out later it had all been a facade. On that subject, he had some painful, personal experience from which to draw.

He opened the envelope the security team at the community center had sent over and took out the photographs.

Earlier he'd enlarged the fuzzy picture of the man Susan had identified as Todd. But even with all the subsequent computer enhancements, the face had remained blurry. He compared the photo now to the batch of video stills.

Andy, the head of the security team at the community center, had been happy to help. When David was a practicing psychologist, he'd helped Andy and his wife through a tough time in their marriage. Andy hadn't forgotten.

David had learned from Andy that the center had sponsored several other seminars in the past six months that might have attracted vulnerable females—and an opportunistic male ready to take advantage of them. If anybody looking like Todd had attended one of those seminars, David wanted to know.

He spent the next hour and a half studying the hundreds of faces on those security video stills. When he got to the last one, he was still unable to pick Todd out of any of the attendees. Which told him that either Todd had attended only the bereavement seminar, or the photograph of his face was too blurry to make a match.

The laptop computer let out a distinctive *beep*.

He set down the stack of photographs that he'd been studying and swung his chair toward the computer, then hit the keys to display his new e-mail. The reporter in Texas was responding to the message sent to him earlier. David quickly scanned the reply.

The two killed in the private plane crash were male, both locals. No women on the plane. Neither victim left a family member by the name of Todd.

He wasn't surprised his inquiry had resulted in a dead end. Still, being thorough was important. Identifying the roads that led nowhere was a necessary part of staying on the right path. He positioned his mouse on the reply button and typed in his thank-you.

As he was gathering up the community center stills, his computer beeped again. He glanced over at the screen and saw that the message was from Susan. Dropping the photographs, he swung his chair in front of the computer to open the e-mail.

She'd sent him a listing of the times, locations and subjects of her shoots for the rest of the week. No personal message. A brief glance at the header told David that his address was not among those employees at the magazine listed as recipients of her schedule. She must have added his e-mail address as a blind carbon copy.

She'd handled the matter both discreetly and professionally.

He leaned back in his chair, picked up the enlarged picture he'd made of her from the seminar. The print was grainy and slightly out of focus, but he could see a sadness on her face that he'd never seen in person, even when she'd talked of her dead husband. She masked her emotions well. He wondered why she thought she had to. What had happened to make her such a private person?

He had no good excuse for having enlarged her picture. She wasn't the one he was trying to find. He had no good excuse for a lot of things he'd been doing lately.

Last night Gabrielle had stared meaningfully into his eyes. She'd invited him to come in for a nightcap. She'd let her breath blow across his cheek while she put her key into the door lock. No man with even a drop of red blood in his veins should have been able to turn her down.

And yet David had.

She'd told him to call her if he changed his mind. He knew that wasn't going to happen. Being with her should have been so simple. Two, free, consenting adults giving and taking pleasure from each other, no strings attached. But he hadn't felt right being with her. And he didn't know why.

He found his eyes being drawn back to the photograph of Susan. The hidden security camera had caught that rare, vulnerable look on her features. Was that what Todd had seen that night, as well? Was his getting up to leave at the same time just coincidence? Or had he been watching her, waiting to make his move so he would deliberately collide with her?

David was still staring at her photo when the telephone rang. He saw the light flashing on his private line, the one that didn't get screened by Harry. He reached for the phone and answered with his name.

"You ready for that info?" Jared's voice asked.

Jared, Jack's twin, was the only one of the four Knight brothers who wasn't working at the firm. Jared was a deputy in the detective unit of the county's Sheriff's Department. His job came in handy for the rest of them.

David grabbed a pen and a pad. "Shoot."

"There were two cars ticketed for overnight parking on the streets boarding the community center on that Friday night you asked about," Jared said. "One was a 1994 black Ford Ranger registered to Jeffrey Alfred Wald of Silver Valley. The other was a 2002 beige BMW registered to Vance Todaro Tishman of Falls Island."

David recorded the names. "When were they ticketed?"

"The BMW at midnight. The Ford a few minutes later. Those side streets are posted No Parking from ten at night to six the next morning. The Ford is a frequent offender. Owner drinks too much at the local watering hole. But at least he has enough sense to take a cab home. You on anything hot, David?"

"Not in the criminal sense. This should be a routine missing person case."

"Your *routine* missing person cases have a tendency to take interesting twists," Jared said. "Not that I'm complaining. You've handed me three solid busts over the past couple of years. Keep 'em coming."

"Always glad to help out with your career."

"Speaking of helping out, I hear Jack set you up with Gabrielle last night. I'm envious as hell. She was voted the sexiest soap opera actress a couple of years ago. So, is she as good as she looks?"

"You know I don't kiss and tell."

"That's a damn shame," Jared said. "Sometimes the telling can be as much fun as the doing."

"If that's true for you, then all I can say is you haven't been doing it right."

Jared laughed and signed off.

David hung up. Neither of his fun-loving twin brothers had ever dated the same woman regularly nor did they seem inclined to. He had a hard time picturing either of them giving up his wild single life.

David had never been one to engage in all that. Even as a young adult, he was more interested in pursuing a good education, getting established in his profession and finding the woman with whom he'd spend his life.

However, now that he'd taken his shot at commitment and missed, he could see that steering clear from emotional entanglements did make things a damn sight easier. Maybe his younger brothers had the right idea, after all.

The private line on his desk rang again. He answered with his name.

"I'll meet you at Chez Bistro in fifteen minutes," Lew said. "You're buying me lunch."

David checked his watch. "At eleven o'clock? Why am I buying you lunch this early at the most trendy place in town?"

When Lew answered, his voice suddenly sounded muffled, as though he had cuffed the phone with his hand so as not to be overheard on his end. "Because what I'm going to tell you is worth a lot more than the most expensive item on the menu."

"I'D LIKE THE ASSIGNMENT," Susan said.

Greg Hall looked at her with his shrewd, deep-set brown eyes. Her editor was short, fifty, with a cloud of curly gray hair on his head, a paunch around his middle and an expression on his face that said he was nobody's fool.

"Tremont is our specialist on sea life," Greg said. "The assignment should be hers. Where in the hell is Tremont?"

Greg's eyes scanned the faces of his senior staff, seated around his desk. His eyes came to rest on the one empty chair.

"Ellie had an appointment," Susan said quickly. "I'll take the assignment. I can leave from home first thing in the morning. I have nothing else scheduled."

Out of the corner of her eye, she could see the disapproving shake of Barry's head. He knew she was covering for Ellie again. He probably figured the reason had to have something to do with Ellie's love life hitting another speed bump.

"No offense, Carter," Greg said, "but the last time I sent you in Tremont's place, you got seasick and threw up all over the tugboat."

"The Sound was rough as hell that day," Susan said, which was true, even if the real reason she had thrown up had been from the morning sickness that had seemed to last that entire day.

"Which is why Tremont should go," Greg said. "She's got sea legs."

"Even Ellie would have gotten sick on that trip," Susan protested. "The tugboat operator was blowing cigar smoke in my face the entire time. Besides, I still got the pictures. You even slated one of them for the next issue.''

Greg frowned at her, but she knew she had him. Her boss had been a two-packs-a-day man until nine months ago when he'd been hit by a heart attack. He had literally taken the warning to heart and quit smoking cold turkey. He was the first one to admit he never looked or felt better. Now there was no bigger antismoker than Greg.

''Okay, Carter,'' he said. ''The assignment's yours. But for everyone's sake, take along a breathing mask and some Dramamine. I don't want that idiot tugboat operator sending us another cleaning bill.''

''Thanks, Greg,'' she said, trying to imbue her voice with some animation.

In truth, she was looking forward to another rocking boat trip with about as much enthusiasm as she was looking forward to her next gynecological exam. But she didn't want Ellie to get in trouble for missing the assignment meeting.

Susan couldn't help but be worried about her friend. Ellie had gotten her stuff out of Martin's apartment and had moved back into her own place. But she hadn't been very chipper over the past few days.

She hoped to hell Ellie hadn't missed the meeting because she'd gone to see Martin. The last thing her friend needed was to forgive the louse.

The senior-staff assignment meetings always came at the end of the workday. When Susan left her boss's office and headed toward Ellie's cubicle, the clock on the wall read forty minutes past quitting time. The deserted desks and chairs showed everyone else had left for the day.

She wanted to leave Ellie a note to let her know she was taking the assignment the next morning in case she came back to her desk. She also wanted to invite her for dinner on the weekend. What Ellie needed right now was company.

But as soon as Susan turned the corner of Ellie's partition, she could see that a note would not be necessary. Nor did Ellie need her company.

Ellie's arms were securely wrapped around the waist of a tall, slender guy with short reddish-brown hair. From the way his head was bent and her hands were clutching his back, Susan had no doubt that the kiss they were sharing was hot. She didn't recognize the guy from the back. But she knew he wasn't Martin.

And for that, she was thankful.

She leaned against the edge of the partition, folded her arms across her chest and smiled. "Am I interrupting anything?"

The kiss ended, and the guy turned, revealing his young face and Ellie's red one. Susan recognized him now. He was the new assistant in the darkroom, probably a dozen years Ellie's junior. Not that he seemed bothered by that fact or the fact that he'd been caught kissing Ellie. On the contrary. He wore a cocky expression. Ellie, however, was clearly embarrassed.

"The meeting's over?" she asked quite unnecessarily, grabbing for some tissue to wipe her smeared lipstick. She handed a piece of tissue to the darkroom assistant, who was currently wearing more of that lipstick than she was.

"Yeah, the meeting's over," Susan said as she stepped into the cubicle and addressed the young man. "Hi, I'm Susan Carter."

"Skip Dunn," he said, still grinning as he worked to get the red streaks off his face.

"Skip was just…uh…" Ellie faltered.

"Leaving," Skip finished for her. But before he did, he turned back to Ellie and gave her a quick, hard kiss. He was whistling as he passed Susan on the way out of the cubicle.

Once he had gone, Susan turned back to Ellie. She tried to make her voice sound serious. "I hope you checked his ID. I'd hate to have to bail you out of jail for contributing to the delinquency of a minor."

Ellie fell into her chair as though her knees were too weak to hold her up. "You know perfectly well that the company doesn't hire minors. Besides, Skip told me he's twenty-one."

"Well, at least he's tall enough to get on the scary rides at the amusement park," Susan said, enjoying the opportunity to rib her friend.

Ellie sent her a warning look

"Okay, I'll stop. When did this all start?"

"This morning. I stopped by the darkroom to get some prints, he told me to come in while he got them, he barely touched my hand, and suddenly we were in each other's arms. Susan, he's so hot!"

And a light-year away from the kind of guy Ellie kept saying she wanted—a mature man who was ready to settle down and have those half dozen kids Ellie had already named. Once again, she'd chosen wrong.

Still, Susan liked seeing the happy glow on Ellie's face. Could be a new, uncomplicated love affair was just what her friend needed to get over her old heartache.

"So, tell me about Mr. Hot," she said.

"I don't care that he's younger. I don't care that he's making minimum wage. I don't care that we probably don't have a thing in common. When he touches me, I don't care about anything except the fact that I want him to keep touching me. I don't know what's gotten into me."

"Lust," Susan said, quite amused and just a mite envious. She rested a hip against Ellie's desk.

Ellie flashed her a grin. "I'm sorry about missing the

meeting. Skip dropped by my cubicle with some prints, and I just couldn't tear myself away.''

''Yeah, I could see that.''

Ellie chuckled as she leaned back in her chair. ''Anything happen I need to know about?''

''That orphaned baby seal they rescued off the beach last November is now hale and hardy and scheduled to be released early tomorrow morning, if you're interested. Or will you and Skip be up too late tonight?''

Ellie rubbed a hand through her mussed black curls. ''I won't be able to see Skip tonight. He's staying at home to attend his twelve-year-old sister's birthday party— Okay, I know what you're thinking. He's just a baby.''

''From what I saw, I'm thinking he's no baby,'' Susan said.

''Damn, you're good for me. Have I ever told you how great you are?''

''Right back at you, El. So, you want the baby seal story?''

''Definitely. I haven't taken a decent photo all week. Time I started pulling my weight around here.''

Susan tore off the sheet with the place and time from her notepad. She handed the information to Ellie. ''See you Monday,'' she said as she headed out of the cubicle.

She was relieved not to have to be covering the shoot, and to see Ellie enthusiastic about work again. Could be Ellie's sudden attraction to Skip would turn out to be a positive thing. A little lust could do a gal good. If only Ellie didn't try to complicate things by expecting Skip to be something he wasn't.

Susan put thoughts of her friend aside as she contemplated heading home and spending a relaxing evening and weekend with Honey. Since she'd found out she was pregnant, she'd searched the Internet for helpful information. But there was still so much she didn't know. A large bookstore was in the mall. On the way home, she'd stop in to see what they had. Time she did some serious reading on the subject. Today marked her seventh week.

She put her hand on her tummy and smiled. *In a little over seven months, sweetie, you are going to make your entrance into this old world. I still can't quite get my mind around it. But don't you worry. I'm not one of those people who puts things off to the last minute. I'll be prepared for you.*

She was so preoccupied with her internal monologue that when she turned into her cubicle and saw David sitting there, she gave a start, knocking over the sign on her wall. But whether her sudden clumsiness and racing heart was from surprise or pleasure at seeing him, she wasn't sure.

"Sorry to startle you," he said as he stood. He stooped to pick up the sign she'd knocked down.

"'Susan Carter. Someday My Prints Will Come!'" he read aloud. "Cute."

As he positioned the sign back on her wall, she found herself focusing on his hands. She remembered the warmth that had rushed through her body when he'd touched her.

*A little lust could do a gal good.*

Susan heard the replay of her earlier thought with considerable alarm. This might be a good time for Ellie to be engaging in a little lust. But not for her.

"What brings you by?" she asked with a casualness she did not feel.

"I left several messages on your voice mail," he said, turning to face her. "I became concerned when you didn't respond."

"Sorry, I haven't checked my messages. I've been in meetings most of the day. Has something happened?"

"I believe I've found out who Todd is. I need you to look at something. Do you have anything pressing now?"

She checked her watch as she laid her notebook on her

desk. So much for her plans of a nice, relaxing evening. Still, she'd give up those plans gladly to have this matter resolved.

She reached for her shoulder bag. "I just have to get home and feed Honey."

"Then, we'll go there first," David said, as he lifted her coat off the coatrack and held it open for her.

They ran into Greg at the elevators. She introduced David as a friend, thankful she hadn't met up with Ellie. Susan and Greg didn't share the kind of relationship that generated questions about their personal lives. Ellie, on the other hand, immediately would have expected an unabridged history on David.

As Susan drove home, she watched the headlights of David's truck following behind her in the dwindling light. She was normally aware of the cars and drivers around her. Such considerations had become second nature to her long ago. But tonight, she wasn't concerned about being a woman driving home alone. Because David was behind her. Kind of a nice feeling.

By the time she had parked her car in the garage, he was waiting for her at the front door.

Honey greeted them both with his typical happy exuberance. When Susan went into the kitchen to get Honey's dinner, David followed her. There was an assumption and familiarity to the action that normally would have bothered her.

But his presence didn't bother her. She wondered if that was because they'd shared a meal in this kitchen. Or because after that meal, she had told him so many personal things. Or because he had accepted those things with such understanding.

"What I need to show you is at my office. We'll stop for a bite to eat on our way. Do you need to walk Honey first?"

She leaned down to pet him. "No. I'll leave his doggie door out to the backyard unlocked. Not that he's going to be too thrilled when he realizes I'm leaving him. He looks forward to our evenings together. We won't be out too late?"

"We shouldn't be."

Although Susan seldom dined out, she had lived in the vicinity of Silver Valley all her life and was pretty certain she'd eaten at all the restaurants. But David drove to a part of the city she'd never been to, and parked on a street surrounded by warehouses. The entrance to the restaurant was off an alley. No sign adorned the door.

"What's this restaurant called?" she asked.

"Meli's," he said, pulling open the door and moving aside for her to enter.

Once inside, she was pleasantly surprised to see the pastel flowered wallpaper and the creamy tile floor. The room was bright, not at all like the dark, subdued atmosphere of most restaurants. Diners dressed in casual clothes occupied the dozen or so tables. The smells drifting through the air were heavenly.

"David, good to see you." The man who greeted them was short, in his sixties, with a long nose, a mass of gray hair and cheery brown eyes that skipped from David to Susan. His eyes crinkled at the corners.

"Mort, this is Susan Carter," David said, as he helped her off with her coat.

Mort bowed his head toward her. "Delighted to meet you. David hasn't brought a lovely lady with him in a long time. Come this way."

Mort led them through the crowded room to a private corner and settled them at a small table for two, draped with a plain white cotton tablecloth. Then he was off.

"There are no menus here," David said. "Mort will

serve us whatever his wife, Meli, has prepared for this evening.''

"What about beverages?''

"Water, coffee, tea, milk. Mort will ask you which you prefer when he returns with the food.''

She looked over at the other tables in the room. All were close together, occupied by either couples or families chatting away. The atmosphere was bright, warm and inviting.

"This seems more like someone's extended family all having dinner together than a restaurant,'' she said. "If you don't like the food on a particular night, do Mort and Meli scold you for not cleaning your plate?''

"Don't know of anyone who's ever left anything but a clean plate.''

"How did you find this place?''

"Mort and Meli are friends of my folks. When their seven kids left home to make their way in the world, Meli found she didn't know how to cook for just two people. They decided to open this little restaurant three years ago.''

"They appear to have a hit,'' she said, once again eyeing the full tables.

"They don't have to advertise. From six-to-nine, six nights a week, the twelve tables in here are filled. Normally, you have to reserve several weeks in advance.''

"You made tonight's reservation that long ago?''

"I eat here every Friday.''

And Mort had said he hadn't brought a ''lovely lady'' with him in a long time. She had already surmised that David worked a lot of evenings, if his meeting with her on two nights were any example. Was he seeing someone? Had he ever been married?

*Forget it, Susan. You have enough things to be thinking about. You don't need to be thinking about a man. Especially not this one.*

"What do you want to show me in your office?" she asked.

"Let's wait until we're there."

Mort arrived with the food, two steaming plates full of a wonderful smelling stew. He scooted away and returned a moment later with a small, freshly baked loaf of bread and butter. She asked for a glass of milk and David ordered coffee.

She found the stew full of savory cooked vegetables and tender meat. The gravy was rich with fragrant spices like nothing she had ever tasted. She was full after finishing the stew, but couldn't resist breaking off a small piece of the bread for a taste. It melted in her mouth. No wonder David said that people who ate here only left a clean plate.

When Mort returned after they were finished, she looked up at him. "Your wife is a marvelous cook. Please tell her for me. Also tell her that if she ever decides to publish a cookbook, I'll be her first sale."

Mort beamed. "Would you like her recipe for the stew?"

"Just tell me who I have to kill," she said.

"I like your Susan," Mort said as he turned to David. Then he leaned down toward David's ear as though to impart a confidence, despite the fact that his voice was hardly a *sotto voce* whisper. "Even better than the other one."

When Mort had left the table to return to the kitchen, she found herself unable to resist teasing. "The other one?"

David sipped his coffee. "Someone I brought here a long time ago."

The change in his voice and the deepening of the lines around his mouth suddenly put her in mind of what he had said to her when he came to her home a couple of nights before. Something about understanding how hard losing a loved one could be.

Had David lost the woman he loved? Was she the woman he had brought to this restaurant?

She wanted to ask him, but she did not. Answering the questions he'd asked of her had been difficult, even when his voice had been gentle. She'd only cooperated because he'd said the answers could help him with her case.

Any questions she asked of him would be prying. She doubted he'd answer them, anyway. Were she in his position, she wouldn't.

She liked him more each time they were together. But theirs was a professional relationship. As he had said on the first day they met, he would be in and out of her life in as short a time as possible.

She sat back, finished her milk and silently vowed to leave the subject of his personal life strictly alone.

"Dinner was great," she said. "Thanks."

He studied the inside of his coffee cup as though he were reading an engrossing message. "Not a problem."

Yet she could see that he continued to have a problem accepting thanks from her. Why?

Mort returned and handed Susan a four-by-six inch card with the recipe for the stew. She stood and gave him a hug.

"Bring this one back, David," Mort said, beaming at them both.

"See you next week," David said, as he handed Mort the money to pay for their dinner.

They were in David's truck and on their way to his office before he spoke again.

"You'll have to excuse Mort for assuming we were a couple. He can't help himself. He's a romantic."

She sighed dramatically. "Now my reputation has been ruined because I was seen eating dinner with you."

The corner of his lip lifted. "I was going to give you the restaurant's number until that remark."

"Too late," she said, smiling. "Mort put their number on the back of the recipe card. But don't worry. I won't show up on a Friday night."

"Some reason you feel the need to assure me of that?"

"You once told me I was a very private person," she said. "I could say the same about you. I very much doubt you would appreciate a former client showing up at a special restaurant where you choose to eat every Friday night."

He was quiet for a moment, concentrating on his driving. "None of us is ever exactly what we seem."

"Oh, I think you probably come close."

"Close to what?"

His question surprised her. Was he really interested in her personal opinion? Or was this simply his way of challenging her assumption that she could read him as well as he could read her?

She studied his profile, lit only by the truck's instrument panel and the occasional streetlights. The subdued illumination gave his strong features an even more unapproachable look.

Still, she remembered the concern he had shown for her at Camp Long. How nice he had been to Honey. The gentle way he had listened to her the other night. How his face changed when even a small smile lifted his lips.

She decided to take the challenge.

"I think you are exceptionally strong-willed, precise, sure, self-sufficient, intelligent and intense," she began. "You've never done anything halfway in your life. You get results because you demand absolute perfection from yourself. And yet..."

She stopped because she suddenly realized she was letting herself get carried away.

''And yet?'' he prompted.

She was glad he was inviting her to go on. She wanted to tell him this. ''And yet you can be very understanding of other people's failings.''

''What makes you think that?''

''Because of how understanding you have been of mine.''

He swung the truck into the parking lot of his office building and switched off the engine. He didn't get out. Instead he swiveled to face her.

''Even if you weren't my client, I would have to be a pretty callous person not to have sympathy for your situation.''

She was amused at this equivocation and the fact that her compliment was making him ill at ease. Despite his carefully projected calm, his left hand was gripping the steering wheel.

''No, you're not callous at all,'' she said smiling. ''You're actually quite considerate and kind. But you needn't worry, David Knight. I won't tell anyone. Girl Scout's honor.''

She held up some fingers.

''That's not the Girl Scout sign.''

She laughed as she dropped her hand to unfasten her seat belt. ''You damn Eagle Scouts know everything. What do you want to show me in your office?''

''First, I need to tell you the curious story of a missing plane.''

# CHAPTER SIX

DAVID SWITCHED ON his office light and moved aside for Susan to enter the room. The delicate scent of her drifted to him as she passed. He vividly remembered the last time she'd been in this office.

He'd behaved unprofessionally that morning. He thought he'd overcome that problem, but he had acted just as unprofessionally tonight when he'd sought her assessment of him.

She'd been surprisingly accurate about several of his personality traits. However, the moment she'd called him "understanding," and he heard the appreciation in her voice, he knew he'd made a mistake. When she had added "considerate" and "kind," the implications became more serious. He had no idea that such simple words could carry such emotional impact.

David dragged a guest chair closer to his desk. "Four months ago, a pilot of a Cessna 150 was returning to his hometown airfield when a Skyhawk nearly collided with him."

"These are private planes?" she asked as she took the offered chair.

"Manufactured by the Cessna Company. The 150 is an older, two-seater model. The Skyhawk is newer, seats six."

"Why were the planes so close to each other?"

"They were flying over the Hood Canal, going in opposite directions. The pilot of the 150 banked to the right to follow the water. The Skyhawk didn't make a similar adjustment. It came right at the 150.''

David paused as he circled his desk and sat down to face her. ''When the pilot of the 150 veered to get out of the way, he got a quick look into the other plane's cockpit. The Skyhawk's pilot was slumped over the controls.''

''Passed out?''

''Appeared that way to the pilot of the 150. He immediately placed a distress call. The weather was turning bad and he was low on fuel, so he had no option but to head back to the airfield.''

''What happened to the Skyhawk?''

''Disappeared into a cloud bank. A search and rescue team was dispatched. Several days later they spotted the wreckage of the plane in a deep ravine within the Olympic Mountain Range. Officials of the county's Sheriff's Department rappelled from helicopters and recovered the three bodies inside—the pilot and two passengers.''

He was giving her a lot of details because he wanted to draw as clear a picture as possible of the events. Being able to visualize them would help her to make more sense out of what was to come.

''I don't remember hearing anything about this plane crash on the news,'' she said.

''It didn't make the news.''

''Don't all plane crashes automatically get written up in the paper?''

''They should. Unless someone with a lot of power exerts the right kind of pressure to prevent them from making the news.''

''You're saying that's what happened in this case,'' she guessed. ''Who would have that much power?''

''The pilot of the 150 radioed in the identification number on the Skyhawk. The plane's registered owner was Lucy Norton, co-owner of Norton's Aviation Academy, a small business located in a county south of here. When the sheriff's office contacted the company, Lucy Norton's husband verified that his wife had taken up the plane a half hour before, with two passengers, Steve Kemp and Molly Ardmore Tishman.''

David paused for a moment to see if she would recognize the name. The expression on her face told him she didn't.

"Molly Ardmore Tishman is—was—Robert Ardmore's only child,'' he explained.

"Robert Ardmore, the billionaire industrialist?'' she asked. "Are you saying Ardmore prevented the news of his daughter's death in a plane crash from reaching the media?''

David nodded.

"But how could even a prominent man like Ardmore keep his daughter's death a secret?''

"Her death was recorded quietly, as was Steve Kemp's and Lucy Norton's, all proper and legal. None of the facts got into the news, however. The cause for each death was shown simply as 'accident.'''

"I don't understand why anyone would want to keep an airplane accident quiet.''

"The crash might not have been an accident.''

Susan came forward in her chair. "What do you mean?''

"The cause still hasn't been determined by the NTSB. Even when they know, the results will be quietly recorded and filed away, thanks to Ardmore's considerable money and influence. But a student that had taken flying lessons from Lucy Norton said she was a lush and often took a flask along with her when she went up in a plane.''

Susan took a moment to digest the news. Her expression was thoughtful, almost sad. "Will the people who investigate be able to determine if Lucy Norton was at fault?''

"If they recovered enough of her body. That information wasn't available."

"How did you find out about the rest?"

"I have a friend on the inside."

"On the inside, meaning someone who knows Robert Ardmore."

"No, a reporter who knows several of the people Ardmore paid off to keep this out of the news."

David had been carefully giving her this information one piece at a time. He waited until she asked the question he'd been leading her to.

"Are you saying Todd's mother was on this plane?"

"Only you can say for certain."

"How can I do that?"

He opened his desk drawer and drew out the blown-up driver's license photo Jared had faxed to him earlier. He rose from his chair and circled the desk until he stood beside Susan. He set the photo on the desk in front of her.

"Recognize him?" he asked.

She picked up the picture. "It's Todd."

David had been ninety-nine percent certain it would be.

"Now I understand why he was so unhappy about the way she would be remembered," Susan said. "If she were drinking that day, she might have caused her own death and the death of two others. Lucy Norton was Todd's mother."

"No," David corrected. "Molly Ardmore Tishman was his mother."

Susan's eyes shot to David's. "What?"

"That's a copy of the driver's license photo of Vance Todaro Tishman of 2100 Crest View Lane, Falls Island. His car was ticketed for overnight parking on a side street adjacent to the community center on the night of the seminar you attended."

"But his name's not Todd."

"Either he lied to you about his first name, or he goes by the name of Todd. I haven't had a chance to discover which."

"Wait a minute. If Molly Ardmore Tishman is his mother, then Todd's…"

"The grandson of Robert Ardmore," David finished when Susan's voice faltered.

She sat back in her chair, stared straight ahead and slowly shook her head. "This is very hard to believe."

"In what way?"

"If Todd is the grandson of a billionaire, what was he doing at a bereavement seminar at a local community center?"

"You mean, why wasn't he seeing a private psychologist to help him deal with the death of a loved one?"

She nodded.

"Why weren't you?"

"Like I said before, I thought I could handle it."

"Until your dreams of Paul made you show up at the seminar at the community center that night. Where you didn't have to give your name and could be just an anonymous face in the crowd. Where if you failed at whatever task they set for you, no one would know."

Her eyes rose to his. "You do realize that your uncanny assessment of human nature can be very disturbing at times."

"I never want to make you feel uncomfortable."

The small nod of her head told David she believed him. "Do you think that Todd attended the seminar for the same reason I did?"

"Hard to tell without knowing him."

"I'd like to find out," she said. "I'd like to know everything I can about him. How will you go about getting the information?"

"The easiest way would be to approach Todd directly."

"No, please don't do that. I don't want him to know about the baby."

"You're going to have the baby?" David asked, although he'd known the answer the moment he'd seen the pictures on her kitchen walls.

She nodded.

"Will you ever tell Todd?"

"Only if that would be good for the baby."

"How do you mean?"

She looked away from him to gaze out the window at the soft blackness of the night, but what she was really seeing came from within. The intensity of that inner focus captured his attention.

"Paul was thirty-three when he asked me to marry him. He was steady, settled, ready to become a husband and father. Still, I persuaded him that we should be engaged for a full year before getting married. Then I convinced him we should wait another two years before starting a family. I wanted to be sure that our love would last. I *had* to be sure."

David could guess why. "For the sake of the children you would have."

She nodded. "Children have a much better chance with two loving, committed parents they can count on. But both parents have to feel that way. If not, the child is better off without them."

"So, you'll only tell Todd about the baby if he turns out to be the kind of man who will be a loving, committed father."

"That's why I have to know everything I can about him."

David understood. What she told him also explained why Susan hadn't had any children with her husband. Paul Carter had died fourteen months into their marriage.

Nearly three years ago. And she still dreamed of him.

Was it because she had never allowed herself to fully mourn him while she was awake? Would she ever be over him?

David reminded himself that wasn't his concern.

"Time I drove you home," he said.

She rose and stood before him, looking directly into his eyes. "You'll find out about Todd?"

She was so lovely. But all he could do was the job she'd hired him for.

"Starting bright and early tomorrow morning," he promised.

"May I come along?"

Her request startled him. "Private investigation can be long and tedious work."

"So can nature photography. Still, the one good shot you have a chance to get is always worth all the effort."

"I don't think—"

"The alternative is I stay at home unable to focus on anything else. Now that I know who Todd is, I have to know what kind of man he is. What do you say?"

"All right" was what he said, because standing so close to her he found saying anything else impossible.

But the moment the words were out of his mouth, he knew he had made another mistake.

PAUL HELD SUSAN'S HAND as they walked down the aisle lined with automobiles. She hadn't been that thrilled about coming to the Antique Car Show. Cars were not her thing. But Paul just loved this stuff. He had insisted they do the tour before the doors were officially opened. She agreed because she knew his instructing her on the background and features of all the makes and models would give him pleasure.

"Now there's a '32 Auburn Model 8-100A," he said.

As far as she was concerned, the car could have been

any one of the hundred old models sitting on pedestals in this auditorium. But she tried to look impressed.

"In 1932 Auburn offered two different motors," he went on as he released her hand to examine the car. "A straight-8 carried over and an all new V-12 like this one," he said, pointing to the blue bumper. "The street value on this baby is one hundred and twenty thousand dollars."

"Doesn't appear to have a heater," she said, wondering what would possess someone to pay that much money for such an impractical car.

"Hey, I didn't know they'd have one of these here," he said, whirling around and hurrying to the next car on display. "Now this is a '41 Cadillac convertible Series 62. Isn't that egg-crate grill amazing? Just look at those classic lines. Have you ever seen anything like it?"

Actually she had. The car looked like every other gangster's car she'd seen in those old black-and-white 1940s movies Paul enjoyed watching so much.

"You are not going to believe this, but this beauty is only sixty-five thousand dollars."

"A real steal," she said, trying her best to keep a straight face. "So you think you'll be trading in your cherry-red '57 Chevy Belair convertible?"

The look he sent her said that such subjects were not for joking. He walked up to his car, which was the next one on display, and caressed its bumper with all the tenderness of a lover. "I'll never sell this baby. We're going to be buried together. Come here, Suz."

She strode over to him and slipped her hand into his outstretched one. He quickly opened the Chevy convertible's door and stepped inside. "Let's make out in the back."

She laughed. "Paul, we can't. They're going to be opening the doors of the auditorium soon. This place will be filled with people."

A devilish grin drew back his lips. "We've got twenty minutes."

"So what will we do with the extra nineteen?"

"Oh, you're going to pay for that," he said as he pulled her with him onto the back seat.

"Seriously, Paul," she said. "This isn't a good idea. We're in a convertible."

He started to unbutton her blouse. "Yeah, a sexy, hot, red convertible."

"But what if someone—"

"Don't worry, Suz," he said as he nuzzled her neck in that way that always drained her of coherent thought. "We've got plenty of time."

Susan reached for Paul, but realized as consciousness overtook her that she had wrapped her arms around a pillow.

Just another dream.

She opened her eyes to the darkness of her bedroom as she clutched the pillow to her breast. She remembered going to the Antique Car Show. How excited Paul had been over all the cars. Even his comment about his classic Chevy being buried with him.

His prediction had been chillingly accurate. The car had gone up in flames along with him and their home.

But there was something else about that day that she also remembered. When she and Paul were making out in the back seat of his convertible, the event coordinator had come upon them unexpectedly. She'd barely covered herself in time. She'd felt so embarrassed.

Strange how she'd forgotten that until the dream reminded her.


"I'M A LITTLE CONFUSED as to why we're driving to the middle of nowhere," Susan said, valiantly attempting to squelch a yawn.

David glanced over at her in the passenger seat of his truck. She looked soft and sleepy this morning in a bulky teal sweater and gray slacks, her eyelids at half-mast. When she'd opened the door for him a few minutes before, he'd had the strong urge to tell her to go back to bed, and an even stronger urge to invite himself along.

He had suppressed both of those urges instantly.

"Todd is a graduate of the University of Washington," he said. "That's why we're going to Seaview."

She stroked Honey, who was curled into a white ball on her lap. David hadn't planned on the dog being part of this expedition any more than he'd planned on Susan being his passenger. But the little terrier had appeared so distraught when she'd started to leave him that morning that David had found himself suggesting she bring him along.

The look of pleasure on her face was worth any inconvenience. He knew he needed to find out about the father of her child and soon. These reactions she evoked in him were growing more uncomfortable with each passing day.

"I went to U-Dub, as well," she said. "Since when do they conduct classes in tiny communities on this side of the Sound?"

"They don't, as far as I know. But Todd's former U-Dub advisor comes from Seaview. This morning he'll be at a white elephant sale there to raise money for a local family in trouble."

"You're going to ask him about Todd?"

"That's the plan."

"He might not want to discuss one of his students."

"Getting people to talk is part of a private investigator's job."

"How do you manage that?"

"Best way is to find a topic they're interested in. Once you have them talking, steering the conversation to another subject is just a matter of waiting for the proper moment."

"I'd like to be there when you speak to Todd's advisor."

"If you wish."

"What was Todd's major?"

"He has a masters in biochemistry."

Her eyes opened a little at that. "A master's degree?"

David felt a lick of discomfort at the sound of approval in her tone. He tried to reason with himself. Why shouldn't she be relieved that the guy she'd slept with had a brain in his head? The child she was carrying had a better chance of inheriting good genes. But the thought that she might be happy for another reason made him uneasy.

She'd told him last night that she wanted her children to have two committed parents. Was she hoping she and Todd would be more than just parents together?

*Not your concern,* he firmly reminded himself.

"How did you find out about Todd's education?" she asked.

"All universities keep records of who graduated and when. Having his full name, date of birth and current address make it fairly simple to check these things."

"Other than his education, what else have you found out?"

"He has no criminal record. He's been involved in no civil cases, at least not in this state. He's never served in the military. I could find no record of his having been married in any of the state's counties."

"You checked all this out after you dropped me at home last night? Don't you ever sleep?"

"I uncovered most of the information yesterday afternoon," he admitted, "after I made the connection of the Tishman in the plane crash to the Tishman who owned the vehicle that had been ticketed near the community center."

"You knew he was Todd even before you showed me his picture."

"Nothing was certain until you identified him. But the facts fit. The general description on his driver's license was also close to the description you gave me. When I compared his driver's license photo to the photo from the videotape, they also appeared to be a match."

"Well, everything's good news so far," she said. "He doesn't appear to be a criminal or married. He's well educated. He didn't lie about his mother being killed in a plane crash."

"Should you feel like celebrating over the news, there's a café up ahead that makes good cappuccino and raisin muffins."

"No, please," she said immediately. "Don't even talk about such things to me at this early hour."

"So the morning sickness is sticking around? How long is that going to last?"

"I wish I knew. If you want to stop at the café and imbibe, though, go right ahead. Honey would be happy to get out and read the postcards."

"Postcards?" he repeated. "As in, the scent stamp left by other dogs?"

"You are quick."

"Isn't there anything you can do for the morning sickness?" he asked, doing his best not to feel pleased by the small compliment.

"Only thing I haven't tried after reading all the advice posted on the Internet is intravenous feeding."

He held back his smile.

"The old hands at this keep saying you're supposed to keep something in your stomach at all times," she said. "But the only thing eating crackers before getting up has done is make me sick at the sight of crackers."

David drove past the café a few minutes later. He hadn't had breakfast because he'd planned on stopping here. But eating when Susan couldn't did not feel right.

Some blue sky was actually peeking through the billows of morning clouds. He sat back, trying to ignore the gnawing in his stomach, and enjoyed the view out the truck's windows.

The Hood Canal was a long, natural fjord carved by glaciers and filled with seawater from the Pacific Ocean. Some called the canal the crown jewel of the region, and for good reason. The scenery was breathtaking. Thick forests of fir, hemlock, cedar and alder, shimmered along its banks like diamonds in the sunlight.

As David followed the curving road, the thick curtain of trees suddenly parted, revealing an open vista of deep blue water splashing onto a rocky beach. Two sea lions lay on the shore, sunning themselves.

Honey jumped up on Susan's lap, rested his paws on the edge of the half-open passenger window and let out an excited bark.

"He smells the sea lions," she said, glancing out her window in their direction as she stroked Honey's back.

"Would you like to stop and let him out?"

She shook her head. "He'd only want to chase them. Lots of fun for Honey, but I doubt the sea lions would appreciate having their sunbathing interrupted."

She obviously loved her little pet. But she would not indulge his whim at the expense of disturbing creatures in the wild. David respected her for that.

They arrived at their destination in under an hour. Although he'd never been to Seaview, he saw that it was very similar to many other rural communities in western Washington State.

For location, Seaview couldn't be beat. It sat in the center of some rising hills, continuing down to a half-moon expanse of unbroken beach. The towering Olympic Mountains curled at its back.

Spindly Douglas firs lined the country road leading off

the highway into the heart of the town. Well-kept, modest homes with lovely gardens were interspersed with homes whose yards were overrun with wildflowers.

Seaview's main street began with a single-pump gas station attached to a convenience mart and went on to include a small post office, an open pizza stand, a café, an antique shop, a pawn shop, a tavern and about a dozen other small businesses.

At the very end of the main street, a bed-and-breakfast sign hung out the window of a pretty little house that stood at the top of a soft grassy mound on which curly-coated sheep grazed. Across from the bed-and-breakfast was the Seaview Elementary School.

David pulled into the school's half-full parking lot and switched off the engine. He did a quick assessment of the surrounding side streets and the vehicles parked there.

"This is where the white elephant sale is taking place," he said, staring at the elementary school, which obviously had been a barn at one time. "Todd's advisor is the auctioneer."

Susan unfastened her shoulder belt and drew the dog's leash out of her large shoulder bag. "Don't wait for us. I'll take Honey on a walk and meet you inside."

She was busy fastening Honey's leash to his collar when David slipped out of the truck. He entered the school and found himself looking into a central hallway with an open classroom on either side. Both were empty. A big sign that said This Way had an arrow pointing to the back door. He walked down the central hall and stepped outside into a green meadow.

A crowd had gathered in the center of the meadow. On several wooden tables, set end to end, was an eclectic assortment of objects. About four dozen uncomfortable-looking metal chairs had been arranged in rows in front of the tables.

People who reflected the modest, casual nature of Seaview occupied the chairs. Some had children on their knees. Others, walking canes. These weren't people who had come looking for a bargain. They had come to help out a neighbor.

Behind the table of white elephants sat a hefty lady with silver-white hair, wearing a flowered dress, comfortable shoes and a warm sweater. Beside her stood a short man with thick gray hair, a ruddy complexion and a bumpy potato for a nose. David recognized him from his picture on the University of Washington Web site. He was Professor Edwin Bateman. Bateman was holding what looked like an old candlestick-style telephone as if it were a priceless sculpture.

Bateman's voice was high and lilting, as excited as that of any kid finding a surprise gift under the Christmas tree. "Look at this beautiful antique telephone with a genuine dial! None of those silly push buttons that can get stuck on you. See here on the bottom? That right there tells you it's a Ma Bell original. Why, they just don't make this kind of quality anymore."

If David didn't know better, he would have guessed Edwin Bateman was a used car salesman. The man's enthusiasm was infectious. Several hands were already being raised to bid on the old telephone. He sold it in less than two minutes for twenty-five dollars.

As the lucky bidder went up to claim his prize, David caught sight of two people who didn't fit the scene—a middle-aged couple sitting in the back row on the far left. Their clothes were deliberately mismatched and casual, but he recognized them as designer label. Her shiny blond hair had seen nothing but the finest salon.

Neither had bid on the candlestick phone. Nor were they interested in the next two, relatively worthless items Bateman managed to make sound like priceless heirlooms. But something had brought them here.

When Bateman's hand reached past a teddy bear on the table to pick up an iron rooster weather vane, the man flinched. He shot a nervous glance at the woman seated beside him as he wiped his sweaty palms on his designer jeans.

That was when David knew what they had come to bid on. And why.

"We're going to take a fifteen-minute break," Bateman announced. "There are drinks and cookies right over there. Everything's just fifty cents. All the money goes to the Meyerson family."

As the chairs were pushed back and people got up to stretch or head for the beverage table, David looked around for Susan. He saw her sitting on a fallen tree trunk at the very edge of the fenced meadow, some thirty feet away.

She was holding a camera she must have brought in her large shoulder bag. Honey sniffed at the shrubbery along the fence. She securely held his leash while she focused on what she was seeing through her camera lens.

David headed in her direction. When he was about fifteen feet away, he stopped.

She lowered her camera and extended her arm, a black sunflower seed on her palm. A foot away on the fallen log, a tiny brown bird eyed the seed.

For a moment Susan and the bird remained motionless. Then the bird hopped onto her palm and snatched the seed. It remained perched there for a moment, before finally spreading its wings and flying away.

David could only see Susan's profile from his position, but he didn't miss the smile that teased her lips. He started forward. She must have sensed his movement because she instantly turned toward him.

"Hi," she said.

"Always carry a camera and birdseed with you?"

"You never know when a special shot may come your way." Her eyes lifted to the sky where the bird had disappeared. "Except that no camera in the world can capture the magical feeling of having a bird perch on your hand."

There was an expression of wonder on her face that he wished he could capture.

Honey trotted up to David and nudged his leg. He leaned down and gave the dog's head a quick pat. "Our auctioneer is taking a break," he said. "No telling how long this white elephant sale will be going on. Now is probably the best time to catch him. Still want to be there when I ask him about Todd?"

"Absolutely," she said, putting her camera into her shoulder bag.

David straightened and held out his hand to help her off the log. She slipped her hand into his without hesitation. He felt the smooth warmth of her skin against his, the firmness of her grasp.

He was suddenly aware that this was the first time she'd accepted an offer of physical assistance. He knew that her giving him her hand was a sign of trust. And that felt very good. As he pulled her gently to her feet, he silently vowed never to do anything to lose her trust.

But as she stood before him and looked into his eyes, he felt that vow already being tested.

"You have big hands," she said.

Only then did he realize he'd enclosed her hand within both of his. He released his hold immediately and stepped back. "Time to go talk to Professor Bateman."

## CHAPTER SEVEN

SUSAN AND DAVID FOUND Professor Bateman at the beverage cart. He was clearly thirsty, chugging down whatever was in his cup.

Susan decided to use the cart as a shield so she could observe what was going on without being too obvious. As she got into position, the memory of David's pulling her to her feet returned.

Whether he was attracted to her or not, she had no idea. But she was certain that he felt something. His hands had held hers far longer than necessary. Still, she realized that even that action could have been just another example of his courteous nature.

David was one of a rare breed—a man who opened doors for women, assisted them out of vehicles, helped them up from fallen logs and even carried them and their camera equipment a mile and a half through thick brush when they fainted.

With every moment she spent with him, she saw more of the caring, considerate man he was.

David dropped a dollar into the collection box, poured himself a cup of coffee and picked up a chocolate chip cookie. He turned to Bateman, who was finishing the drink in his cup. "Buy you a refill?" he asked, holding up another dollar.

"Yes, thank you," Bateman said.

David dropped the bill into the container and pointed to the drinks in front of him.

"The cola," Bateman said in response.

David filled Bateman's cup and then recapped the cola bottle.

"I understand the Meyersons have had some tough breaks recently," David said.

"Very tough," Bateman agreed. "Joe took a bad fall on the job a month ago and hurt his back. He's still bed-ridden. His wife Margie was hit broadside by a drunk driver two weeks ago. She's just out of the hospital. Her shoulder and arm will be in a cast for another five weeks. They have four little ones depending on them."

"Their friends and neighbors have certainly come through with donations," David said, gesturing toward the tables.

"They're good, decent people," Bateman said. "But even if we manage to collect a thousand dollars for Joe and Margie today, I'm afraid that will only cover a few utility bills and this month's payment on their mobile home."

"You'll do better than a thousand dollars," David said as he gently scooped up the teddy bear from the table. "This is an original 1905 Steiff teddy bear. One sold at auction a few years ago for $185,000. That bear wasn't in nearly as good condition as this one is."

Susan was startled as she listened to David. She knew what he said had to be true. He wouldn't lie about this.

Bateman stared dumbfounded at the bear. "That's an antique?"

David gently held out the bear. "You might want to wrap the bear in some protective material."

He took the bear and gathered it close.

David gestured toward the other side of the meadow. "If the middle-aged couple over there doesn't offer you at least $185,000 for the bear, get in touch with me. I'll put you in contact with someone who will pay that much."

Susan watched David pull a business card from the shirt pocket beneath his sweater.

Bateman looked at David's card. Then he shot a glance over his shoulder at the couple standing close together, hugging the wire fence and sipping coffee.

"They offered me fifteen dollars for the bear before the auction started," he said, anger clear in his tone. "I told them there were families here with young children who might want a chance to bid. They told me I was a fool. Said no kid wanted an old, used teddy bear."

"In that case, make sure you don't sell the bear to them for less than $200,000," David said.

"I'd rather tell them that I threw the bear into the garbage dump and let them go rooting around in *that* for a few days," Bateman said as he pocketed David's card. "The dump here is three miles wide, half again as deep and smells worse than a cesspool."

Susan smiled.

"Who donated the bear?" David asked.

"One of our elderly ladies found the bear wrapped in a trunk in her attic," he said, his eyes swinging back to David. "The bear had been her mother's. Both girls preferred to play with dolls, which explains why the bear is in such good condition."

"Think they'll be any problem there?"

"No," Bateman said. "I'll tell her about the bear's value, but I'm certain she won't want it back. She's a wonderful old gal—kind who'd give you the orthopedic shoes off her feet. She's going to be delighted when she finds out her donation helped so much. The Meyersons will want to thank you personally for what you've just done, Mr. Knight."

"Their thanks is unnecessary, Professor Bateman. But I could use your help."

Bateman's eyes widened in surprise. "You know who I am."

"I know you were Vance Tishman's advisor at U-Dub."

Confusion dug furrows into Bateman's brow. "Vance?"

"I should have said Todd Tishman," David amended quickly. "That's the name I believe he goes by."

"Of course, Todd," the other man repeated, his confusion immediately clearing. "Yes, Todd was a graduate student of mine a couple of years ago."

*He didn't lie to me about his name,* Susan thought.

"Why are you investigating Todd? Has he done something wrong?"

"Not at all. I'm just trying to understand the kind of man he is. Can you help me out?"

Bateman didn't have to think about David's question long. "Yes, I can help *you* out. What would you like to know?"

Susan wasn't surprised at Bateman's response. David had done both him and the Meyersons a very good turn. He was presenting himself openly and honestly to the professor. She liked that about him.

"Was Todd a good student?" David asked.

"Very conscientious, very hardworking, very bright. Grade-wise he was always in the top quarter of his class."

"And otherwise?"

"Our department is known for its friendly, interactive environment. We're on a first-name basis with the students from the start and encourage them to work as a team. We believe a free exchange of ideas results from students and faculty getting to know one another well. Todd had…difficulty in this area."

"What kind of difficulty?"

Bateman looked around to see if anyone might be overhearing their conversation. Despite the fact that he had no problem talking to David about this, he clearly was not a man who spoke about his students and their problems to just anyone.

Susan was out of his immediate line of sight, but she dropped to a squat and began to pet Honey to make herself even more unobtrusive. Honey was only too happy with the attention. He lay on his back, paws up in the air, encouraging her to rub his tummy.

"Todd's introverted, quite shy," she heard Bateman tell David.

Yes, she had been sure he was.

"He has strong ideas, has difficulty communicating them verbally and doesn't know how to negotiate a compromise," Bateman continued. "He'd just go off and do what he thought best, despite what the group had decided."

"He doesn't know how to be part of a team," David said.

"That about sums it up," Bateman agreed. "When he had to get up in front of the thesis committee to speak, he'd stare down at his notes and his voice would drop so low you could hardly hear him."

She remembered Todd's soft voice, how he only briefly met her eyes. Nothing that Bateman was saying surprised her.

"Did his shyness have anything to do with why he didn't go on to get his Ph.D?" David asked.

"No, I had trouble with his thesis. When we couldn't come to an agreement, he chose to drop out."

Bateman was quiet for a moment before going on. She figured he'd paused to take a drink of his cola.

"We emphasize the value of using interdisciplinary approaches to attack important biological problems in our department. But Todd's approach was unrealistic. Frankly, I doubted his thesis was doable, forget publishable, within a reasonable time frame."

"What was his thesis?"

"Biological pest control through augmentation."

"Increasing the population of a natural enemy to control a pest," David said.

"Yes," Bateman agreed, his tone telling Susan that David's understanding of the technical term had surprised him.

David's understanding had surprised her as well. She knew what augmentation meant from her wildlife studies. How did he?

"What part of Todd's thesis struck you as unrealistic?" David asked.

"Todd believed he could simultaneously breed half a dozen variations of a more efficient natural predator that would jointly find and attack a single pest and wipe it out in one life cycle."

"Isn't work like that already taking place?"

"Work *like* that, yes," Bateman agreed. "In well-funded laboratories with dozens of qualified scientists working together. Natural predators are often susceptible to the same insecticides that kill the pests, so using them successfully takes great care."

"How did Todd's approach differ?"

"His required an insecticide-free environment for his superior predator species to survive. Even if farmers were willing to stop using insecticides, the residue would remain in the soil for years. I tried to get Todd to consider a modification of his premise that would introduce his predator species along with a reduction of pesticide. But he wouldn't compromise. He was adamant against insecticide use of any kind."

Susan heard a couple of women interrupt the conversation at that point as they walked past Bateman and asked him when the auction would resume. He checked his watch and told them in just a minute.

"I won't take much more of your time," David assured him after the women had moved on. "Who were Todd's friends at school?"

"He didn't make friends with any of the other students in the department. Never attended any of the social functions. Kept very much to himself. No friends. No girl. No family. No, wait, I take that back. His mother picked him up after class once. At least, I think she was his mother. The physical resemblance was there."

"Did Todd go to work after he received his master's degree?" David asked.

"I told him I'd be happy to give him a reference for any of the job openings posted on our bulletin boards. He thanked me but said a relative was getting him a research position at a chemical company."

"Did he tell you the name of the relative or company?"

"No. Todd was quiet about his personal life, especially his family. I'm sure he comes from money, though. He was one of the few students we had who never needed financial assistance."

David thanked Bateman, shook his hand and wished him luck with the rest of the auction. As Susan rose she saw Bateman carefully wrap and then hide the Steiff teddy bear in a cardboard box before he returned to the auction podium. She wondered if he really would announce that the teddy bear had been thrown in the garbage dump.

David nodded to her as he headed toward the truck. She slipped into step beside him, Honey trotting along happily on his leash.

"That was great," she said with enthusiasm.

"No, that was luck," he said, but she could see that he was pleased.

"How did you know about the Steiff bear?"

"Successful private investigators learn anything and everything they can. You never know when a piece of information will come in handy.''

''Where did that piece of information about the bears come from?''

''A collectors' magazine. I read all about Steiff teddy bears while I was waiting in the dentist's office one day. The article had a picture of the 1905 original that had sold recently at auction.''

They reached the truck, and he opened the passenger door. Honey hopped in. Susan turned to face David. ''If you'd only seen a picture of the original, how could you be sure the bear wasn't just a copy?''

''That couple waiting to bid told me the bear was an original. Another thing you learn as a private investigator is to watch people…and note vehicles.''

He paused as he gestured at a side street. ''See that van over there with the antique store logo on the side?''

She followed his finger until she caught sight of the van. There was plenty of space to park in front of the school, but the van was almost hidden beneath the drooping branches of a tree on that side road. She realized the driver had parked the van there deliberately to hide the logo on its side.

She also understood that David wasn't just observant. He was able to make sense of what he saw by putting the pieces together.

She slid onto the passenger seat of the truck.

*Watch people,* he'd said. She did that as he walked around the vehicle to get to the driver's side. He wore casual clothes today—faded jeans, a soft-looking blue sweater over a sports shirt—both appropriate for the small auction they'd just been to.

He looked good, just as he always did. But today she noticed how he moved—with the confidence of a man who was sure of himself.

She'd sensed that quality in him the first day they met. Now she was witness to the caring way he treated her and others. The honest way he presented himself. With every day that passed, she liked and respected him more.

"You were right about Todd," David said when they were a few miles down the road. "He was the shy griever you took him to be."

"And those are the three hardest words a man can ever say to a woman."

"What three words are those?" he asked, clearly puzzled.

*"You were right,"* she repeated with hearty emphasis. "The heck with this 'I love you' stuff. Any man can get up the courage to say that."

His lip twitched upward. "You may be right."

"Sorry," she said with feigned disapproval. "Maybes don't qualify. It has to be the specific words *you are right* or *you were right.* Anything else is an equivocation."

David chuckled—a deep, warm rumble. She liked the feel of the vibration against her ears.

"There are a couple of nutrition bars in the glove compartment," he said after a moment. "Mind handing me one?"

"You didn't eat breakfast, did you," she said, striving to mimic what he'd said to her a few mornings before at Camp Long. "I thought you were a professional. You should know better than to begin a long morning assignment without any food in your stomach."

His chuckle was even heartier this time. "Touché," he said. "You think your stomach is up to some food?"

"Please, don't use the words *stomach, up* and *food* all in the same sentence."

This chuckle made the seat shake. She decided that the sound was fast becoming one of her favorites.

"If you can keep something *down,*" he said carefully,

"there's a place a few miles from here that offers a good, hot breakfast. Or a bowl of fresh fruit if you'd prefer."

"You seem to know a lot about where to eat in this area," she said. "Do you come out here often?"

"Only traveled this way a few times. But since I'd rather starve than go grocery shopping, and I'm the worst cook this side of the Cascades, I try to know where the best places to eat can be found, no matter where I am."

"I'm glad you told me."

"That I'm the unofficial restaurant guide of Puget Sound?"

"No, that you're the worst cook on this side of the Cascades," she said. "I was beginning to think you knew how to do everything. Believe me, that was wearing thin. So, burned a lot of pots, have you?"

"You don't have to seem so happy about my shortcomings."

He glanced over at her briefly, his expression a mixture of annoyance and amusement that she decided to find charming. He really was very good company when he let himself relax a bit.

Of course, she supposed a private investigator had to keep his mind on business and not let himself relax too much. And she had to remember this *was* business.

But that was becoming more difficult by the moment. The sun was out and she was with a man who was smart, courteous, kind, great-looking, and charming when he chose to be.

Her stomach told her she wouldn't be able to eat. But if all he had so far was that cup of coffee and a chocolate chip cookie, she knew he needed a lot more nourishment to keep his body going. His big, strong, handsome body.

*Okay, Susan. Enough of those thoughts.*

"I could go for a bowl of fresh fruit," she lied.

DAVID WASN'T FOOLED when Susan ordered the small bowl of fresh fruit and a tall glass of water. He knew that she'd only suggested they stop so he could get something to eat. Not that he was complaining. He appreciated her consideration. As he dug into his steak and eggs and buttered English muffins, he realized that there was a lot about her that he appreciated.

She was sweet, funny, damn good company. He'd gotten used to working alone. Preferred it, actually. But having her along on this trip was nice.

When he had finished his food, he looked up to catch her watching him. She quickly turned to stare out the window to where the truck was parked, as though she were checking to be sure that Honey was all right.

But he hadn't missed the approving expression on her face. He quickly reminded himself of all the reasons why her approval shouldn't matter to him. He wasn't quick enough.

"I love the feel of the sun," she said, squinting into the slanting light. "I suppose that's because sunshine is so rare at this time of the year." Her eyes returned to his. "Rare things are always so much more precious."

He watched the bright light warm her hair and skin. Rare and precious. He took a deep, steadying breath and gave himself a mental kick.

"So what do you think about Dr. Bateman's reaction to Todd's thesis?" he asked as he set down his coffee cup, determined to get his mind back on the case.

"Wouldn't be fair of me to venture an opinion without having read the thesis first."

"But if you had to?" he pressed.

"I favor augmentation. Using natural predators is far superior to pesticides that are as harmful to humans as the pests we're trying to eliminate. But biological control takes more intensive management, planning, time, and a lot of education and training. Plus pesticides are less expensive initially. Getting a farmer who is relying on selling his crop to stop using the pesticides that are working for him in favor of a slower, more expensive approach is hard.''

She was being grounded and real about her reservations. She wasn't going to allow thoughts of her and Todd getting together cloud her judgment about his professional competency.

''So how would you sell augmentation?'' David said.

''I think Dr. Bateman had the right suggestion for Todd,'' she said as she leaned her forearms on the table. ''If he started out with a reduction of the pesticide along with the simultaneous release of his superior predator species and got good results, then he could reduce the pesticide until he was able to eliminate it and the pests altogether. I'd like to be rid of all pesticides tomorrow myself. But sometimes gradual change is the only kind that has a chance.''

''Hard to be patient when you see natural things being harmed,'' he said, enjoying the sharpness of her mind.

She nodded as she leaned back. ''One of the first things a nature photographer learns is not to tamper with the balance of life. Even removing dead leaves from around the base might kill a plant, if the plant is relying on the decay of the leaf materials for nutrients. If that plant dies, so, too, might the animal that uses the plant for food. Life is wonderfully resilient, surviving in the harshest environments. But it's also fragile and can be forever lost beneath the boot of a blundering human.''

He liked the calm way she said that, with the quiet strength of belief but without the heated passion of blame. She wasn't a born-again zealot with tunnel vision. She was as balanced as the nature to which she was so deeply attuned.

"When did you decide to become a wildlife photographer?" he asked.

"I'll make you a deal. I'll tell you when I decided to become a wildlife photographer if you'll tell me when you decided to become a private investigator."

David wished she hadn't said that. He had been thoroughly enjoying their conversation up until then. Her expression was open, friendly. Her "deal" had been delivered in a light, uncomplicated, conversational tone. But she had no idea what she had just asked of him.

Sharing that time of his life with her would be inviting her to become a part of something that had been shatteringly personal to him. Even if he wanted to, he could not engage in such an extreme act of intimacy with Susan. She was his client—his very likeable, very intelligent, far-too-attractive client.

He had made yet another mistake, asking her a personal question that had nothing to do with the job she had hired him to do.

David finished his coffee in one gulp. "If you're not going to eat that fruit cup, I think we should be going."

Without waiting for Susan's answer, he signaled to the waitress to bring him the check.


ALICE KNIGHT LOOKED AT her son with the surprise caused by his uncharacteristic two-hour early arrival to Sunday dinner and his out-of-the-blue question. "Morning sickness?" she repeated.

"Yes, you had it, right?" David asked.

"And how. Most pregnant women do."

"What causes it?"

Alice studied her son as she strolled on the cobblestone path weaving through her garden. Of her four sons, David was the most like her in coloring—the same dark hair and gray eyes. He'd also inherited her organizational abilities, about which she harbored a secret pride.

But her heart broke to see how much his solidly handsome features had sobered over the past couple of years. She couldn't remember the last time she had seen him happy.

"I'm not sure anyone knows," she said in response. "Why the sudden interest?"

"I just wondered how you kept things down," he said as he kept pace beside her.

She fingered a pink rhododendron bud as they turned a corner. David wasn't one to ask idle questions. His interest in morning sickness could only mean one thing. He knew someone who had it.

"When I was carrying your older brother," she said, "I was just miserable until about the fifth month when my stomach finally settled. When I was pregnant with you, I learned that sipping a thin milk shake in the early morning helped."

"Any particular flavor?"

"Peppermint," she said, then added conversationally, "So, who do you know who's pregnant?"

"A client."

A client? She found that surprising. David didn't take on the personal problems of clients. Oh, he was good at solving their cases. Very good. But ever since his disastrous experience with Theresa, he'd steered clear of any involvement with a woman.

Was that changing?

"So, you're concerned about this pregnant client," Alice said carefully. She knew she was going to have to be careful not to appear too eager. David was not a man who shared personal information easily.

"I don't want her throwing up while we're trying to conduct business."

She wasn't buying her son's explanation. Ever since he was a child, David had been Mr. Cool when being open with her. But when he was even a little evasive, he developed an endearing clumsy streak. She hadn't missed the fact that he'd just stepped into a bed of fresh fertilizer.

Alice stopped to point at his shoe. "She's a new client?"

"As of last week," he said, leaning against a tree and attempting to use the bark to scrape the muck off the bottom of his shoe. "Did you drink the milk shake all morning?"

"Sipped it," she corrected, hiding her smile. David was making a mess of his shoe cleaning. Mr. Meticulous never made a mess of anything.

"Tell me more about her."

"Nothing more to tell."

She was pretty certain there was a lot more to tell. So, David was finally showing interest in a woman again. Well, well. This could be either really good news or really bad. All depended on the woman.

"Who's the father of her baby?"

"Grandson of a billionaire no less."

Ah, was that a touch of jealousy she heard in his voice? If this were one of the twins, she would have had no trouble teasing the truth out of him. But David was not someone you teased about a woman.

She heard a familiar twitter and looked up. "Oh, look, the swifts are trying to coax their babies out of their nests. When the baby swifts start to fly, you know summer is on the way."

From her peripheral vision, she could see her son's head was tilted upward. But his troubled expression told her he wasn't thinking about birds.

"Is your client going to marry this billionaire's grandson?"

"Haven't a clue."

"You think she should?"

"She hardly knows him."

"So you *don't* think she should."

"I don't care one way or the other. She's just a client."

Alice watched David trying to elude a bee that was buzzing him. He hopped sideways, collided with a low-lying branch and stumbled onto the grass.

Like hell he didn't care. He was a complete klutz today. She held her smile as she walked over to offer him a hand.

"No, no, I'm fine," he said, holding out his palm like a traffic cop, forestalling her approach.

Well, he might have been fine if the sprinkler beside him hadn't gurgled and turned on at full blast. David rolled onto his side, struggled to get a firm footing, gave up and crawled out of the spray.

She had to pretend to cough loudly to hide the chuckle that erupted in her throat. Any woman who could turn David into this she had to meet.

"Invite your client to have lunch with us tomorrow," she said as soon as she had gotten herself back in control. "I'll tell her all the trade secrets of how to get through a pregnancy with panache."

Water dripped off his hair as he turned toward his mother. "You're suggesting I bring a client *here?*"

She drew a handkerchief out of her pocket and offered it to him. "Or we could all meet at a restaurant if you prefer."

"Thanks," he said, taking the handkerchief and drying his hands and face. "But there's no reason to meet her. She's just a client."

Yeah, she was *just* a client and Mr. Meticulous was *just* smearing mud all over his forehead.

"Been a while, of course," Alice said, carefully pursing her lips and drawing her brows together in a thoughtful look. "But if I remember correctly, that milk shake had some other important ingredients."

"Like what?"

"I'm sure if I concentrate, they'll come to me in time."

"How much time?"

He was clearly so eager for her to start concentrating right now that Alice had to struggle to hold back her smile once again. "After dinner tonight I'll take a few minutes to jot them down for you. Would that be helpful?"

"Yes," he admitted, clearly relieved. "Thank you."

So she was right. Her son was smitten.

*Ah, David, I just hope that she's not another Theresa. You do not need another woman who is hiding from the truth.*

SUSAN HAD JUST BRUSHED her teeth and slipped on her cotton nightgown when the telephone rang. She looked at the clock on the nightstand. After ten. No one *she* ever wanted to talk to called at this time of night.

She decided to just let the answering machine pick up the call. After the fourth ring, her brief recorded voice message came on, followed by a *beep*.

"It's David Knight." His deep baritone filled the room. "I know you're home. I know you're awake. Please pick up."

She padded over to the phone and snatched the receiver. "And how do you know I'm home and awake?"

"I'm a detective, remember?"

She was in no mood to let him off that easily. "Well, Sherlock, you'd better explain exactly how you detected those particular pieces of information."

"Your SUV is in the garage, and a light is shining behind your bedroom drapes."

She sat on the edge of her bed and digested that bit of news. "Where are you?"

"In your driveway."

"What are you doing in my driveway?"

"I have something for you. Meet me at the front door in two minutes."

"Uh—"

She didn't get a chance to finish. The dial tone blared in her ear, and she dropped the receiver on the base.

What could he possibly have to give her that couldn't wait until tomorrow?

She shook her head as she headed for her closet and a robe. Sometimes she wondered if David weren't two men. Driving out to Seaview with him the day before had been so nice! Watching him work, listening to him, talking to him. Hearing his warm, throaty chuckle.

But the moment she'd asked him when he had decided to become a private investigator, pleasant Dr. Jekyll had instantly transformed into a closed Mr. Hyde.

Such a simple everyday question. One of the first questions even a casual acquaintance asked. One he'd just asked of her!

What bothered David so much that such a simple question like that had him shutting her out? He'd said not a word to her on the drive home. He'd barely even said goodbye when he'd dropped her off.

Now here he was, showing up at ten o'clock on a Sunday night with something she had to have before the next morning. She let out a frustrated breath. Trying to figure him out was a waste of her time.

She closed her bedroom door on her way out, not wanting Honey to jump off the bed and follow her downstairs. If the dog discovered David on her doorstep, he'd want him invited in. Susan had no intention of doing that.

She stomped down the stairs and reached the door exactly two minutes from the time he'd hung up on her. She switched on the outside light and checked through the peephole. He was standing on the porch.

Taking a deep breath, she unlocked the door and pulled back on the knob with pent-up irritation.

But her irritation immediately fizzled at the sight of him. He was soaking wet. His hair and shoulders were dripping. A thick rain beat noisily on the walkway behind him. *Damn.*

She sighed in defeat as she stepped aside. "Come in."

"No."

He held out a paper grocery sack.

She stepped forward. "What's this?"

"Read the directions," he said as he placed the sack firmly in her hands. "You may already have some of the ingredients, but just to make sure, I got them all. Good night."

He turned to leave.

She stared at the bag in bewilderment. "Directions for what?" she asked. "Wait!"

But she was talking to herself. He was already halfway to his truck.

She closed the door with a perplexed shake of her head, turned off the outside light and threw the lock into place before heading into the kitchen.

When she looked inside the bag, she found milk and an assortment of other items. Then she caught sight of a piece of paper. She unfolded it and found a handwritten recipe scribbled inside.

At the top of the list of ingredients was the heading, "For the Relief of Morning Sickness."

Susan sunk onto the nearest chair and let out a deep, disconcerted sigh. She tried to picture the man—who had confessed he'd rather starve than go grocery shopping— walking up and down the aisles, picking up the ingredients on this list, and then delivering them to her late at night in the pouring rain. Just so she'd have them before the next morning.

David wouldn't tell her when he'd decided to become a private investigator. But he'd gone to all this trouble to try to help her feel better.

He was so damn confusing.

And so damn sweet that he made her heart ache.

## CHAPTER EIGHT

DAVID FOUND A DOZEN e-mails waiting for him when he returned to his office Monday afternoon. He quickly checked the senders, noting that two were from Susan. He clicked on the first and found a copy of her weekly shooting schedule.

Her second e-mail had been sent a few hours after the first. He assumed she'd sent him an update to the earlier schedule. But when he opened it, he discovered she'd written him a personal note.

The recipe worked! I've sipped the milk shake all morning and not a twinge of nausea. Just to show you how much I appreciate what you did, I am *not* going to tell you how wonderful you are for having done it. I know that would just make you uncomfortable.

Susan.

David reread her short message at least a dozen times. Even after that, he was still smiling. He tried to tell himself there was no reason to feel so good just because he'd helped to cure her nausea.

The intercom buzzed. He reached over and pressed the button. "Yes, Harry?"

"I've completed that Internet search of scientists involved in biological pest control, sir. I found only one small reference to Todd Tishman."

"Bring it in," David said.

Harry gave his perfunctory knock on the office door a moment later, before marching up to David's desk and laying a multipage printout on top.

"I thought you said you found only a small reference," David said as he looked at the thick printout.

"The reference said Todd Tishman was a member of a team studying a new method of integrated pest management at Ardmore Chemical Company," Harry said as he pointed to the first line on the printout. "I thought you might want to read the research paper the team authored."

That was Harry. Thorough as always.

"Good job," David said. "Thanks."

Harry did his typical one-eighty and left the office.

The published article from the scientific journal was entitled, "Pesticide Plus New Predator Puts End To Pesky Beetle." He checked the date. The article had been published five months before. He next checked the bylines. The authors were six Ardmore research scientists. Todd Tishman was one of them. David sat back and read the article.

An accidentally imported beetle that had been attacking and decimating local crops for the past two years had finally been brought under control. Although a genetically strengthened lizard had initially reduced the beetle's numbers, an application of an existing insecticide produced in the labs of Ardmore Chemical Company had been required to eliminate the pest.

Seemed odd to David that Todd Tishman was part of a team that had resorted to using a pesticide, considering what Dr. Bateman had told him.

David had talked to three people that morning about Todd. One had been an administrator at the military school Todd had attended. The other two had been University of Washington professors that Todd had taken classes from while earning his undergraduate degree. All of these people had described Todd as being quite stubborn about his beliefs.

David had visited the Ardmore Chemical Company in the industrial complex of Ardmore Hills that morning. He learned a lot about the subjects of his investigations by listening to the people who knew them. But whenever possible, he always tried to meet with people he was investigating. Even the way a person shook hands said a lot. The way he or she met David's eyes, or didn't, often said a lot more.

He had developed a plausible cover story for seeking out Todd. But when he'd arrived at the lab, David had found the facility gutted and in the process of being rebuilt.

Over the noise of sawing and hammering, the receptionist had told David that Todd and the other scientists had left on an expedition for South America five weeks before. She could not—or would not—tell him anything more.

David had called Jared and asked him to use his position in the Sheriff's Department to check out the passengers on the plane that had taken the Ardmore employees to South America. He wanted to know the date on Todd's return ticket. But Todd Tishman's name was not on the passenger list.

Todd wasn't at the lab, and he wasn't on an expedition to South America. Where was he?

Before David checked his other e-mail to see if he had any responses to the questions he'd sent out early that morning, he hit another command.

Susan's two messages came off the laser printer. He put them in his pocket. He needed her schedule in case he had to get in touch with her. He told himself he needed a copy of her personal note as a reminder to thank his mother for her help.

But there was a nagging voice inside his head that told him that second excuse was a pretty poor one.

"BARRY, WAIT UP," Susan said as she hurried toward her co-worker.

He stopped and turned toward her as she approached. "Everything okay?"

"Fine," she assured. "Just want to switch assignments. I'll take yours tonight, you take mine tomorrow."

A frown turned Barry's forehead into an exact replica of an old car's radiator grill. "Let me get this straight," he said, crossing his arms over his barrel chest. "You want to sit in a cold and drafty, old lighthouse shooting bats at night instead of lying on a lounge chair in the sun taking photos of sweet hummingbirds?"

"What sun?" she said. "Forecast calls for overcast skies, maybe even some rain tomorrow morning."

"Oh, so you want *me* lying out in the rain shooting those damn birds."

"A moment ago they were sweet hummingbirds," she said, trying not to grin.

Barry tilted his head at her like someone trying to understand an obscure painting. "Hummingbirds are one of your specialties. Greg is going to be pissed if I switch assignments with you."

"Look, if Greg gives us any grief, I'll take full responsibility. I haven't had a chance at any low-light shots in months. I'm forgetting how. The bats will present a real challenge."

All of that happened to be true. But the real reason she wanted to trade with Barry was that the lighthouse was on Falls Island where Todd lived. Assignments came up at the exclusive, gated community of Falls Island very rarely. She wasn't sure what she expected to find once she gained entry, but the opportunity seemed too good to pass up.

"I bet you'll do a dynamite job on the hummingbirds," she said, giving Barry's arm a nudge.

"You think flattery is going to turn my head, don't you."

"On a dime," she said, smiling.

"What if your pictures of the bats turn out so terrific Greg decides you get to do all the low-light shots from now on?"

She laughed. "Yeah, like that could ever happen. You know perfectly well no one captures the *creepy* in night creatures the way you do. One day you're going to have to let me in on your secret."

"It's my Romanian blood," Barry said as he hunched his shoulders, spread his sweater sleeves like wings and swooped toward her neck. She was giggling from the tickle of his mustache when Ellie came around the corner.

"Well, well," Ellie said, an eyebrow rising. "What's going on here?"

"I'm sucking her blood," Barry said in his best Dracula imitation. "Would you like me to suck yours?"

"IRS already beat you to it," Ellie said, sounding somewhat less than amused. "Hey, Suz, do you have a minute?"

"Sure."

Susan smiled at Barry. "Thanks for switching. I'll hug you later."

"That's four hundred and sixteen hugs you now owe me," Barry said as he headed toward his cubicle.

"He's always hanging around you," Ellie said as she watched Barry walk away. "I think he has a thing for you."

Susan laughed. "No way. Barry's just a friend."

"Oh, I know you'd never fall for *him*. Barry couldn't hold a candle to Paul. Paul was one of those perfect guys who only happen along once in a woman's life. You'll never find another man like him.''

''What do you need?'' Susan asked, ill-at-ease over Ellie's comment.

''Oh, yeah,'' Ellie said, obviously having forgotten she'd asked to speak to Susan. ''Skip is going to take me to this concert tonight, and I really don't have a thing to wear. Go shopping with me after work and help me pick something out.''

Actually, Ellie had two big closets in her apartment bursting with clothes. But Susan understood. When you wanted to go someplace special with someone special, only a new outfit would do.

''I'd really like to, El, but I have a shoot tonight.''

''Don't tell me you took Barry's assignment?'' Ellie asked in disbelief. ''Have you gone batty?''

''I've watched you photograph a bloody shark-feeding frenzy without so much as flinching, Ellie Tremont. What could possibly bother you so much about bats?''

''They're ugly.''

''Bats are shy little creatures, and not ugly at all. They have these enormous ears, soulful brown eyes, and cute claws on the ends of their wings.''

Ellie was making a wonderfully disgusted face. Susan reached around her cubicle wall, grabbed her camera and snapped her friend's picture.

''Now I have a photo of you to give to Skip for his wallet,'' she said.

Ellie laughed. ''You develop that shot, Susan Carter, and I'll shoot you. Only I won't be using a camera.''

DAVID WAS PARKED down the block from Todd's condo on Falls Island when Susan's SUV turned the corner. The surprise of seeing her froze him for several seconds. He barely managed to scoot down in the front seat of the delivery truck he was using for camouflage before she passed by his window.

He watched her closely in his rearview mirror. She drove slowly, clearly checking the numbers on the buildings. When she came to the condo complex where Todd lived, she stopped.

She sat in her idling SUV and stared at the building for a full minute, then finally drove off.

David started the engine of the delivery truck and pulled away from the curb, following her down the street. He was determined to find out just what the hell she thought she was doing.

SUSAN WAS GLAD she'd worn a jacket when she reached the top of the lantern-shaped lighthouse tower and found the windows missing.

Falls Island Lighthouse hadn't been in operation for at least half a century. The electric lamp that had once warned ships away from the rocky cliffs below had apparently been removed to a museum somewhere. As she looked around at the stripped space and felt the chilly breeze, she decided that aside from the historical value, the place was only fit for bats.

She carefully set up her equipment. Then she spread out the thick blanket she'd brought to cover the cold and dusty stone floor. She sat in the center, called Honey over to settle beside her and curled the blanket ends around them both to keep warm. All she had to do now was wait until dark for the bats to become active.

She wasn't sure what she had hoped to learn by driving by Todd's place. The fact that it was in a nice neighborhood? Everything on Falls Island was nice, exclusive and so laughingly expensive that only the very wealthy could afford to live here.

Todd's condo was in a complex that sat on the top of a

hill. His view of the Puget Sound waterway had to be gorgeous. Still, she far preferred the warmth of her old town house's weathered wood siding and native rhododendrons. The steel and glass of Todd's building and the stylized Italian cypress trees that surrounded the structure seemed cold and formal.

Why had Todd chosen that building over the more traditionally styled and warmer-looking condo units available on the island?

Maybe where he lived didn't matter that much to him. Most men weren't nearly as picky about their living quarters as women. Of course, the cars they drove were another matter. They selected them as though their very masculinity was at stake.

As she stroked Honey, she began to question whether the things David would find out about Todd would help her to make a decision about him. What was she looking for? How did you see the potential of a loving, committed father in a man?

"What are you doing here?" David asked.

Susan whirled around to see him climbing the last stone step. Honey jumped up and ran over to him, barking in welcome.

*Oh, great.* Now *he barks. Some watchdog.*

"I'm working," she said, not able to keep the surprise out of her voice.

He leaned down to pet Honey as his eyes swept over her blanket, the tripod, the silvered reflectors and the flash guns.

"This location was not on your shooting list," he said.

"A last-minute change at the end of the day. I didn't have a chance to update my schedule."

What she didn't say was that even if she'd had a chance, she wouldn't have made the change. She didn't want to alert Greg that she was going to be at the lighthouse this evening instead of shooting hummingbirds tomorrow.

"What are you doing here?" she asked.

"I'm working," he said in a repeat of her words as he sat down on the edge of her blanket.

Honey hopped onto his lap. David let him settle there, giving his ears a rub.

That was when Susan got a closer look at what David was wearing, something she had missed before in the dim light. Of all the uniforms she might have pictured him in, this would have been the last.

"Delivering pizzas? I didn't realize the private investigation business paid so poorly you had to moonlight. Will it help if I order a large one with everything on it?"

"Very funny." He didn't sound amused.

She tried not to laugh, but quickly lost the battle. Several moments passed before she'd gotten herself under control again.

"I'm going to enjoy billing you for this evening," he said. "The rates are double for overtime, and triple for ridicule."

But she could see the flash of his teeth and knew he was smiling.

"You want some soup?" she asked. "I have an extra cup."

"Something hot would be welcome about now," he admitted. His shirt with the Papa and Mama's Pizza emblem on the lapel was a short-sleeved, lightweight cotton. Not much protection in the open tower.

She poured the soup into an extra cup and handed it to him along with a plastic spoon and paper napkin. Then she lifted Honey out of his lap so he could enjoy the meal unmolested.

David scooped out some of the soup and tasted a spoonful. "Beef and fresh vegetables. You made this from scratch."

"I don't like the taste of canned or packaged soups."

"Neither do I," he said, before eating more soup. "How long is this assignment going to take?"

"Few hours probably. The bats should be coming out soon."

"Bats," he repeated in disbelief. "*You're* going to shoot those things that swoop through the night sky baring their teeth?"

"They're not baring their teeth," she corrected, "they're echolocating—using their ultrasonic cries to find their way and their food. Bats are a great natural pesticide. As a group, they eat two hundred tons of insects every night."

She noticed his cup was empty. "More soup?"

"Not after that appetizing picture you just put into my head, thank you."

She laughed.

"What kind of picture are you looking for?" he asked.

"I'm not sure yet. A shot of them flying through that window up there with the crescent moon rising in the background would be just another pretty picture. I'd rather hold out for something that would show what they're really like."

"And if you don't find that something?"

"Then, I'll probably be fervently wishing I was shooting hummingbirds. So, what are you doing on Falls Island?"

"Checking out Todd's condo."

"You saw me drive by," she guessed.

"I'd rather you left the detective work to me," he said gently.

"Since I had to come out here for the shoot, anyway, I thought I'd take a look at where he lives," she said, trying not to sound defensive but knowing she did.

"If Todd had seen you, were you prepared to tell him why you were stopped outside his condo?"

"Okay, you've made your point. So, have you found out anything else about him?"

"What would you like to hear first, past history or current events?"

"Let's start with his history and work to current events."

"He's an only child," David said. "He was put in a military boarding school when he was five and stayed through high school. The administrator admitted Todd hated his time there, despite the fact that he did well academically. He didn't like sports, didn't fit in with the other boys. He made only one friend, Warren Sterne, another outcast."

"If he was so unhappy there, why did his parents insist he remain?"

"His mother took Todd out after he'd been beaten by a couple of the other boys, but his grandfather returned him a week later. As the administrator explained to me, his grandfather was paying for Todd's education. He believed the military school to be the best and would settle for nothing less than that for Todd."

"Even if his grandson was battered and miserable there," Susan said with a shake of her head. "Todd must have liked U-Dub a lot better. Maybe that's why he chose to go to a public university after that private military school. Did Warren Sterne go there, too?"

"No, he went to a private college and then to work at his father's computer firm. Sterne started his own Internet company a few years ago on the coast. He's still Todd's best friend—only friend that I could find, actually."

"I wonder why Todd didn't make new friends."

"Once a child sees himself as an outsider, his behavior

often continues to conform to that image, even when his environment changes.''

"Yes, hard to get rid of those early images," she said, thinking about the struggle she'd had with her own.

"I did confirm that Todd has neither married nor had any children, so no example of his fathering skills currently exists. His credit is good. No evidence he's much of a drinker.''

"I didn't think he would be," she said. "I may be wasting both our time. Just before you got here tonight, I was trying to come up with a series of qualities that would make a man a good father. I'm not even sure I know what they would be, or even if I did, how to discover if a man had them.''

"Are you asking me to stop the investigation?''

"No. I just…well, Paul was hardworking, stable, and he wanted children. What other qualities would a good father have to have?''

"Drawing on my own father's example, I'd have to say intelligence, integrity, a commitment and loyalty to his wife and children, and a willingness to let his children see his mistakes as well as his successes.''

"So they can love as well as respect him," she said, immediately understanding. "Your father sounds terrific. What's your mother like?''

"I never feel grown-up around my mother. I mean, she's great, but somehow I always feel like she's caught me with my hand in the cookie jar.''

Susan laughed. "My grandmother could make me feel like that. She always saw right through me.''

"What about your father? Was there anything he did that you especially admired?''

She looked out at the darkening sky. "I never knew my father.''

"Sorry, I—''

''No reason to be,'' she said quickly, and then just as quickly changed the subject. ''You said there were some current events you've learned about Todd. Anything important?''

David was quiet for a moment before answering. She felt him studying her face. ''Todd has two books overdue at the library.''

''Oh, well, that's a serious flaw,'' she said lightly.

''They're on nature photography. Todd took them out right after you two met. According to the Falls Island librarian, he's a regular customer but has never been interested in the subject before. Did you mention your profession to him?''

Had she? She tried to remember.

''I moved some of my camera equipment out of the way in order to roll out the sleeping bag in the back of SUV that night,'' she said as she replayed the events in her mind. ''I might have said something then. But he can't have taken out those books on nature photography because of me.''

''I think he did,'' David said, handing her a white envelope. ''I found this lying on Todd's writing desk.''

''How did you get access to his writing desk?''

''If I tell you all my secrets, you might decide to chuck photography and give me competition in the private investigation business.''

''Very funny.''

''Go on. Take a look.''

The envelope he'd given her was open. She slipped her hand inside. Empty. She peered at the writing on the face of the envelope, but she couldn't make out the words in the dim light. ''What does it say?''

He flicked the beam from a tiny flashlight across the handwritten name.

*Susan Carter,* she read to herself.

"He knew my last name," she said in surprise. "I didn't tell him."

David turned off the flashlight. "Your name's on your camera equipment along with the name of the magazine. He might have seen them both that night."

He might have, she supposed. Had Todd really taken out those books because he'd learned of her profession? But why would he? They had shared only one night together. He hadn't even waited for her to wake up the next morning. She had no indication that he'd tried to contact her since.

What did her name on this envelope mean?

"Todd hasn't been at the research lab where he works for a few weeks," David said. "I haven't been able to find out where he is. But I do know that a moving van is coming for his stuff tomorrow morning. The moving company's supervisor was up in his condo this afternoon doing a survey of the job, when I happened to be delivering a pizza to the condo next door."

"That must be a good cover," she said, still unable to keep from smiling every time she looked at his uniform.

"Don't know many people who can resist the smell of a hot pizza."

"That's how you got into Todd's apartment?"

"When I showed frustration at no one being home next door, the supervisor was very sympathetic," David admitted. "Clearly, he's faced similar situations."

"And since he was giving you such a sympathetic ear, you reciprocated by offering him the pizza."

"Like I said, hard to resist the smell of a hot pizza. We walked through Todd's condo, while the supervisor complained about the job he faced between bites of pizza. Todd's refrigerator was full of spoiled food. Nothing was packed. There was also a mound of unopened mail on the desk. From the postage marks on the bills and letters, I'd say that Todd hasn't been home for at least a month.''

''Where is he?''

''That's what I intend to find out. The supervisor's moving order shows the contents of Todd's condo are going to his grandparents' home on the other end of Falls Island.''

''That's the explanation, then,'' she said. ''He's moved in with them.''

''Except that doesn't explain why he hasn't been at the lab, or joined the rest of his research team when they went to South America five weeks ago.''

''Maybe he's working on his part of the project alone,'' she said after giving the matter some thought. ''Dr. Bateman did say that Todd wasn't much of a mixer.''

''Dr. Bateman also said Todd was adamantly opposed to pesticides. The team he's been a part of at his grandfather's chemical company has just used a potent one to get rid of a new pest.''

''If I were Todd, I think I'd be pretty upset over that. Could be he's angry at the team and that's why he's not with them.''

A movement caught her eye. She looked up at the fluttering shadows on the ceiling of the lighthouse. ''I'd better get to work.''

''Where are the bats?'' he asked.

''They nest up there within the pockets of wood that keep them in shadows.''

''Do you use a nightscope to see them?''

''If I tell you all my secrets, you might decide to chuck your profession and give me competition in the photography business.''

''Very funny.''

''I don't need a nightscope,'' she said as she got on her knees and positioned herself beneath the camera she'd secured to the tripod. "The light's dim but there. With a high-speed film, the right exposure, a soft flash and a lot of luck, I should be able to get the right image at the right moment."

She cupped her hand around her eye as she looked through the lens and focused on the tower's ceiling. When the stirring bats were properly framed, she leaned aside. "Have a look."

He squatted beside her, and she felt a small shock as his nearness registered on her senses. She knew she was too close, but she didn't move away.

"Amazing how tightly they huddle together," he said. "Looks like they're starting to take off. You might want to get this."

When he leaned back so she could reposition herself in front of the camera, their shoulders brushed. She sucked in a breath.

"You all right?" he asked, his breath warm against her cheek.

"Fine," she said, her voice barely audible. His face was in shadow, and he smelled of the rich spices in her soup and warm, healthy male. Her heart thumped in her ears.

Honey let out a sharp bark. She knew he was probably upset at being ignored. But at the moment, all her attention was on David.

She could feel the heat of him against her skin just as though he were touching her. She knew he could have moved away, but he hadn't. They were so close.

And she wanted nothing more at that moment than to lean closer until she was kissing him. Until she was touching his shoulders and finding out firsthand if they were anywhere near as muscular as they looked. Until—

"What's going on here?" a gruff male voice demanded.

Without warning, a torch blazed in her eyes. She let out a startled cry and fell back on her heels, trying to shield her eyes with her hand. Above her, the telltale flutter of wings were taking off out the window.

"Turn off your light," David said. "You're scaring the bats."

"Who are you?" the man asked, shining the light toward him.

"He's with me," she yelled, "and if you don't turn off that damn thing right now, I'm calling the Island security. This is a photo shoot. You're scaring my subjects!"

"I'm the Island security," he said, finally switching off the light.

Susan still couldn't see anything but the unmoving blob of brightness that had been burned into her retina. "Well, then, you should have known that this lighthouse tower is off bounds tonight," she said in angry indignation. "Damn it, you've blinded me!"

"They said one photographer," the security guard answered in a sulky voice. "No one said anything about a pizza delivery van."

"I suppose *you* wouldn't care if your wife were all alone at night in a remote lighthouse shooting bats where any creep could come along," she said. "*You'd* probably just leave her there all by herself!"

Her shouting was probably scaring away more of the bats than the security guard had. And although she was directing her anger at him, she was really angry with herself. For if the guard hadn't come along when he did, she would have kissed David.

She should be hugging this guard instead of yelling at him. He'd just saved her from humiliating herself.

"This is my fault," David said. She could hear him getting to his feet although she still couldn't see anything. He must not be as blinded as she was.

"She wasn't expecting me tonight or she would have told the people in charge there would be two of us," he explained calmly. "I was just concerned for her safety. You understand."

"Yes, of course," the guard said. "But you gotta understand my job is to check these things out."

"I'm glad you feel that way," David said. "Your presence has reassured me. I feel I can leave her now to take her photographs, and you'll be watching out for her safety."

"You can count on that, Mr...?"

"I'm David. And your name is...?"

"Fred."

"Good to meet you, Fred. This is Susan Carter. You've probably seen her photos in *True Nature* magazine."

"I don't subscribe to any magazines."

"You don't know what you're missing. Her work is unforgettable. We'd better go, so she can concentrate— Would you like me to take the dog home, or would you like to keep him with you for company?"

A silent moment passed before Susan realized that David was addressing her. No doubt, Honey had gone with him to the stairs. "Uh...I'd like to keep him with me."

She heard David's footsteps coming toward her. A moment later Honey's warm little body was being put into her arms.

"Don't be out too late," he called back to her as he retraced his steps to the stairs. He sounded just the way a concerned husband should.

She cuddled Honey in her lap so he wouldn't follow David.

"Will she be able to get the photos she needs?" Fred asked as he and David descended the stairs. "I didn't mean to scare away the bats."

"She'll figure something out, don't worry," David said. "She's very resourceful."

"She was really mad."

"Photographers are perfectionists," David said. "Especially the really good ones. Takes them a while to set up just the right shot. I'm sure you understand the feeling. You're obviously very concerned about doing your job properly, as well."

"You bet I am."

"You hungry, Fred? I have some cold pizza in the truck."

"Cold is my favorite kind."

As their footsteps faded away, Susan found herself letting out a deep sigh. She was glad David was being nice to the security guard. She hadn't handled that well at all. Damn, she used to be so calm in a crisis. What was happening to her?

She gave Honey a hug. "You did try to warn me someone was coming."

He licked her hand.

"I'm sorry for ever thinking you weren't a wonderful watchdog."

Honey woofed his acceptance of this much-deserved apology.

She was finally beginning to regain some of her vision. She doubted she had a prayer of getting any shots of the bats tonight. But she did know that she wasn't going anywhere for a while. She needed time to get herself back in control.

She had come close to making a fool of herself over David tonight. She was going to have to be more careful around him from now on. Much more careful.

DAVID PARKED ACROSS the street from the Falls Island estate of Robert and Nancy Ardmore and waited for the vanload of furniture from Todd's condo to arrive. He couldn't see much of the mansion. Tall, carefully groomed hedges hid even the massive stone walls surrounding the property.

But he knew from having checked the county assessor's file that the house had fourteen bedrooms, fifteen baths, two kitchens, an outdoor and indoor swimming pool, four saunas, two hot tubs and a tennis court.

He also knew from having talked to Fred, the friendly Falls Island security guard, that billionaire industrialist Robert Ardmore had the latest in security systems installed behind those hedge-lined walls.

But his conversation with Fred wasn't the only event from the night before that was still very much on his mind.

When Susan had invited him to look through her camera lens, he'd been very aware of how close she remained. When their shoulders brushed, he'd heard her startled intake of breath. And still she had stayed where she was, so close to him that he could smell the scent of her hair.

To David, that had been a startling, welcome invitation, an invitation that had taken every ounce of his control not to accept. He'd tried to make himself move away, but he hadn't been able to. He'd barely been able to keep himself from closing the small distance separating them.

Except it wasn't a small distance separating them. It was an abyss.

For the hundredth time he reminded himself that she was not only his client, but also mourning her dead husband and facing an unexpected pregnancy. To take advantage of her vulnerability would be a breach of every ethic he possessed.

He would not touch her.

But it was costing him. When she so boldly implied to the security guard that he was her husband, he had to restrain himself from wrapping his arms around her and kissing her for such an inspired explanation. After waiting outside the Falls Island gates and following her home to make sure she got there safely, he had lain awake the rest of the night, trying *not* to imagine what kissing her would have been like.

He had to find out where Todd was and close this case. Fast.

He heard the engine of a heavy vehicle and saw the moving van approach the gate. He watched as the driver leaned out of the cab and pressed the intercom button at the entrance to the Ardmore mansion. After an exchange of conversation, the entry gates swung open to admit the van. David was trying to decide whether he should head to the top of the hill to see if he could get a view of the front of the house with his binoculars, when Todd's BMW suddenly drove out and took off down the road.

He couldn't see who was driving, but chances were good it was Todd. Part of being a successful private investigator was luck. Some of that luck seemed to be with him today. He followed the BMW.

Tailing cars was not one of his favorite pastimes, especially on two-lane rural roads where there were no other vehicles to hide behind. But the driver of the BMW gave no sign of noticing the dark-blue van David drove today with the logo of a nonexistent cellular company on the side.

He had used the van and his dark-blue overalls to get him through the security gates at Falls Island today, just as the logo for the nonexistent pizza place had gotten him past the security guard the day before.

Both were good covers. But both were also easily remembered, and, hence, not the best for tailing.

The BMW followed the winding road to the island's main thoroughfare. David followed the car through the exit gates and off the island toward the adjacent industrial complex of Ardmore Hills. He was beginning to wonder if Todd was on his way to work, when the BMW suddenly took a right turn onto a side road.

Giving the car a slight lead, David followed. The BMW maintained speed down the narrow tree-lined road for two miles before finally slowing and entering the driveway of a small, private hospital. As he watched, the BMW headed for a vacant parking spot. David pulled into an empty space, picked up his camera and aimed it at the BMW.

As he stared through the telephoto lens, he was surprised to see a woman open the driver's door and get out. She was petite and looked to be in her seventies, with a puff of white, meticulously groomed hair and powdered skin. He clicked off several quick shots of her face. She was dressed in a long, warm coat and walked with a steady, focused gait toward the entrance.

He stowed his camera, turned off the engine, picked up a clipboard and a blue cap that matched his uniform, and jumped out of the van to follow her inside. The older woman went directly to the elevator. He hurried to catch up, stepping in just behind her. She pushed the button for the second floor. He pushed the button for the third floor, then retreated behind her once again.

The woman was clearly preoccupied. She neither looked at him nor gave any sign she was even aware he was there. When she got off on the second floor, he gave her a small head start before following.

But he had no sooner stepped off the elevator than he was suddenly challenged by two enormous orderlies wearing white jackets and black scowls. They charged up to him like bouncers at an exclusive club.

''This is a restricted area,'' one of the orderlies growled as he laid a restraining hand that felt like an anvil on David's chest.

He let all the surprise he was feeling claim his features before pretending to look down at the notes on his clipboard. The brim of his cap helped to hide the fact that he was actually following the path the elderly woman was taking down the deserted hallway.

"Sorry," he said, after he had gotten a fix on where she was going. His eyes rose to the two orderlies. "Looks like I got off on the wrong floor."

He backed into the elevator, sending an apologetic look toward the two grim faces as the doors closed. He rode the elevator to the third floor and got out. He wasn't challenged this time. No one paid any attention to him at all.

This floor looked perfectly natural, with a busy central nurses' station next to a family waiting area and a few ambulatory patients mingling in the halls with the medical personnel.

He made his way to the stairwell at the opposite end. When he had descended one flight, he tried the door leading from the stairwell to the second floor. It was locked. He took the next flight down to the lobby and quietly exited the building.

David stood outside, looking up at the room on the far right end of the second floor—the room to which the elderly woman had been heading. The drape was open. That was good.

He needed a look into that room.

And he knew he'd better do that before someone closed the drape.

# CHAPTER NINE

SUSAN BALANCED THE TRAY of lemonade in her hands as she shouldered open the screen door and stepped out into the backyard. The bright hot August sun hit her in the eyes. Paul had been working at digging the irrigation ditch for several hours. She knew he had to be thirsty.

She paid careful attention to where she was stepping in her strapless, open-toed sandals, intent on not tripping over the dirt and debris. But when she looked over at the irrigation ditch, Paul was nowhere to be seen.

Strange. She walked over to the patio table and set down the tray. She shielded her eyes with her hand as she surveyed the backyard. No Paul. She headed toward the irrigation ditch. Maybe he was on his hands and knees down there, trying to dig out a stubborn rock.

She stopped at the edge and leaned over to peer down the dark channel he'd dug, squinting to see in the sun. "Paul?"

Without warning, arms circled her waist from behind, wrapping her in a tight embrace. "Gotcha!"

She whirled around to see Paul's face covered in mud and an enormous grin. "Paul, you scared me. Good thing I don't have a weak heart."

"Good thing *I* don't, after seeing you bending over in those shorts."

He pulled her to him. "Let's take a shower together."

"I don't need a shower, Mr. Mud Man," she said, trying

to wiggle away from his dirt-covered chest. "I just got out of one ten minutes ago."

"I can fix that," he said as he picked her up and slid down the side of the tunnel he'd dug. The next thing she knew, they were rolling around in the muddy ditch together, and she was laughing so hard she hurt—

"Susan, you there?"

Susan awoke with a start, the sound of someone calling her name echoing in her ears. She was disoriented, a part of her still connected to her vivid dream.

"Oh hell, I thought you were home by now," Ellie's voice said.

Susan looked around and realized that she'd fallen asleep on her bed, fully clothed. Honey was stretched out near her feet. Ellie's voice was coming from the answering machine.

"I have some exciting news, and I wanted you to be the first to hear. So, when you get home, please give me a—"

She grabbed the telephone receiver. "I'm here, Ellie," she said, pulling herself into a sitting position and trying to stifle a yawn.

"You sound strange. You okay?"

"Yeah, just too many late nights trying to get a decent shot of bats."

"Any luck with the creepy critters?"

"I think the ones I shot in an old barn last evening will do the trick. But the darkroom was backed up, and I was too tired to wait around for the contact sheet. I left the office at three today and came home to crash. So, what's this exciting news?"

"Skip's going to move in with me."

Uh-oh.

"Oh, I know there are a lot of things we'll have to work out," Ellie said. "But he hates living at home. They treat him like such a child. We haven't known each other that long, but we've just stepped right into love.''

Ellie had stepped into something, all right.

"I know I'm not being logical," she went on. "But I can never be logical about these things. I'm one of those women who just has to follow her heart.''

Actually, Susan believed that her smart, savvy friend only knew how to follow her fantasies when it came to men. But Susan knew better than to say that to Ellie.

"Suz, you there?''

"Yeah, I guess I'm still a little groggy.''

"I'm sorry for waking you. But I was just bursting with the news.''

"I understand. So when's the big move?''

"This weekend. He's telling his folks tonight.''

"Let me know if I can do anything.''

"You've already done it, Suz. You haven't put me down or tried to lecture me. You've just let me be me. You're the best friend ever.''

Susan said goodbye to Ellie and hung up the phone. She didn't feel like the best friend ever. She felt depressed. Ellie was repeating her unhealthy pattern, and she was going to end up getting hurt.

Susan didn't want that. But there wasn't a thing she could do to prevent Ellie from making this mistake.

She headed for the shower. As she stood beneath the warm spray, shampooing her hair, she thought about the dream she'd been having when Ellie called. She'd had this dream of Paul before. A lot of the dreams of him were repeats. She wondered why the scenes that kept playing over and over in her dreams weren't the ones that came to mind when she was awake.

When she was awake, she remembered the first time she and Paul had met. She'd gotten stuck in the snow with a flat tire, and he'd stopped to change it. Then there was the time after they were married when he had surprised her by cleaning the house and cooking dinner for her on her birthday.

But this dream had once again brought back that hot day in August when she'd gone out to the backyard with the lemonade she'd made for him and ended up getting tackled and rolling around in the mud.

That was Paul. Always so full of life. And mischief.

But he really should have been more careful that day. Now she remembered the reason her laughter had hurt so much was that his horsing around had cracked one of her ribs.

Susan stepped out of the shower and dried herself and her hair. She wished she could stop these dreams of Paul. He was gone. She accepted that. She always thought of him with unqualified love, and gratitude that he'd been part of her life. Why was she being haunted by these dreams?

She didn't want to be pulled back into a past she had laid to rest. She had enough to deal with, getting ready for the baby.

And not just the baby. Two days had passed since she'd talked to David. He'd been in contact with her every day since he'd taken the case. Now, suddenly, silence. Ever since that night in the lighthouse.

Had he known she was about to make a fool of herself? He was so damn good at reading her. If he had read that about her, she'd just as soon not see him again. The embarrassment would be intolerable.

A woman throwing herself at a man was a pitiful thing to witness. She knew. She'd watched her mother's displays often enough.

She pulled on a pair of old jeans over her panties, shoved her arms through a bulky white sweater and went downstairs to feed Honey and cook her dinner. But her thoughts were still churning.

She'd learned to hide her feelings as a way of protecting herself as a child. But hiding things from David was proving difficult. She didn't like the way he had of making her feel so exposed.

Maybe she was wrong to pursue this investigation. Todd seemed like a pretty nice guy. Did she really have the right to withhold the information that he was to become a father? If someone were checking into her past and using what they found as criteria to judge her ability to be a good parent, would she pass? Probably not.

She should write to Todd, tell him about the baby, explain that she expected nothing from him but would be willing to have him play a role in the life of his child if that was his wish.

What was the worst that could happen? He wouldn't answer her letter? Well, if he didn't answer, that would *be* her answer. A man who didn't want to be involved in his child's life was clearly one who shouldn't.

The idea was sounding better by the minute. The post office would forward Todd's mail to wherever he was staying. Once he read her letter and got back to her, or didn't, the matter would be resolved.

Tonight, she'd compose the letter. First thing tomorrow, she'd mail it. Then she'd call David and ask him to drop the case. She would never have to see him again. That would be the ideal solution to these inappropriate feelings she was having for him.

She finished her dinner and settled herself on the living room couch, pen and pad in hand. *Dear Todd,* she wrote. *I'm Susan Carter. We met almost two months ago at a bereavement—*

The doorbell rang. Honey barked and hopped off the couch, making a dash toward the door. Susan resented people who dropped by unannounced. But whoever was there must have seen her light and knew she was home.

She put her pad and pen down on the coffee table and went to answer the door. When she turned on the outside light and looked through the peephole, she was very surprised to see David standing there. And immensely dismayed at the sudden thrill that shot through her.

She took a deep, steadying breath and reminded herself that she was a levelheaded woman. She could handle this. She calmly opened the door. Honey immediately rushed out to greet David, barking happily.

As she watched David bend down to pet her dog, she let out a private sigh. Less than five minutes before, she had convinced herself that she never wanted to see him again. Now here he was, and she was glad.

He rose to his considerable height, made all the more considerable since her feet were bare. He wore dark dress slacks and a light-blue sweater. Not a strand of his hair was out of place. No stubble lined his chin.

She wished she had slipped into something prettier than her faded, old jeans and sweater. She hadn't even put on a bra. Her hair was an untamed mass around her shoulders.

"May I come in?"

She realized with tardy dismay that she'd been staring at him the whole time she'd been inventorying her hopeless personal appearance. She quickly stepped aside. "Of course."

He entered with Honey trotting after him. She closed the door, reminding herself her appearance didn't matter. David was just her private investigator, soon to be her ex-private investigator. But none of her self-talk was helping. All the logic in the world didn't take away the disappointment she felt. Around him she wanted to look her best and be her best. Tonight she was neither.

And this would be the last time she saw him.

Maybe that was a good thing.

She led the way into the living room. He had come to

report. She would listen politely. When he was finished, she would thank him and tell him of her decision to stop the investigation. That would be the end of that.

"Is there anything I can get you to eat or drink?" she asked in what she hoped was a polite, detached manner.

"No, thanks."

His tone seemed as polite and detached as her own. She was glad. She gestured for him to have a seat.

She sat back on the couch and called to Honey to join her. When he leaped up beside her, she wrapped an arm securely around him. She didn't want Honey jumping up on David's lap. She was determined to keep everything cordial but businesslike between them. The way she should have kept things all along.

He rested back in the chair. She waited for him to start, but he was quiet. She could feel his eyes on her face. A few days ago, she would have boldly returned his gaze. But tonight, she was not feeling up to it. Nor was she going to take any more chances with him. She couldn't afford to.

Susan concentrated her attention on Honey, stroking his ears and back, patiently waiting for David to begin.

"I called earlier," he said, "didn't get an answer."

"I was probably in the shower. Did you find out where Todd is?"

"Yes."

She waited for him to continue. When he didn't, she finally looked over at him. But he wasn't looking at her. He was staring at the note she'd begun to write to Todd.

His eyes rose. "You were writing to him."

There was no point in trying to deny the obvious, nor did she see the need to defend her actions.

"What have you found out?" she asked, dropping her eyes back to Honey.

"Why were you writing to him?"

"Doesn't matter."

"It does," David insisted, not but ungently. "Please, tell me."

She knew then that he was not going to let the subject go until she told him. She might as well. She wasn't up to a verbal sparring match. Not tonight.

"I'm going to tell Todd about the baby. He's not a criminal. He's not married. He's not a bum. He has a right to know, even if he chooses not to be a part of his child's future."

There was no missing the stress in her voice. So much for maintaining her cool. She let out an internal sigh and fervently wished David hadn't come.

"He won't answer your letter."

Oh, great. She could tell more good news was on its way. "Why not?"

"Shortly after meeting you, Todd deliberately set an explosion in the lab at the Ardmore Chemical Company."

Her head came up in alarm as her eyes sought David's face. "Are you telling me he destroyed the lab because he was upset over their using the pesticide?"

"No. It was a suicide attempt."

She slumped against the couch cushions. "Oh, no," she said. "Is he badly hurt?"

"He's in a coma."

Susan suddenly felt small and ashamed. Here she'd been worrying about how she looked, and all the time the father of her unborn baby was terribly injured.

"Did they let you see him?" she asked, wondering if she'd be able to.

"They don't even know I'm aware he's hurt or how he was hurt. I followed his grandmother when she went to see him in the private hospital where he's being kept under tight security."

Honey nudged Susan's thigh.

''What are his chances?'' she asked as she absently stroked the dog.

''Slim to none.''

Honey kept nudging her thigh despite the fact that she was petting him. When he finally jumped off the couch and headed toward the kitchen, she realized that he was telling her he had to go out. She stood and followed him to unlock his doggie door. But her movements were automatic, her thoughts entangled with what she had just learned.

She replayed the events of the night she'd met Todd. His quiet manner and shy smile. His offer to buy her a drink when he saw she was sad. His confessed inability to write the goodbye letter to his mother. His genuine unhappiness and upset over her death and how she would be remembered.

Had that unhappiness contributed to his suicide attempt?

Todd was so young. He had so much life ahead of him. Had he known they had conceived a child together that night, would he have thought twice about taking such a drastic action?

She dragged herself back into the living room, plopped onto the couch and lay back against the cushions. ''I didn't even really know him. I'm not sure why this is making me feel so awful.''

''The missed opportunity of getting to know him, perhaps,'' David suggested.

''No, I think I feel bad because of all the opportunities he'll be missing out on now.'' Sorrow squeezed at her heart. ''He'll never see his baby.''

She heard her voice break, noticed the dampness on her cheeks and realized suddenly that she was crying. She fumbled for the tissue on the side table. But the tears blinded her and she knocked over the tiny figurine of a dolphin Ellie had given her at Christmas. The figurine broke in two and fell to the floor.

"Damn!" she said, and was dismayed to hear the high, unhappy sound of her youthful voice reverberating in her ears. So much for all her voice training.

"Here," David said. He took her hand and placed a tissue in her palm.

She brought the tissue to her eyes. "I don't know why I'm crying. I haven't cried in twenty years. I read hormonal swings in pregnancy can make you cry for no reason. But this feels crazy."

A shameful, jerking sob escaped through her throat.

She felt him move beside her on the couch, his hands urging her closer as he nestled her securely against his chest.

"Go ahead and cry," his deep voice said as his arms wrapped around her. "You don't need a reason. Feel crazy if you want. You have the right."

The gentleness in his voice undid her remaining restraint. She collapsed against him and gave in to the useless, idiotic tears. Since she was eleven she'd been aware that crying did no good. No damn good at all. But that awareness didn't keep the tears from coming now.

When the tears finally subsided a few moments later, he was still holding her against him while he stroked her hair in the same soothing way he'd stroked Honey. She wiped her eyes with the tissue, realizing she'd soaked his sweater.

"I'm sorry," she said. "I've never cried in a man's arms before. Must feel awful against your skin."

"What?" he asked, surprise in his voice as his hand halted in mid-stroke.

"I've drenched your sweater," she said. "Probably ruined it."

"No, tears are good for sweaters," he said. "I try to get someone to cry on mine at least once a week."

Her laugh was soft and shaky. How wonderfully silly he was being. And how genuinely nice. She knew she should move away. But being next to him felt good.

"So, were you in the dentist's or the doctor's office?" she asked after a moment.

"The dentist's or doctor's office?" he repeated, clearly confused.

"When you read the magazine article on how to be nice to crying women."

"Oh, that," he said, his tone far too quick and casual. "I was in the psychiatric wing at the hospital. The title of the article was 'Comforting Crazy Female Photographers Who Only Cry Once Every Twenty Years.'"

She placed her palm on his chest as she pushed back to look up into his face. His eyes sparkled with mischief. He was trying not to smile.

She imbued her tone with too much sweetness. "And did the authorities finally release you from that psychiatric wing or did you escape?"

He chuckled, that throaty sound she loved so much. She looked down at her hand as the chuckle rumbled through him, tingling through her palm.

She was so focused on the feel of him that for a moment she wasn't aware of his arm tightening around her.

"Susan."

His voice was a husky whisper, nothing like the normal baritone she was used to. She suddenly became conscious of what she had been doing. Lying intimately against him, she'd been rubbing his chest with her hand.

She yanked her hand away. He captured it and put it right back. His heart pounded beneath her palm.

Her heart had begun to pound, too. As she looked into his eyes, she knew two things. She had not imagined what she'd seen that first night he'd come to her home. And she was so very glad she had not imagined it.

He bent his head and gently placed his mouth on hers, his lips softly questioning. A delicious shiver snaked through her.

The kiss deepened with a sudden heat that stole the breath from her lungs. His free hand inched under her sweater. When his fingers spread over nothing but her bare skin, a groan escaped his lips.

The telephone suddenly screeched beside her. She jumped.

He instantly released her, pulling his hand away. He grabbed both of her hands and held them tightly in front of him. He struggled for breath, his voice barely a whisper. "Susan, I'm so…sorry."

She searched his face as her pulse raced.

He was sorry for kissing her? *No, please don't let him be sorry.*

But regret had already etched itself into the hard line of his mouth. He was sorry, all right.

And that damn telephone was still ringing.

She couldn't look at him anymore. As she leaned over to pick up the telephone, she sensed him rise off the couch. His eagerness to flee from her left her feeling hollow and cold.

She brought the telephone receiver to her ear. "Hello?"

"Thank God you're there," Barry's voice said on the other end of the line. "My ex-wife intends to move in with me."

"What?" Susan asked, trying to get her thoughts aligned to Barry's problem.

"The psycho is on her way!" he yelled.

Susan forced herself to concentrate. "I thought she was in Florida harassing her third ex-husband."

"He just called," Barry said. "She made bail after violating his restraining order a second time, packed her bags and is on her way here. She arrives sometime tomorrow."

"Move out tonight, Barry. Don't leave a forwarding address. Have your landlord store the stuff you don't have time to take with you. Warn him that she might break in and that he should call the police on her."

"She still knows where I work."

"You can move your desk into the old storage room, the one with a lock on the door. We'll reroute your calls through me. If she tries to get in contact, I'll tell her you took a job in Chicago at this terrible magazine I've heard is run by hoodlums. It operates out of a condemned building in the worst neighborhood imaginable. They don't have a telephone so she won't be able to verify whether you're on staff. If she goes there, she'll probably get mugged."

"I pity the poor mugger who tries to tangle with her," Barry said. "Any chance I can crash there with you for a while?"

"I know you mean that in a platonic way, but the answer still has to be no. I converted my half-bath into a darkroom and my guest room into a study. That leaves just one bedroom and one bath. When Ellie stays over, she has to sleep on the couch."

"I hate motels, but I guess one will have to do."

"Or you could give Ellie a call," Susan suggested, as the new possibility presented itself. "Her apartment has two roomy bedrooms, each with a bath."

"You've got to be kidding," Barry said.

"Absolutely serious." Actually, the idea was sounding better by the second. If Barry were in one of Ellie's bedrooms, maybe Skip would think twice about moving in, and maybe Ellie would think twice about letting him.

"Ellie's never going to let me stay with her."

"I've never known Ellie to turn down someone in need. You've never been in trouble before or you'd know this about her. She's an absolute sweetheart."

"You really think she'd take me in?"

"Call her. Tell her what's happening. Remember, Ellie knows all about the knife wound the psycho inflicted when you told her you were divorcing her. Ellie will understand what you're up against."

She could hear Barry's deep exhale on the other end of the line. "Guess it's worth a try."

"Don't forget that tomorrow you need to see a lawyer and start on your restraining order."

"The picture is clear, Susan. Thanks for sharpening the focus. I owe you a hug. Cover for me tomorrow if I'm late getting in?"

"Consider it done," she said.

Susan said goodbye to Barry and hung up the phone. She leaned back on the couch to see that David was sitting across from her in the chair. A part of her was surprised he hadn't left.

"Problem?" he asked, nodding toward the phone. He was back to his composed self, as if nothing had happened between them.

"Just a friend needing some advice."

She was thankful for Barry's call. Concentrating on his problem had cleared her mental fog and helped her get her emotions under control.

David rested his forearms on his knees and made a point of meeting her eyes. "I deeply apologize for what happened tonight, Ms. Carter. My actions were inexcusable."

So, he was back to calling her Ms. Carter. How formal. How correct. How gallant to accept all the blame.

How sad it made her feel.

"I have no defense for my behavior," he continued. "I can only ask that you try to forgive me, and I promise... Please be assured that it will never happen again."

Well, he'd made his intent very clear. Nothing personal beyond this point. She told herself she was glad.

"It was just a kiss," she said. If he could walk away from this so easily, damn him, so could she. "Your professional integrity didn't even come into play since our business relationship was already concluded."

"You consider the case closed?"

"Is there any chance that Todd will recover?"

"There's no sign of any brain activity," David said gently.

Which meant that even if they kept his body alive, his thoughts, personality—everything that made Todd who he was—was gone. Susan felt the new sadness settling in. She'd handle it. She had handled worse.

"Then, that definitely closes the case," she said.

"There is another consideration," he said. "Todd was Molly Ardmore Tishman's only child. You are carrying the great-grandchild of Robert and Nancy Ardmore—the only great-grandchild they will ever have. You should think seriously about telling them."

"Tell the Ardmores? No, definitely not."

"Why not?"

"If Todd weren't in a coma and chose to tell them about the baby, that would be his decision. But he and I didn't have a real relationship. There was no courtship. No commitment. None of the things that should have come before conceiving a child."

"So what you're saying is that you think those things would be important to the Ardmores."

"No, what I'm saying is that those things are important to *me*. Conceiving and bringing a child into the world shouldn't just be an act of biology. It should be an act of intent, and of love."

Susan let out a deep sigh before she continued. "I behaved like a brainless boob on the night I conceived this baby. But I'm consciously choosing to bring my child into the world now with the full intent of being its loving parent. Todd isn't going to have the opportunity to make that choice."

"The Ardmores might want the opportunity."

"Oh, right," she said with sarcasm. "I'm sure they'd be just thrilled to have some stranger show up on their doorstep claiming to be carrying their great-grandchild, especially after having lost their only daughter a few months ago and having to watch their only grandchild lying in a coma in a hospital."

"Those are the very things that could make them grateful for news of a baby."

"More likely they'd think I was just some crackpot trying to scam them."

"DNA testing would prove your claim."

"I don't want to claim anything. Nor do I want to get into the legal and emotional hassles such testing would entail, or the media involvement that would most certainly ensue. I have no intention of allowing my private life and that of my baby's to become entertainment on the ten o'clock news."

"Are you going to tell anyone about your baby's father?"

"I'll tell the baby, when she or he is old enough. I have a firm belief that children have a right to know who their parents are, or were. But I must insist that you keep everything about the baby's parentage strictly confidential."

"If that's your wish. But what of your family, friends, co-workers?"

"I have no family. As for my friends and co-workers, when I start to show, I'll tell them I was artificially inseminated." She shook her head at the thought. "I hate lying. But sharing the truth in this case is not an option. They'll believe that explanation. None of them would ever imagine I'd had a one-night stand."

"No, I don't suppose anyone knowing you would," he said quietly.

"But as you once pointed out, Mr. Knight, none of us is what we seem. Here I am, living proof."

Susan rose. "I apologize for crying on your shoulder. It was stupid. Please include the cost of laundering your sweater in my bill. And please accept my sincerest thanks for all that you've done."

She stood tall and erect before him as she held out her hand. He got up but did not take her hand.

"The pleasure has been mine," he said.

He swiftly made his way to the door. A moment later she heard the door open and close behind him.

DAVID DROVE HOME from Susan's telling himself he was glad the case was over. But there wasn't a cell in his body that was agreeing with him.

Holding her in his arms as she cried, touching the tangled silk of her hair, feeling her soft body against him—he couldn't put into words how good that had made him feel.

She hadn't cried in any man's arms before. But she had let him hold her and had cried in his. The gift of her trust had been the greatest high of all. Taking advantage of her vulnerability at that moment had been the last thing he'd thought he would ever do. But all it had taken was the light caress of her hand across his chest to totally erase every good intention he'd ever possessed.

He'd had to kiss her. And she hadn't just let him. She'd kissed him back with brain-numbing enthusiasm.

*Just a kiss,* she'd said later.

Not just a kiss. Not by any stretch of the imagination. If that phone hadn't rung, he wouldn't have stopped at a kiss. He wouldn't have stopped at anything.

The stark reality of that fact had his hands shaking on the wheel.

Two years earlier, David had left his psychological practice because he'd come to the conclusion that he'd been kidding himself. No amount of training and no number of degrees had helped him predict or even understand how his own fiancée would react, the woman he'd thought he knew better than anyone else in the world.

He'd finally realized that the only person's behavior he would ever be able to predict was his own. And now, he had to admit that he couldn't even predict that. He'd been so sure that no matter what he felt for Susan, he would do nothing because he had his emotions under control. Tonight had shown him just how out of control his emotions really were. How out of control *he* was.

Thankfully, he was being saved from himself. The case was over. He didn't have to see Susan again. The thought should have comforted him but didn't. Because he so badly wanted to see her again.

He knew he needed time. And distance. And work. A lot of work. He had to bury himself in another case. Fast. Something difficult and intricate and engrossing. Something that would leave no time for thoughts of anything, or anyone, else.

He'd talk to his father first thing tomorrow and see what was available. As to how he'd get through tonight, he didn't know.

Despite the turmoil of thoughts and emotions bombarding his brain, David's training had him constantly checking his rearview mirror. He'd noted the dark sedan, two cars behind him. When the sedan suddenly made the same turn as he did, then switched over into the same lane, his spine stiffened. Was that the same dark sedan he'd caught a glimpse of when he was on his way to Susan's?

He spied an all-night convenience store coming up on

the right. Slowing, he pulled into an available parking space on the end, where the inside of his truck's cab would be in darkness. Putting the nightscope to his eye, he watched as the sedan drove by the convenience store.

A midnight-blue Toyota. Female driver. Long hair. Tall. Eyes straight ahead. Alone in the vehicle. He focused the nightscope on the back bumper and made the license number before the car drove out of sight.

Either she was tailing him or she wasn't. Only one way to find out.

David got out of the truck and went into the convenience store. He bought a couple of soft drinks, a purchase bulky enough to require a paper bag. If she was tailing him and she was a professional, she would be watching to see if he came out of the convenience store with something. Otherwise, she'd assume he had used the stop as a ploy to spot her.

He had no intention of letting her know he'd made her. He casually threw the paper bag on the passenger seat, got into the truck and headed for home.

Four blocks later, he caught sight of the sedan, three cars behind him. The nerves tightened at the back of his neck.

She was following him, all right. Now the only question was, why?

## CHAPTER TEN

SUSAN ATE HER LUNCH at her desk as she read the newspaper article about the mint-condition, 1905 Steiff teddy bear that the Meyerson family of Seaview, Washington, had just received $195,000 for in a private auction. She smiled.

"He's driving me crazy," Ellie said as she came into Susan's cubicle and plopped onto her side chair.

"What's he done now?" she asked as she put the newspaper aside.

Susan knew Ellie was talking about Barry. Every day since he'd become Ellie's roommate, Ellie had called or dropped by to complain about some new blunder he'd committed to spoil her romantic bliss.

"You know what he prepared for dinner last night?" Ellie complained. "Lasagna and garlic bread."

"I'm failing to see the problem here. You love that combination."

"And so does Skip! He had three helpings and two glasses of the imported wine Barry served. Skip was so over-carbed he fell asleep on the sofa. I had to wake him up to go home at midnight. Some romantic evening that was."

"So Skip is still living with his parents," Susan said, trying not to sound too happy.

"Yeah, I guess I told you they weren't too thrilled about the idea of his moving in with me. When they heard that I'd let Barry move into the second bedroom temporarily, things really hit the fan. They agreed to pull the restrictions off Skip if he agreed to remain at home.''

"Good of Skip to be concerned about their feelings.''

"I guess,'' Ellie said as she gnawed on a cuticle. "I just wish he'd start being a little more concerned about mine.''

"What do you mean?''

"Well, like the other night. Skip argued with Barry all through dinner about some stupid ball game.''

"Too much friction?''

Ellie shook her head. "They get along *too* well. When I see them together...well, Barry treats Skip almost like a son. And Skip likes it!''

"Barry's just trying to be nice. He told me you were great.''

"*Barry* said I was great?'' Ellie repeated, clearly surprised.

"His exact words,'' Susan confirmed. Of course, the full content of his sentence had been that Ellie was great to help him out. But she didn't see any reason to add that last part.

"He does clean up after himself,'' Ellie said grudgingly, as though Barry's compliment deserved reciprocation. "Maybe he does have a few of Paul's qualities.''

In truth, Paul had only cleaned the house that one time. But she let her friend's comment pass without challenge.

"Things will work out,'' Susan said as noncommittally as possible.

She was pleased with the way they were working out already. If this got-to-have-commitment obsession of Ellie's could be stopped with the unsuitable Skip, maybe the inevitable heartbreak could also be avoided.

She sometimes wondered whether Ellie's selection of unattainable men had anything to do with how hard Ellie had tried to get close to her emotionally aloof father.

As useless as Susan's effort to win her mother's approval.

"You okay, Suz? You've been looking a little tired lately."

"Just working too hard, I guess," Susan lied.

"You ever need me to cover an assignment, you know all you have to do is ask."

Susan's telephone rang. "Thanks, El."

Ellie left as Susan picked up the phone and answered with her name.

"Ms. Carter, this is Harry Gorman returning your call."

"Yes, Mr. Gorman. Did you get my bill straightened out?"

"I checked with Mr. Knight as you requested. He has not had an opportunity to give me his time and expenses on your case. He told me to tell you not to be concerned if you don't receive a bill for a while."

"He worked for nearly two weeks on my case, including the weekend and nights," she said, trying to keep her voice low. "Why don't you give me a ballpark figure, and I'll send you a check. Then when the bill is prepared, we'll make the adjustment."

"I cannot bill you for anything without Mr. Knight's authorization."

"May I speak with him?"

"He's unavailable at this time."

Just as he'd been unavailable the last time she'd called about this matter. Well, this was getting her nowhere. She thanked Harry and hung up.

Nearly two weeks had passed since David had walked out the door. She needed to close that chapter in her life.

She was going to be bringing a child into the world. The awesome responsibility of her decision had to be the focus of all her waking thoughts. There was so much to think about and plan for, with a baby on the way.

Which was why she had put David out of her mind.

And yet, there had been times while she was at a shoot that she'd had the strongest feeling he was close by. Once, the feeling was so strong she had even whirled around expecting to see him. But she hadn't seen him because he wasn't there.

David was gone.

"SIR, MS. CARTER called again," Harry said over the intercom.

"What did you tell her, Harry?" David asked.

"Exactly what you told me to, sir."

"Good."

"Sir?"

"Yes, Harry?"

"Are we ever going to send Ms. Carter a bill?"

"I doubt it, Harry."

"Yes, sir. Thank you, sir."

David released the intercom key. He realized Harry didn't understand. He didn't completely understand himself. Not in any logical, analytical way. He just knew that sending her a bill felt wrong. Doing the things he'd done for her had given him pleasure.

He opened the new issue of *True Nature* magazine and skimmed through the pictures. Every time one caught and held his attention, he knew that when he looked at the photo credit, he'd see Susan's name.

But when he came to the two-page center spread containing the bat pictures she'd taken, not even he was prepared for their impact.

In the first photo, a furry female Brown Bat was hanging by her claws, forming a basket with her tail to receive her baby. The next photo showed the baby bat being born feet-first, clutching the mother's fur with its tiny toes. As the baby fully emerged, bare and pink in the next picture, the mother cradled her infant under her wing. In the final picture, the baby bat nursed securely at the mother's breast while she carefully and lovingly cleaned its tiny body.

With talent, integrity and the perfect focus of a gentle heart, Susan had captured the rare, pure love that radiated between this mother and her baby, and had exposed the true nature of this winsome creature.

A knock came on his office door. He put down the magazine. "Come in."

Richard Knight entered. Richard was the eldest of the Knight brothers. He was also the tallest, besting David by an inch. He'd joined his parents' private investigation firm right after college, and David knew he was the best.

"Madeline McKinney won't tell me why she was following you," Richard said, his expression clearly conveying his own displeasure with the news. Richard was a man used to getting results. He didn't accept failure well.

"I thought you two were friends," David said.

"We spent some time together at an investigator's convention a while back," he said. "But as Madeline took pains to inform me a few minutes ago, we are definitely not friends."

David was a little surprised at the expression on his brother's face. Richard was a great deal more than displeased. He was pissed. Obviously, he *had* thought that they were friends.

"She kicked me out of her office just now, right after vehemently denying she'd even been following you."

"Oh, she was following me, all right," David said. "Right up until last week. I made her two weeks ago, although I had trouble tracking her identity down because she was driving a rental. Had to jump through hoops to get her name out of the clerk at the car rental agency."

"I believe you. But you have to understand that Madeline was probably annoyed that you'd seen her at all.

She's a damn good investigator. Great at tailing. Even under torture she'd never tell you who her client was."

David couldn't keep the disappointment out of his voice. "So you're telling me I'm at a dead end?"

"Not necessarily. Madeline must have or has had a client who's interested in your recent activities. Just ask yourself where those recent activities have taken you, and who might have had a reason to have you followed."

David had already asked himself those questions. He just didn't like the answers.

Whoever hired McKinney might have been someone connected with his earlier missing person case. But he didn't believe that. He was sure that the person who'd hired McKinney was someone connected with Todd Tishman.

What bothered him most about that was the fact that McKinney had followed him to Susan's town house.

He had deliberately visited the homes of several unattached females on the nights after he'd spotted Madeline. He wanted to leave the impression that the reason for his visit to Susan and the others had been casual romance rather than casework.

But he couldn't be sure his subterfuge had succeeded. That made him edgy.

David thanked his brother for his help and advice, and Richard left.

David knew he should get back to his current case—a man looking for the brother he'd lost track of after a heated argument twenty years before. His client wanted to mend the rift between himself and his brother. There were few clues as to where the lost brother might be. David had a lot of looking to do.

This was exactly the kind of case that he'd needed to get his mind off Susan.

But he didn't go back to his search. Instead he went to

his e-mail file and pulled up Susan's schedule, which was still being sent to him. She'd forgotten to take him off her recipient list. He could have blocked her address so he wouldn't receive her schedule, but he hadn't. As he read about the subjects of her next shoot, he couldn't wait to find out how she'd picture them.

SUSAN HAD NEVER SEEN an all-white black bear before. Such miracles of nature gave her a special thrill. The bear's white coat was rare and beautiful, especially when contrasted against the shiny ebony of the other black bear in the wildlife refuge. She knew that shooting the white-coated bear and the dark-coated one together would emphasize the unusualness of the white coat.

But after watching them silently for the past forty minutes, she still wasn't happy with the scene. These bears seemed as flat personality-wise as the gray rocks that they covered with their furry, slumberous frames.

The wildlife refuge provided a clean and spacious environment that was designed to mimic the natural habitat of the animals. But these were wild creatures, and she knew that captivity to them—however benevolent—was still captivity.

If she had to guess why these bears were lethargic on this brisk spring day, she would have said they were bored. They looked exactly like Honey did when Susan was too busy to play with him and he had grown tired of all his toys.

*Toys?* Susan rose from the stool she'd positioned in front of her tripod and headed for her SUV at the curb of the maintenance road. She rooted around in the back until she found the big, red, rubber ball Honey loved to chase around the park, despite the fact that the ball was far too large for him to catch in his jaws.

She returned to the enclosure, pitching the ball over the

tall, chain-link fence toward the bears. Then she quickly positioned herself on the stool in front of her camera and watched through the telephoto lens as the ball bounced enticingly on the rocks before the animals.

The dark-coated bear sat up. He leaned forward and swiped at the ball with his paw. The ball lifted high into the air and landed with a *plunk* on the chest of the supine, white-coated bear. The other bear grunted, sat up and swatted the ball back at his companion. The ball hit that bear smack-dab in the nose.

DAVID SAT IN HIS TRUCK grinning as he peered through his binoculars, watching the bears having a Ping-Pong match with the rubber ball. He'd been wondering how Susan was going to infuse life into her shots of the sluggish beasts. What she had come up with was ingenious. He was looking forward to seeing these pictures in the next issue of the magazine.

Just as he was looking forward to seeing all the pictures he'd surreptitiously watched her set up and take over the past couple of weeks. He'd shown up at her shoots, sitting out of sight in his truck, observing her work through his binoculars.

Had he been a practicing psychologist treating someone with his symptoms, David knew he would have told him he was a borderline stalker and needed to get some impulse control, and fast.

For his own sanity, he had to put an end to this.

There was just one way. He would put down the binoculars and drive away. He would never show up at another one of her shoots. And when he got back to the office, he was going to block her e-mail address so he wouldn't receive any more of her schedules.

David knew how to map out the directions that needed

to be followed to reach any destination. He had just mapped out these. Now, he was going to follow them.

SUSAN KEPT CLICKING her shutter. The muted sunlight glistened off the thick coats of the bears playing with the rubber ball against the tall evergreens in the background. It was everything she'd hoped for and more. Contrast, color, movement, shape, texture and the bears' playful personalities shone through every frame.

She loved watching nature reveal itself—sometimes sweet, sometimes sad, sometimes fragile, sometimes frantic, sometimes strong, sometimes tender, and sometimes surprisingly whimsical—like these wonderful bears who instinctively knew that a bouncing red ball was a signal to play.

She was so focused on the marvelous images that flowed effortlessly in front of her camera lens that she was unaware of anything else around her.

One second she was clicking away, and the next a heavy hand was grabbing her shoulders and yanking her backward until she hit a man's hard body. Disbelief numbed her. Before she could recover her senses, a large arm encircled her chest in a vice-like grip and a gloved hand clamped tightly over her mouth.

Sheer panic poured adrenaline into Susan, pumping her heart and tightening her muscles. She squirmed with all her might to pull her arms free. But the man was too strong, and she was too off balance. He dragged her backward.

She wanted to scream, but his hand was pressed hard against her mouth, and the pressure of his arm against her diaphragm was making even breathing difficult. Her eyes darted from side to side, looking for help.

But there was no help. The wildlife refuge was off

bounds to the public today. The guard wouldn't be making his rounds again for another twenty minutes.

She dug her heels as hard as she could into the rocky ground to stop from being dragged. The man's pace barely slowed. Still, she continued to struggle. She would not give in, not as long as there was an ounce of strength left in her body.

Then, without warning, the man released her. She fell to the ground, stunned and gasping for breath. She heard running feet behind her. An engine starting. The spew of gravel beneath tires.

Her assailant was fleeing!

"Susan!"

She could not believe her ears. She knew she had to be imagining his voice, just as she'd imagined his presence so many times before. But when she looked up, David *was* running toward her. He slid on his knees to the ground beside her.

"Susan," he said gently as he touched her cheek. He was perspiring, breathing hard. He looked absolutely real and absolutely wonderful.

"David," she said, finally allowing herself to believe what her senses were telling her. He wrapped his arms around her and held her close.

She understood now why her assailant had released her and fled. He'd seen David running toward them.

She had so many questions. But none of them mattered at the moment. All that mattered was that he was here, and she was safe in his arms.


"DID YOU GET ANY PART of the license number on the black van?" Jared asked his brother in his professional detective's tone.

David's hands balled into fists. "No! I was too far away when I saw the guy grab her. His van was at the other end of the roadway. All I could think about was getting to her before he dragged her into that van.''

''The door to the van was open?'' Jared asked in his irritatingly calm voice.

''Yes!'' David said as he paced around Susan's SUV, parked on the access road at the wildlife refuge. ''I've told you that already. Why aren't you out getting this guy?''

''I can't put out an APB on a black van, make, model and year unknown,'' Jared said calmly as he leaned against the SUV. ''There are literally thousands of black vans in the county. I need something more concrete to go on.''

David knew his brother was right. But knowing that didn't help.

All he could think about was what would have happened to Susan if he'd put down his binoculars and driven away a moment sooner. If he hadn't seen the man grab her. If he hadn't arrived in time.

His eyes traveled to Susan's pale face. She was talking to a female paramedic at the back of the ambulance, parked about twenty feet away. A male paramedic was checking her vital signs. She kept insisting that she was all right.

But David had seen what she'd been through. He'd held her trembling in his arms. He knew she was not all right.

''All I can give you is a sketchy description of the bastard,'' David told his brother, fury underscoring his words. ''He had a ski mask over his head. His jacket was black leather. So were his gloves. He appeared to be over six feet and stocky.''

''That's a lot better than what Ms. Carter gave us,'' Jared said.

''What do you expect? He came at her from behind. He never let her see him.''

Jared's hands came up. ''Whoa, David, back off. I'm not attacking her. I'm just stating the facts here. What's wrong with you?''

David met his brother's eyes. Jared and his twin, Jack, were identical in features and coloring. But despite the fact Jared shared Jack's fun-loving lifestyle and devil-may-care attitude, there was a hardness in him that Jack didn't possess.

David took a deep breath and slowly exhaled. "I can't be detached about this."

"No one said you had to be."

"That's who I am, Jared. At least, that's who I used to be."

"Hell, none of us are who we used to be," Jared said as he slowly straightened. "So what were you doing here?"

"That's not important."

Jared looked at his brother closely as he tapped his pen on the notepad in his hand. "That'll do fine for me, bro, but I'll need to have something a little more definitive for the official report."

"I was just passing by."

"Okay, you were a passerby. Saw a lady in trouble. Helped her out. Where exactly were you when this started to go down?"

David waved at a point behind him. "In my truck, parked on the other side of that chain-link fence."

Jared followed David's wave. "You scaled that twelve-foot fence and ran through a quarter mile of heavy brush and still got here in time to scare off the guy? I'm glad I stopped competing with you in those local Ironman races."

"How did he get in, Jared?" David asked, ignoring his brother's comment. "The refuge is closed today. There's a steel gate in front of the entrance."

"Security guard says someone removed the barrier he set across the maintenance road after he let Ms. Carter in for her photo shoot."

"The bastard must have been following her," David

said. "He saw the security guard let her in and then let himself in later when the security guard left. Jared, this was too well planned to have been a random abduction attempt. Someone was specifically after Susan."

"I'm inclined to agree. Were you here because you expected something like this?"

"No."

"She was your client."

"How did you know Susan was my client?"

"All part of my skillful interrogation techniques. I told her I was your brother. She told me she was your client. So give me something to go on."

David intended to. "A private investigator by the name of Madeline McKinney was following me when I was working on Susan's case. Find out who McKinney was working for, and odds are that's the bastard who tried to abduct Susan today."

"I know McKinney," Jared said. "She's a tough lady and normally pretty careful about who she takes on as a client. She's not going to give up a name without a court order. For that, I need probable cause. Can you give me anything I can take to a judge?"

"My gut feeling is telling me McKinney led this bastard to Susan."

"If I walk into McKinney's office with only your gut feeling to back me up, she'll have *my* guts on a platter. I told you, the lady's tough."

"Then, *I'll* talk to her," David said quietly, but there was nothing quiet about the look in his eyes or the clenched fists at his sides.

Jared stared at his brother as though seeing him for the first time. "Damn, and I always thought you were the *tame* one in the family."

"Make sure Susan is taken to the hospital," David said as he turned toward his truck. "And make sure someone stays with her until I get there."

THE OFFICE BUILDING was in the oldest section of Silver Valley, a hilly region heavy with history. Early settlers had staked their claim at the inlet of a then flourishing salmon stream. The salmon were long gone, but the descendants of the settlers remained.

The sign on the solid mahogany door said, McKinney and McKinney. David knew the two McKinneys were Madeline and her father. They were a reputable firm and the only real competition White Knight Investigations had on the peninsula.

Although David had often heard his parents and brothers speak of them, he had never met either of the McKinneys. That was about to change.

He entered the reception area of their nicely appointed offices. He noted the door to his right was open, the office beyond empty. The door to the office on the left was closed. He walked up to the young woman receptionist who was typing on her computer keyboard and asked politely, "Is Madeline in?"

The receptionist stopped typing and smiled up at him. "Do you have an appointment?"

He glanced at the phone on the receptionist's desk. The button beneath the third line was lit.

"She'll see me without one," he said.

Before the receptionist could react, he had turned the knob on the closed door to his left and stepped inside. He immediately recognized Madeline McKinney as the woman who'd followed him.

Madeline sat behind the large mahogany desk with her stocking feet resting on top. A phone hung from her ear. She had long, red hair, brown eyes and an expression filled with mirth. But the moment she saw David marching up to her desk, all hint of humor fled from her face.

She swung her legs to the floor and came to her feet in one graceful swoop. Even without shoes she was at least six feet tall. "I'll have to call you back," she said to whomever was on the phone before slamming down the receiver.

"Just what in the hell do you think you're doing barging into my office?" she demanded with considerable heat.

"Someone just tried to forcibly abduct Susan Carter," David thundered, in a voice so deep and deadly that Madeline flinched. He deliberately leaned his bulk across her desk. She fell back in her chair.

"If I hadn't been there, he would have succeeded. You tracked me to Susan, and then you gave away her identity to this bastard. I'm going to have your license, McKinney. If anything happens to Susan Carter, I swear to you, I'm going to have your head."

He straightened, turned and stomped out of her office, slamming the door so hard behind him that the walls shook and books fell off the shelves. The receptionist was cowering in her chair when he passed by. He gave the outer door an equally resounding slam.

He couldn't ever remember slamming a door before in his life. But then, he couldn't ever remember feeling so furious before in his life.

Poor impulse control. He was beyond caring. He had wanted to strike fear in the heart of Madeline McKinney. And from the look on her face, by God, that's exactly what he'd done.

"YOU CAN'T STAY HERE," David said after having checked the locks on the doors of Susan's town house and rejoining her in the living room.

She sat on the couch, Honey snuggled beside her, looking up at the solemn expression on David's face.

"This is my home," she said simply.

"Susan, you're not safe here. Anyone who's determined enough could get in. Don't you understand how close you came to..."

He turned away, shoved his hands into his pockets and began to pace. The tension in him was tangible. She knew he was angry. She also knew he wasn't angry *with* her. He was angry *for* her.

She was too full of gratitude to be angry. The paramedics had taken her to the emergency room to be checked over by a doctor. She and the baby were fine, just as she knew they'd be. She'd had a considerable fright but she hadn't been physically hurt.

She was home. She was safe. And she was with David. An unbeatable combination.

He had rescued her, held her close. But the moment the paramedics had arrived, he'd pulled away. She felt certain that were she to try to put her arms around him now, he would pull away again.

He cared for her and wanted her. But he was keeping his distance for a reason, and that reason was more important to him than whatever he felt for her.

She accepted that because she had no alternative.

"David, thank you for saving my life. The words are inadequate, of course. But they're all I have to offer. I don't know what made you come by the wildlife refuge today, but if you hadn't, I—"

He took his hands out of his pockets and irritably waved away her words. "Stop thanking me. I'm the one who put you in jeopardy."

She sat up straight. "What?"

He stopped pacing and looked at her for a moment before responding. "There's something I should have told you sooner."

Her heart gave an odd beat at the unhappiness that clouded his handsome features.

"While I was investigating Todd, I was being followed by another private investigator."

She tried to understand the significance of what he was telling her. "Why would another investigator follow you?"

He shoved his hands back in his pockets and started to pace again.

"I was asking questions about Todd, his father, his grandparents, his best friend, the people involved in the accident that killed his mother. Somewhere along the line someone got nervous. So they hired this other investigator to follow me."

"Who hired the investigator?"

David stopped pacing once more and stood in front of her. "I don't know. But that person was looking for my client. I led him right to you."

"You believe that man today was after me specifically?"

"The attempt to abduct you was carefully planned. He's probably been watching you for days, maybe weeks, waiting to get you alone in a secluded place before making his move."

A chill shot through her. Being the victim of a random attack was bad enough. Being the specific target was far worse. She leaned back on the couch, fighting to remain calm.

"David, this doesn't make sense. Why come after me? I'm no threat to anyone."

"There's only one thing in your life that could be generating this kind of attention."

"Not the baby," she denied in instant protest. "I've told no one I'm pregnant."

"When was the last time you went to the obstetrician?"

"About a week and a half ago. But my doctor's also a gynecologist. Even if someone followed me to her office, how would they—"

"Think about that last visit. Did the doctor's receptionist or nurse ask you anything about your pregnancy while you were in the waiting room where someone could overhear?"

"No."

"What about other patients waiting to see the doctor? Did you talk to them?"

"Well, yes. I asked the woman sitting next to me where she'd bought her maternity blouse. Then we talked a little bit about morning sickness and being tired."

"Was there a tall woman with long red hair in the waiting room at that time?"

Susan carefully thought back to that day. "A very tall woman came in after me, but as I recall, she had short dark hair."

"More than likely, she was wearing a wig. The private investigator following you was a woman. All she had to do was eavesdrop on that conversation you had in the waiting room of your doctor's office, and she'd know you were pregnant."

David had made a good point, but Susan wasn't yet sold. "Even if the investigator was there and learned I was pregnant by eavesdropping on my conversation, how could she know I was carrying Todd's child? I didn't even know who Todd was until you told me."

"But Todd knew who *you* were. Remember the envelope with your name written on the front? The books on nature photography he took out of the library? If Todd told someone about your night together, and they later learned that you were looking for him *and* that you were pregnant, connecting the dots wouldn't be difficult.''

"This is so hard to take in.''

"I know. But you must believe me when I tell you the threat against your life is serious.''

She believed him. The dreadful memories of the attempted abduction were still quite fresh in her mind.

"You can't stay here,'' David said. "He knows your address.''

"I don't know of any motel that would allow Honey to be with me.''

"Motels also require names and credit cards, which can be traced,'' he said, thinking aloud. "What's worse, you have to leave your car in plain view where anyone driving by can see it. They are definitely out. Besides, you can't stay anywhere alone.''

"Well, my best friend's apartment is currently filled to overflowing with her boyfriend and another friend of mine. There's no place else but here. I have good door locks. I won't be alone. I have Honey.''

"You don't have a security system. Even if your door locks are adequate, all someone would have to do to get in is break a window. And despite the fact Honey is a great companion, let's face it. He's not a rottweiler.''

Honey's head came up in dismay. Susan rubbed his chin reassuringly. "I'm very glad you're not, Honey. You're perfect just the way you are.''

Honey licked her hand and lay his head back on her knee. "We're staying here, David.''

"You're not safe here.''

"I'll be okay.''

He blew out a breath. "Do you have a gun?''

"No.''

"If I leave one with you, would you use it if necessary?''

"I've never even held a gun."

"Susan, what are you going to do if someone breaks in?"

"Call 9-1-1 and beat the intruder over the head with my tripod until help arrives."

## CHAPTER ELEVEN

THE SUN STREAMED DOWN on Susan's bare skin as she dug her toes into the warm sand. She picked up a handful of the damp soil and deftly formed a turret on the castle that she and Paul were building together on the beach. He grinned at her.

"Bet I finish my side before you finish yours," he said.

She rolled onto her knees, immediately rising to the challenge. "You're on." She grabbed another glob of sand, quickly fashioning a blunt tower with her hands. No more time-consuming turrets for her. She scooped out the moat, used some of the sand to begin making the bridge.

She worked feverishly, feeling sure she would win. But less than five minutes later Paul jumped to his feet and yelled, "Finished!"

She sat back on her heels and squinted up at him. "You can't be finished. We barely started."

"Come see," he said.

She got up and stomped over to his side of the castle. What she saw were three words dug into the crude wall where towers and turrets should have been.

*I Love You,* Paul had written.

She turned to face her husband of three days, wrapping her arms around his waist. "Great-looking castle."

"All in the technique," he said, waving his sand-encrusted index finger as an orchestra leader waves his baton. "Let's go for a walk."

"I'd better put on some more sunscreen first," she said.

"You don't need to. We won't be gone long." He started to lead her away.

"Susan can't go for a walk now," a deep voice came from behind her. "She has to get out of the sun."

The shadow of a big man covered her. She stiffened. Two strong hands gently cupped her bare shoulders, hands that warmed her even more than the sun's full rays.

"Come with me," the voice said as the hold on her shoulders tightened. "I won't let you get burned."

She looked to Paul for his reaction. But his face was an emotionless mask.

Susan awoke with a start. She sat up in bed, shaking from more than just cold. She pulled her comforter around her shoulders. The illuminated clock read three forty-eight.

*Just a dream.* She let out a long, shaky breath.

She remembered that day. She had dreamed about this before. Building the sand castle. Paul spelling *I Love You* in the sand where the castle details should have been.

She remembered it all.

But she didn't remember *his* deep voice interrupting them. Or the shadow of *his* body behind her. Or *his* large, warm hands on her shoulders.

David's voice. David's body. David's hands.

David had been in her dream of Paul. No one had ever been in those dreams before. They were always exact re-enactments of actual events. Which was why every other time she'd awakened from one, she had expected to find Paul beside her. But not this time.

There was something else, too. She and Paul had gone for a long walk on the beach that day, and her exposed shoulders and legs *had* gotten badly sunburned. She'd been forced to spend the rest of their honeymoon indoors.

Now David was in her dream, warning her about it.

She gave herself a hearty shake. Honey's head came up on the pillow beside her.

"It's okay, little guy," she said, giving him a gentle pat. "I'm just losing my mind."

But Honey wasn't reassured. He hopped up on all fours and started to growl. That's when she heard a faint rustling beneath her balcony windows, and then the distinct *crack* of a twig.

She tensed, instantly alert. Honey flew off the bed and charged toward the closed balcony windows, barking as he threw himself against them.

She flung the covers aside, jumped to her feet and grabbed the heavy tripod she had positioned against the headboard. But when she reached over to turn on the bedside lamp, she was stopped in mid-motion by a familiar voice.

"Don't turn on the light," David commanded from the doorway.

She jumped, shocked by his sudden appearance in her home. "David! What are you doing here?"

He didn't answer, but swiftly crossed her bedroom to the window. Her heart beat wildly as she watched the gleam of the street lamp reflecting off the nightscope he held to his eyes, and the gun he held in his hand.

Honey had stopped barking. But he was still agitated, whining and circling in front of the windows.

David lowered the nightscope and turned toward the door. "Stay where you are. I'll be back."

As he started out of the bedroom, Honey ran after him. David picked up the little terrier and brought him to Susan. She put down the tripod and gathered the dog into her arms.

"Not a bad little watchdog," David said as he patted Honey's head before swiftly leaving the room.

"A *great* little watchdog," she amended.

She sat on the bed, hugging her pet as she waited for David's return. She was shaking, and she couldn't seem to stop. Was the same man who'd tried to abduct her now here? Despite David's warnings, she'd felt safe in her home. Not any more.

She distinctly remembered closing and locking her front door when she'd said good-night to David at six o'clock. How had he gotten back inside?

In her dream, he'd tried to prevent her from being sunburned. Just as he'd prevented her from being abducted. Just as he had appeared tonight to defend her against an intruder.

She knew a woman had to be strong and stand on her own two feet. That was the only truly safe way to live. But David's care and concern filled her with a protected feeling that she'd never before known.

That feeling was fast becoming addictive.

Minutes later he reappeared in the doorway of her bedroom. He moved so quietly, she jumped, even though she'd been expecting him.

"Your intruder appears to have been a large dog on the prowl," he said, breathing hard as he sank into a chair in the corner of her bedroom. He'd obviously been running.

"That's good news," she said, feeling relieved. "Thank you for being here tonight."

"I told you. You can't stay alone."

Why did he always have such a hard time accepting a simple thank-you from her?

"You missed dinner at Meli's," she said.

"This isn't the time to be talking about food."

"You've probably been awake all night."

"Nor is it the time to be discussing sleep."

In truth, she didn't want to be discussing any of these things. She wanted to put her arms around him and tell him how touched she was by his concern for her.

But she knew that if she did, she would be crossing the line that he'd drawn between them.

"How did you get in?" she asked.

"The window in your laundry room. The latch isn't secure. As I mentioned earlier, your home isn't safe."

"You've been downstairs?"

"On the couch since about eleven. Where are you going?"

She'd risen from the bed and was heading toward her closet. "To get a robe. Since I very much doubt either of us is going to be getting any more sleep tonight, I might as well make something to eat."

DAVID USED HIS FLASHLIGHT to check the ground beneath Susan's balcony for shoe prints. The undergrowth was thick. Even if an intruder had passed here, the possibility he'd left a trace was slim. David wasn't surprised when he found nothing.

He carefully checked all around the outside of Susan's home, ending up in her enclosed backyard. The area was small and private with thick plants along a perimeter wall. But gaining access to the yard was as simple as opening the gate at the front walk.

The stray dog David had chased may have been what caused Honey to bark. But he couldn't be sure. He'd heard the engine of a vehicle starting up a block away when he'd spotted the dog in the street. He'd sprinted to the next street, trying to catch a glimpse of that vehicle, but he hadn't been fast enough.

The person who had started that engine could have been someone with an early schedule. Or he could have been the man after Susan. David was determined she would not be staying another night in her home.

He drifted into the kitchen through the back door, drawn by the smells of food. He hadn't eaten since lunch the day before. Refusing her offer to cook simply wasn't an option, especially not after having sampled her culinary talents.

He found the fluffy cheese omelette and flaky buttermilk biscuits she prepared nearly as seductive as she was. She sat across the table from him while he ate, sipping a glass of water and trying not to yawn. Her eyes were sleepy, her hair soft and loose.

He had tried to talk her into going back to bed and getting some needed sleep. But she had insisted that if he was staying up, so was she. She was so damn stubborn. And so damn beautiful.

He concentrated on his food and tried to get his thoughts back on track. He could handle a few sleepless nights. But he needed all his wits about him to track down the man who was after her. That meant finding a way to keep her safe while they both got some needed rest. He figured he'd better introduce his strategy to her in stages.

"You're going to need to pack a bag with essentials," he said. "Plan on being away from your home for at least a week. I've found a safe house."

A moment passed before she responded. "Are you offering your services as my bodyguard?"

"Unless you'd prefer to hire someone else," he said as casually as he could.

He buttered a hot biscuit and hoped to hell she didn't decide to hire someone else. He couldn't trust anyone else to take care of her. Not now.

"I haven't received a bill for your private investigative services."

"I've been too busy to give the clerk my time and expenses," he lied. "I'll add both services together when this is over."

He moved his food around his plate with his fork and waited.

"Where is this safe house you're taking me to?" she asked.

He let out a relieved breath he didn't even know he'd

been holding. "Close by. I'd like you to stay with my mother today, while I take care of a few things."

Her sleepy eyes blinked open. "Who?"

She'd heard him, so he didn't bother to answer. "It's Saturday. You're not scheduled to work. You can take Honey along. She won't mind."

He munched his biscuit and watched the frown pulling her eyebrows together.

"Unless you're the son of some saint, I think your mother would very much mind having some stranger and her dog suddenly dumped on her for the day."

"She not only doesn't mind, she's looking forward to meeting you."

"You already asked her? When?"

"When I was trying to get comfortable on your couch last night. We're expected at nine."

"David, I can't—"

"She knows you're a professional nature photographer. No doubt she's eager to learn your secrets of getting pictures of birds without scaring them away. Of course, if you're not willing to share your secrets with her..."

He knew the kind of person Susan was, which was why he was certain she couldn't refuse an invitation like this one.

"Of course, I'd be happy to share. But—"

"Good," David said. "It's settled."

ALICE KNIGHT WAS a beautiful, big-boned woman. Her eyes were a soft gray, identical in shade to David's, but filled to the brim with warmth. She carried herself with all the radiant confidence of a woman who would find the calm in any storm.

Her smile was full of genuine welcome as she stepped forward to take Susan's hand into both of hers. "I'm so pleased to meet you. I've been poring over my back issues of *True Nature* magazine. Your pictures are so full of beauty they brought tears to my eyes. Come in. Oh, and who do we have here?''

Alice released Susan's hand to turn toward Honey, who was sniffing at her heels.

''This is Honey,'' David said.

''So this is the stout-hearted little terrier who alerts his mistress to danger,'' Alice said, dropping to her knees and giving him a welcoming rub. Honey rolled on his back, instantly in love.

Susan hadn't realized David had told his mother so much about the previous evening's events. She began to wonder what else he might have told her.

''I may be late,'' David said as he headed toward his truck.

''Take your time,'' Alice said as she straightened. ''We'll be fine.''

She slid her arm into Susan's and led her and Honey up the stairs to the entryway of her high-bank, waterfront home. Once they had stepped through the open doorway, she closed the door behind them and threw the bolt.

The inside was spacious and airy, with stone floors, sparkling white walls and lots of windows. The furnishings were large and looked both comfortable and lived-in. Paintings of colorful flowers covered the walls.

Susan stopped at the floor-to-ceiling windows off the living room and kitchen, drawn by the spectacular view of the Hood Canal below. A pathway bordered by spring flowers, all in bloom, sloped down to the beach.

''This is beautiful,'' she said with feeling.

''Yes, the view is my favorite part, as well,'' Alice said.

She beckoned Susan to have a seat at the center island in the kitchen, as she headed toward the refrigerator. Honey sniffed at the room's corners, clearly intrigued by the new smells.

"David's father and I bought this land right after solving our first big case. We built the house ourselves between babies and working cases over the next few years."

"So, you were a private investigator, too."

"I still get into the action now and then. My mother and I started White Investigations. White's my maiden name. She was a great, gutsy gal. David's father was part of the FBI team sent in to investigate her death."

"Your mother was killed on a case?" Susan asked, unable to hide her shock.

Alice nodded. "Even after all these years, I still get angry when I think of her death. Of course, back then I was reduced to a raving lunatic."

Susan had a hard time picturing this serene, confident woman even ruffled, much less a raving lunatic.

"When I met Charles Knight, it was irritation at first sight," Alice said, chuckling. "He kept telling me to stay out of *his* investigation. I kept telling him to reread the Constitution. We were married six weeks later. He left the FBI to join me at the firm. That's when White Investigations became White Knight Investigations."

Alice placed a milk shake in front of her. *"Bon appetit."*

Susan smelled the peppermint in the drink and realized what Alice had been busy mixing. She suddenly felt very awkward. "David told you."

"It's my recipe," Alice confided as she slipped onto the bar stool next to her. "How's the morning sickness now?"

"Conquered, thanks to you. This milk shake has been an absolute lifesaver. David didn't tell me the recipe was yours."

"He's told me very little about you, as well, apart from the fact that you needed a safe place to stay today."

"I shouldn't have let him dump me on you."

Alice pulled back her cardigan sweater to reveal the gun

resting in a holster strapped to her waist. "You weren't dumped. You're in protective custody. David is very worried for your safety and rightfully so."

Susan felt a small shock as she stared at the huge gun. She had no doubt from the calm expression on the woman's face that she could and would use the weapon, if necessary.

"He told me you wanted tips on how to photograph birds," Susan said, unable to keep the smile from her lips.

Alice chuckled as she pulled her cardigan back into place. "Probably easier for him than saying, 'I'd like you to meet my mother with the .357 Magnum.' I'm relieved to see the weapon doesn't bother you. The last woman he fell for was an emotionally delicate creature who damn near fainted at the sight of my gun."

Susan was startled, not sure she'd heard right. "Did you say *fell for?*"

Alice looked straight at her. "David hasn't even noticed a woman in a very long time. He's doing a lot more than noticing you, Susan."

She wanted to believe what this woman was telling her. But she remembered David's words after he'd kissed her. *It will never happen again.* He was not a man who made idle promises.

"Forgive the mother in me for asking this question," Alice said. "Are you still grieving?"

Alice was looking at the gold band on her finger. Susan shook her head. "My husband's ring was all I had left of him after he died in a fire. I was ready to take the ring off a few months ago—only, then the dreams—"

She stopped herself, surprised she'd volunteered so much. She hadn't even told Ellie about the dreams. Alice was proving far too easy to talk to.

"The dreams of you and Paul started," Alice said gently.

She looked up to find Alice's expression open and understanding. "David may not say much, but he does take very thorough case notes. I had our office clerk e-mail me your file this morning. What do you think the dreams mean?"

"I don't know," she said, embarrassed at the admission.

Alice gave her arm a quick squeeze. "You'll figure it out. What I like most about your photographs is that they go past the surface to seek out the truth. You would have made a good private investigator."

She sensed that was high praise and was emboldened to broach a subject she might otherwise have left alone. "Alice, what happened to the emotionally delicate woman David fell for?"

"He'll have to tell you. But we have all day to discuss the excitement of being pregnant. Are you talking to the baby yet?"

She smiled. "All the time."

"I sang to David the entire time I was carrying him. I was determined he would turn out to be musically inclined."

"Is he?"

She chuckled. "Can't even carry a tune. Would you like to see his baby pictures?"

Susan's smile grew at the conspiratorial look on Alice's face.

"How did it go?" David asked when he picked Susan and Honey up late that night.

"Your mother is charming, gracious and communicative," she said. "Are you sure you two are related?"

David hid his grin.

"She didn't seem surprised that your father didn't show up for dinner. Does that happen often?"

"Dad's out of town on a case he's handling for me."

"One you had to give up to be my bodyguard," she said, her tone growing concerned.

"One I was *happy* to give up to be your bodyguard. Your case is far more interesting. I didn't have my head in the other one. He'll do a much better job."

"You were working on my case today?"

He nodded, carefully watching to make sure they weren't being followed before making his next turn. "I believe I've discovered why Robert Ardmore has been so determined to keep both the plane crash that killed his daughter and the explosion that injured his grandson out of the news. The pilot, Lucy Norton, was flying Molly Ardmore Tishman and Steve Kemp to a weekend tryst at an intimate B&B when the plane crashed, killing them all."

"So Molly and Steve were lovers. How did you find out?"

"Jared got the records from the B&B in the town where Lucy Norton was taking them. Steve Kemp booked them as Mr. and Mrs."

"That must have been what Todd meant when he told me he didn't like the way his mother would be remembered," Susan said after a moment. "She was having an affair."

"If the plane crash had become news, Robert Ardmore's married daughter's affair also would have come to light."

"Did Ardmore pay Steve Kemp's relatives to be quiet, too?"

"Probably didn't have to," he said. "Steve Kemp was also married. I doubt his wife or son were eager to talk to the press."

"This has to be a very painful time for Robert Ardmore. But don't his actions to suppress the truth seem a little extreme to you?"

"Not when you know what he's gone through with the

media over a past scandal,'' David said as he continued to check his rearview mirror. An old pickup had pulled in back of them.

''I don't remember a past scandal involving him.''

''You were only twelve at the time. Twenty years ago, one of Ardmore's secretaries claimed he'd forced himself on her and that she was pregnant with his child. After being crucified in the media, Ardmore was finally cleared of the charges when a blood test proved the baby was not his and eight witnesses placed him at his mother's funeral in Europe at the time of the alleged assault.''

''If Ardmore was exonerated of all wrongdoing,'' she said, ''I don't see why he should fear media involvement in the death of his daughter and injury of his grandson now. He can't be held accountable for their actions.''

The old pickup behind them pulled into a driveway. David relaxed his hands on the wheel. ''I'm not so sure Ardmore sees it that way. Twenty years ago he was innocent, but the papers carried all the accusations against him in bold, front-page headlines. Everywhere he or his family went, reporters hounded them, shouting insensitive questions, trying to get them to react on camera. But when he was cleared, that news barely made the back page.''

Out of the corner of his eye, he could see Susan shaking her head. ''It's a shame that we live in a society where people seem to be so much more interested in hearing about the harm done by others instead of about the good.''

Three miles later they arrived at a set of gates. David pressed the electronic opener. The gates opened and he drove through, checking to make sure the gates closed behind them before continuing. A quarter mile up the narrow, tree-lined drive, the trees gave way to a clearing, in the center of which was a small, two-story home.

As David pulled in front of the house, a motion-sensor light came on. He turned off the engine, got out of the truck and came around to open the door for Susan. Before he could reach her, she opened the passenger door herself.

Her foot had barely landed on the drive when two large Labrador retrievers loped up to her. She quickly closed the truck door to keep Honey from jumping out, then stood absolutely still.

David hurried toward her. "Back," he commanded. The two dogs immediately retreated to the door.

"They won't hurt you. They know the truck and they know that whoever rides in it is a friend. They're just curious."

She nodded as she crouched and held out her hand. After an affirmative nod from David, the dogs approached to sniff her, tails wagging.

She gave their chests a pat. "What are their names?"

"Galahad and Gawain."

"Cute, Mr. Knight," she said, smiling.

Honey gave a bark from the truck, jumping excitedly against the window.

"Honey loves other dogs. What are they going to make of him?"

"Let him out and see."

Susan understood that he was telling her it would be okay. She opened the truck's door, and Honey leaped out. The well-mannered Labradors politely sniffed the little terrier that circled excitedly around them.

David put his key in the lock and opened the door to the house. He switched on the light. Then he quickly punched in a code on the security panel to prevent the alarm from sounding.

Susan stepped inside a large living room with a high ceiling, glowing teak floors, ivory walls and sanded-glass cabinets. A cream-colored couch and chair with straight lines sat in front of a large glass coffee table. The fireplace was white marble. No paintings adorned the walls. The room was an open, uncluttered expanse of simplicity.

"Who lives here?" she asked.

David reentered the house carrying her suitcase, all three dogs trotting after him. "I do," he said as he closed the front door.

She turned a startled look in his direction.

"This is the safest house I know," he said. "The security system is state-of-the-art. The dogs will not just warn you of an intruder, but will also be outside to stop him, if necessary. If for some reason they can't, I can. You'll be safe here. I'll show you to your room."

The room he showed her was upstairs, with the same beautiful teak floors and ivory walls. The attached bath had large emerald towels, lime wallpaper, and a soaking tub lined with white lava rock. David put her suitcase on the white comforter that covered the bed.

"Here's how you lock your door," he said as he demonstrated.

"If an intruder can't get inside the house," she said, purposely meeting his eyes, "I don't need to lock my door."

She knew he wouldn't be trying to enter this bedroom tonight.

He nodded. "The ingredients for your morning milk shake are in the refrigerator. I'll leave you to unpack. Good night."

He left the room, closing the door behind him.

SUSAN TOOK A LONG, hot bath. Honey was already snoozing on the bed when she put on her cotton nightgown and brushed her hair. She caught her reflection in the mirror over the dresser. She had none of Ellie's dazzling good looks. She was really rather plain.

Just as well that she wasn't *seriously* thinking about seducing the man across the hall.

*He's doing a lot more than noticing you, Susan.* Alice's words kept coming back to her. The message in them both thrilled her and made her yearn for what might have been. Falling for David would be so easy. A part of her already had. But he didn't want a relationship with her. He'd made that very clear.

Besides, she didn't throw herself at men. She was not her mother.

It was after eleven. She was tired since she'd had so little sleep the night before. She got into bed, turned off the light and lay her head on the pillow. The sheets smelled freshly washed. The pillow felt soft and inviting.

But she couldn't sleep. After several minutes of tossing and turning, she decided she might as well go downstairs to the kitchen and prepare her milk shake for the morning.

She'd gotten into the habit of keeping a thermos of it next to her bed, just in case she awoke feeling queasy. Taking a few sips always settled her stomach.

She swung out of bed and shoved her arms through the sleeves of her terry-cloth robe, cinching the sash tightly around her waist. She put on her slippers and picked up her thermos on the way to the door.

Slowly twisting the knob and carefully opening the bedroom door, she was happy to see the hallway illuminated by a night-light. David's bedroom door was closed. No light shone underneath.

Well, at least *he* was getting some sleep. She tiptoed down the stairs, determined not to disturb him.

They'd arrived late, and he'd taken her right to her room. When she reached the bottom of the stairs, she didn't know where to find the kitchen.

After flipping a mental coin, she turned left down the hallway. When she opened the first door and pressed the wall switch, the bright fluorescent light revealed a large home gym. The space was filled with a stair climber, several weight machines, a rowing machine, an exercise bike and an enormous treadmill that looked like it could challenge a cheetah.

No wonder David was in such good shape.

She flipped off the light, closed the door and continued down the hall. When she opened the next door she discovered a cozy library.

What a great find. A little light reading was just what she needed to help her get to sleep.

She approached the wall of built-in bookshelves, her eyes sweeping over the titles: *Psychotherapy, Handbook of Psychology Assessment, Human Nature According to Freud and Jung.* These books would hardly do the job.

Then she caught sight of a framed document, shoved sideways between two of the textbooks on the shelf. She set her thermos on the side table and pulled out the document.

A wire had been attached to the back of the frame, telling her that at one time it had hung on a wall. The doctorate degree was in psychology and had been conferred on David Alan Knight.

"So you're the burglar." David's voice came from behind her.

She whirled around to see him standing in the doorway. He was replacing his gun in a shoulder holster. The thin straps were all that covered his massive chest and shoulders, glistening in the subdued light. The sight of all that bare, muscular male flesh did nothing to reduce the racing of her startled pulse.

She swallowed hard and forced her eyes up to his face. "And you're the psychologist. No wonder you're so damn good at reading people and predicting their behavior."

He walked up to her, lifted the diploma out of her hands

and shoved it back on the shelf. "I *was* a psychologist, and I couldn't predict the behavior of a slug."

His voice conveyed a combination of anger and sadness that she had never heard before. She stepped toward him and laid her hand on his arm.

"David, what happened?"

Muscles flexed beneath her fingers as tension tightened his jaw. He was uncomfortable with her touch. She withdrew her hand.

"David, tell me. Please."

He looked away from her entreaty and shoved his hands into the pockets of his black sweatpants. Moments passed. When he did finally speak, his voice sounded different, almost damaged.

"Theresa and I were therapists, partners in what was becoming a thriving practice. She had once been married to a physically abusive man and was full of sage advice for women who found themselves in similar situations. She made a difference in their lives."

"You loved her very much," Susan said with conviction.

He nodded. "A month before we were to be married, she confessed that she'd been seeing her ex-husband secretly for weeks. She told me he'd changed, conquered his problem. He'd begged her to give him another chance. She was going to."

"But she was engaged to you," Susan said, unable to imagine how any woman could give up David.

"She told me that *he* was the only man who could truly love her. She told me she had never stopped loving him."

"She'd never stopped loving a man who abused her? I'm sorry, but I have trouble accepting that."

"Abused women have been conditioned to accept the unacceptable," he said, and that angry sadness rode hard through his words. "Theresa appeared outwardly confident. She spoke with authority to the women she helped. I never saw the depth of her mammoth self-doubt, nor understood how vulnerable that doubt made her.''

Susan had waged her own battles against self-doubt. She understood only too well what David was describing.

"Theresa's ex played on her feelings of inferiority. He convinced her he was the only one who could truly love her, imagined warts and all.''

"But you said she was a therapist," Susan protested. "If she'd counseled other women with this very same problem, how could she not see what he was doing to her?''

"Seeing the mistakes of others is simple. Seeing our own is damn near impossible.''

The way David said that told Susan he was talking about himself, as well.

"I tried to remind her that abusive men did not change, something she had said countless times in the seminars she'd given," he went on. "I begged her to rethink what she was doing. But she kept insisting things would be different this time. She kissed me goodbye and walked out the door. The next month, I learned her ex had beaten her to death and then taken his own life.''

Susan stared at David's profile, the lines of pain etched around his mouth and eyes. She felt an overwhelming sadness.

"Theresa was too vulnerable to know her own mind or heart. I had missed all the clues that should have told me who she really was. How eager she was to please. How easily she gave in on things. She only agreed to marry me because she knew it was what I wanted. I never really saw *her* at all.''

He turned to face Susan. "My supposed psychological expertise was nothing but a sham.''

"So you stopped being a therapist and became a private investigator."

"I figured my training could at least help me find missing persons."

When she'd first looked into David's eyes, she'd wondered whether they had been aged by a life assault or a life assessed. It had been both. That was why he'd refused to tell her why he had decided to become a private investigator. He hadn't been able to share this personal part of his life with her then.

She was so glad that he had shared it with her now.

"I've never questioned my decision to become a private investigator," he said. "I felt confident that whatever mistake I might make, at least the cost would not be a life. But, now, because of me, your life is in danger."

She took a step toward him and laid her hands on his bare chest. He sucked in a hard breath at her touch. "David, you *saved* my life."

His hands came out of his pockets to run up her arms, as though of their own volition. His touch set off an avalanche of tumbling warmth inside her.

"Susan, don't look at me like that."

She knew exactly how she was looking at him, but she wanted him to tell her. "Like what, David?"

"Like you want me to…"

His hands cupped her shoulders as his muscles tensed with strain. She didn't know if he was preparing to hold her back or pull her to him. But she could feel his heart racing beneath her hands.

His voice was a strained whisper. "Susan, please. I gave you my promise I wouldn't."

She stared boldly into his eyes. "I never asked for that promise, David. I never wanted that promise. I'm certainly not going to hold you to it."

He murmured a strangled oath of defeat as he pulled her toward him.

SUSAN LAY BESIDE DAVID in his king-size bed, a bundle of soft, warm woman. He held her close, inhaled the sweet scent of her body, and smiled.

He'd tried to take her slowly, though it had been a long time for him. But she hadn't allowed him to slow down much. She had wanted him nearly as urgently as he had wanted her. The impossible thrill of that knowledge still beat in his blood.

She lay with her head on his chest, her breath deep and even in sleep.

She was even more vulnerable now that she'd been attacked.

He couldn't think of a more disastrous situation for depriving a woman of her deepest defenses. Any man with a shred of conscience would have kept his distance.

David's conscience was in shreds. He brushed his lips against the soft skin of her bare shoulder and sighed. How could this be so wrong when she felt so damn right in his arms?

He had no answer for that. But he did know why he hadn't been able to have casual sex with Gabrielle. He wasn't a casual man. Which was why the sex with Susan was so good. He didn't want just sex. He wanted her.

He had never hesitated to go after what he wanted. But he knew he could not go after Susan. He'd made a disastrous mistake with one vulnerable woman because he'd allowed his desire for her to blind him to everything else. He was determined not to make that mistake again.

She needed both time and space to deal with the challenges facing her. She also needed to feel safe. First and foremost, he had to keep her from harm. That included the harm he could do her.

He had no choice but to back away.

But, God help him, David could not back away from her tonight. She was stirring in his arms, and he had to make love to her again. Nice and slow this time.

# CHAPTER TWELVE

SUSAN LOOKED UP from the stove when David entered the kitchen. He was clean-shaven, his hair wet from his shower, dark jeans lining his long legs, a snow-white T-shirt stretched across his broad shoulders and chest.

"Robert Ardmore wants to see you."

She was still too full of the sight of David and the satisfying memories of their night of lovemaking to pay much attention to his words.

"I'm sorry, what did you say about Ardmore?"

David slid onto a bar stool at his kitchen counter and regarded her steadily. "He knows about you. He called the office last night, left the message on voice mail."

She turned back to the stove, scooped the vegetable omelette from the frying pan onto a waiting plate and turned off the burner. She set the plate in front of him, next to the fresh apple compote she had baked, then poured coffee into his cup. When she'd come down to the kitchen this morning, she had found his refrigerator and pantry stocked with items nearly identical to her own.

He had done that for her.

"Did you hear what I said?" he asked.

She'd heard. But every cell in her body was buoyed and bubbling with the knowledge of what they had shared last night. Concentrating on anything else was very hard.

She wanted to talk to him about so many things. But she knew his concern over Ardmore would have to be addressed first.

"How does Ardmore know about me?" she asked.

"When I called him back this morning, he admitted he'd hired the private investigator who was following me, but denied he had anything to do with the attempted abduction. He would say nothing more, except that he wanted to see you."

"You don't think he was behind the attempt?"

"I don't know. But at least he's come forward and admitted to hiring the private investigator. I'll give him points for that."

She sat down on the stool next to David and took a sip of her milk shake. Robert Ardmore wanted to see her. The billionaire industrialist who'd started out as a lowly clerk in a manufacturing company and had quickly risen to be one of the most powerful men in the Pacific Northwest.

"Do you want to see him, Susan?"

"If he doesn't know about the baby—"

"You can be sure he does. Knowing you're carrying his great-grandchild is without a doubt the reason he wants to see you."

"Then, I should see him," she said. "He needs to understand that I won't be asking anything of him. Did he suggest a time and place?"

"Today at his home on Falls Island, but I'm not comfortable taking you there."

She looked over at him and noticed that he had yet to touch his breakfast. For a man with his appetite, this was serious.

"Why not?" she asked.

"His estate is a fortress. If we went in there, and he didn't want us to come out, we wouldn't."

"You don't really think—"

"I don't intend to take any chances with your life."

He said that very quietly, emphatically. He was being so careful with her. She felt protected, cherished, *loved*.

"Do you want Ardmore to come here?" she asked.

"No. You're safer if no one but my immediate family knows you're staying here with me."

"Then, where? My place?"

"I'd rather set up the meeting in a neutral spot. Meli's is closed on Sunday. That section of town should be deserted. I'll give Mort and Meli a call and see if they'll let me use the restaurant."

She smiled. "Does this mean that you're no longer afraid that Mort will link us romantically?"

She had only meant the comment as a light tease. But David wasn't smiling. Quite the contrary. There was a frown on his face.

"Susan, about last night. We need to talk."

Uh-oh. He'd used the dreaded phrase—the only four words in the English language that could sound like a guillotine blade.

*If he says he's sorry for making heart-stopping love to me no less than three times, so help me I'm going to knee him in the groin and drop him to the floor.*

"I'm not sorry it happened," he said. "God knows I should be, but I'm not."

She let out a soft sigh.

He looked down at the cooling food on his plate. "But you're in an extremely vulnerable position. My job is to protect you, not to take advantage of you. I can't let it happen again."

Her heart squeezed tight. He didn't want what she'd given him. Now she had one of two choices. She could let him continue, or take the initiative and hopefully save her pride.

"Susan, please understand that I—"

She pulled her shoulders straight as she laid a firm hand on his arm. "Look, last night was no big deal. I know I came on pretty strong. You were great to be so…cooperative. But you can relax. I won't be attacking you on a regular basis."

She forced herself to smile at the astonished look on his face. "Now, you might want to eat your breakfast before it gets cold. Excuse me while I call Honey in from his morning constitutional."

She withdrew her hand from David's arm and headed toward the front door.

She was not going to cry. Nor would she rant, rave or beg as her mother had always done when a man could not return her feelings. David had made her no promises. He had shared an intimate part of his past with her last night. She'd jumped to the conclusion that had meant he wanted an intimate relationship with her. She had been wrong.

He had tried to keep their relationship about business. She had been the one to cross the line. Now she had to get back across that line and stay there.

ROBERT ARDMORE'S long limousine pulled in front of Meli's at two minutes after three. Four bodyguards with the solid physiques of wrestlers formed a protective circle around one door.

Robert Ardmore stepped out of the limousine. He was in his seventies, five-ten and slender, dressed in an impeccable gray suit and tie. He had a full head of straight silver hair and a posture as firm as stone. When he saw David standing outside the entrance to Meli's, he nodded.

David nodded back but remained where he was.

Ardmore leaned into the limousine to assist his wife. As soon as she was beside him, he gestured to one of the bodyguards. That man opened the truck and took out a wheelchair.

As David watched, two of the bodyguards lifted a large man from within the vehicle and placed him into the waiting wheelchair.

David had known Vance Tishman, Todd's father, was to be part of the trio meeting with Susan today. But until this moment, David hadn't known Vance was an invalid.

Three of the bodyguards flanked Ardmore and his wife as they started toward David. The fourth pushed the wheelchair in which a slightly hunched-over Vance Tishman sat. Tishman's broad face wore a bland expression, his eyes behind heavy-looking glasses that slipped down his nose.

When Ardmore approached, David held up his hand. "Only one bodyguard inside."

Ardmore stared at him with cold, colorless eyes. "Your lack of trust is intolerable. Just what kind of a man do you think I am?"

"I have no idea what kind of a man you are," David said calmly. "But consider this. If she were under your protection, would you do less?"

Ardmore stared at David a moment longer before pointing to the man who was pushing the wheelchair. "You will accompany us. The rest of you will remain."

David opened the door to the restaurant and stepped back to let the Ardmores and Vance Tishman enter with the lone bodyguard.

Inside, Susan sat at a table, Alice beside her. In front of each of the three walls of the room, one of David's brothers stood. Ardmore noted them with obvious distaste.

"Care to meet them?" David asked.

"Not necessary," Ardmore said. "Ms. McKinney has briefed me on you all."

David had no doubt that she had. His visit to McKinney's office had probably put her on the phone with Ardmore immediately. David was glad he'd made that visit.

He fell into step beside Ardmore as they advanced toward Susan. When they reached the table where she waited, David held out the chair for Nancy Ardmore. Her husband took the chair beside her. The bodyguard pushed Tishman's wheelchair to the other side of Nancy.

David stood beside Susan as he performed the introductions. Only Vance Tishman leaned forward to offer her his hand.

"Nice to meet you," he said in a slightly wheezy voice.

Susan smiled and shook his hand briefly. "Thank you."

Ardmore waved away the bodyguard, who retreated to the door.

Alice stood. "I'll leave you to your private conversation," she said. She gave Susan's shoulder a brief, reassuring squeeze before she went to stand beside her son, Jack, at the far wall.

"Ms. Carter," Robert Ardmore began, his manner brisk, his voice gruff, "I know all about your affair with my grandson."

"How do you know?" she asked, her voice calm, her expression open.

"He wrote to you, Susan," Nancy said, suddenly leaning forward, her bland features coming to life. "We were so surprised when we read the letter. Of course, he'd addressed you only by your first name, so at first we didn't—"

"Please, Nancy," Robert said, interrupting his wife. "Let me do this."

"Yes, of course, dear." Nancy sat back in her chair.

"What letter was that, Mr. Ardmore?" Susan asked.

"Before we speak of the letter or anything else attendant to this matter," Ardmore said without warmth, "you should know that my grandson was involved in a serious accident soon after meeting you and has since passed away."

Susan let out a soft sigh. "Oh."

Nancy's head bowed as she dabbed at the tear escaping

from her eye. Susan rested her hand on the woman's arm. "I'm so very sorry for your loss," she said gently.

Nancy looked at Susan. "Thank you, dear. I can see why Todd was so taken with you. I know you didn't know each other well, but—"

"Nancy, please," Ardmore interrupted again.

His wife shot him a frustrated glance but refrained from further comment.

"Ms. Carter," Ardmore said, "I must speak plainly. I understand that you are pregnant. Was my grandson the one who impregnated you?"

"Yes, but don't be concerned. I have no intention of asking you for anything. Nor will anyone outside of this room ever learn he was the father."

Ardmore frowned at her. "Were you even going to tell us?"

"Truthfully, Mr. Ardmore, I was not. As Mrs. Ardmore said a moment ago, I didn't know Todd very well. My choice to have this baby is—"

"You're keeping the baby?" Tishman interrupted. "What a relief. Ever since learning that my son had left behind this unexpected surprise—"

"Vance!" Ardmore said, his frustration clear. "If you will *please* let me."

"Yes, yes," Vance said, waving his hand in way of an apology. "Sorry."

"Ms. Carter," Ardmore said once again as he turned back to Susan, harshness still evident in his tone, "we are all pleased with your decision to have the baby. But this baby is not *just* yours. You're carrying *my* great-grandchild."

Susan met Ardmore's intense gaze with one of her own. "Since that's how you feel, Mr. Ardmore, then, yes, it most certainly is." She sent him a smile.

The tension visibly eased from Ardmore's body as he

leaned back in his chair. "My grandson made some very serious mistakes in his life, Ms. Carter. I'm glad to see you were not one of them."

"SUSAN TELLS ME she accepted Ardmore's invitation to dine on Tuesday," Charles said as he joined David by the fireplace after their family dinner.

David nodded at his dad. "The entire Sheriff's Department knows she'll be at his estate, and I'll be with her."

"You need any help keeping her safe at other times?"

"No, thanks. When she's in her office, she'll be surrounded by fellow workers. I'll see her there and home. My only other concern is when she's out on an assignment. Jack's just finished his case. He's offered to cover her if I'm tied up with Jared on the investigation."

"She does have lovely, straight, white teeth," Charles said, a small smile playing at the corner of his lips. "Must have been a nice surprise to discover your cat burglar wasn't married."

"Yeah, nice surprise," David agreed, taking a sip of his after-dinner wine. "So, how's the search for the lost brother going?" he asked, determined to steer the conversation elsewhere.

"Hit nothing but dead ends yesterday and today," Charles admitted. "It seems that he was..."

David sipped his wine, nodding attentively, not hearing a word his father was saying. Out of the corner of his eye he could see Susan laugh again at something Jack had just said. Ever since they'd come back from Meli's, Jack had been monopolizing her. He'd sat next to her at their family dinner and regaled her nonstop with his show-business stories.

Now they sat together on the couch, Honey snuggled between them. Jack whispered something in Susan's ear.

Whatever he said made her laugh. David's hand gripped his wineglass.

*Last night was no big deal.* That's what she'd said. Looked as if she meant every word, too.

David told himself he should be relieved; her reaction was just what he needed to help him back away. But the unbearable casualness of her brush-off had thrown him completely. He would have sworn that their time together had been something special for her, too.

He shook his head. Thirty-five years old and a certified specialist in human behavior, and he *still* didn't have a clue when it came to women.

"David?"

He realized with a start that his father was waiting for him to respond to something he'd asked.

"Sorry," David said, setting his half-full glass of wine on the fireplace mantel. "I'm pretty bushed, Dad. Haven't had much sleep lately. Tomorrow will be another long day. Time I rescued Susan from Jack's dubious charm and headed for home."

"JARED HAS KEPT everything about your attempted abduction quiet," David said to Susan on their ride home. "Keeping you safe means saying nothing to the press for the time being. None of your friends or business associates should know."

"Okay," she said.

He took a package out of the center console. "This is a cell phone. There's a soft case and belt clip so you can carry the phone with you at all times. You won't hear a ring but will feel the vibration when a call comes in. Don't give out the number. I've encoded my cell phone number in the memory. All you have to do to get me is press one."

She took the package from him. "Okay."

"If your friends or co-workers see me with you when I

take you to and from work, tell them I'm a distant cousin who just got in touch.''

"Okay.''

"Make sure you prepare yourself a sandwich or yogurt at home and take them to work along with your milk shake so you don't have to go out to lunch.''

"Okay.''

One-word answers. That's all she'd been giving him the whole day.

Earlier he'd attributed her uncharacteristic quiet to her concern over meeting the Ardmores and Tishman. But she'd been animated with his parents and brothers afterward. Especially with Jack.

Now with *him*, nothing.

"Appears your baby gained some relatives today,'' he said, trying again to get a conversation going.

"Yes,'' she said, stroking Honey's back as he lay snoozing in her lap.

David waited a moment, but that was all she was going to say.

"Is something wrong?'' he asked.

"No.''

"Susan, you can't be that blasé about what's happening.''

"I'm just holding back my enthusiasm until I have a chance to spend more time with them. Having relatives can be the proverbial double-edged sword.''

He knew she couldn't be talking about her father, since she'd said she never knew him. "What was your mother like?''

"Why do you want to know?''

He was irritated by her cool and distant response.

"I would think that by now you'd—'' He stopped himself. He had almost said that by now she should know that she could trust him with personal information. But they both knew there was no reason he needed this personal information. At least, no reason associated with being her bodyguard.

He took a couple of deep, steadying breaths and tried to get his emotional balance back. "You don't need to tell me, Susan. But I'd like you to."

A quiet moment passed. When she finally responded, her voice was so emotionless, she could have been reading from the phone book.

"My grandmother was forty-six, my grandfather fifty, when my mother finally came along. They were so ecstatic, they spoiled her silly. She was wild and unwed when she had me at nineteen. They had to bribe her into taking care of me. All she ever really cared about was bar-hopping to pick up guys. I never knew when I came home from school what new creep I'd find living with us."

He winced at the images that brought to mind. "Did they hurt you?"

"I learned to outrun them. You asked me once when I became interested in wildlife. I was eight. I escaped this nasty drunk my mother had brought home by climbing up to the tree house my grandfather had built for me in the backyard."

She paused. When she continued, her tone warmed with soft wonder. "As I lay awake that night in my tree house, I watched a speckled owl at her nest hole, feeding her brood. She was so caring and protective."

*Unlike Susan's mother.*

"That night I decided I was going to learn all I could about wildlife."

He knew that was because they'd seemed so much more humane than the humans around her.

"What happened to your mother?" he asked.

The calm, emotionless voice was back. "She drank herself to death by the age of forty-four."

"Did you ever forgive her?"

"Of course. Not forgiving her would have only hurt me."

She was a hell of a lot smarter than he had even imagined. "I'm sorry, Susan."

"Don't be. My childhood may not have been a wholesome slice of the *Brady Bunch,* but I learned to be self-reliant. Speaking of which, I need to borrow an alarm clock. I don't want to be late getting up for work tomorrow."

He got the message. She was planning on sleeping in her own bed tonight.

*Last night was no big deal.*

He had believed her when she'd told him. But after hearing about her childhood, David began to wonder.

By the age of eight, Susan had learned how to outrun those who could hurt her. Had her casual brush-off just been a way to get away from him?

SUSAN SAW THE SMOKE—greasy black funnels swirling into the light gray sky. Her first thought was dismay that someone was burning trash so near the house. She would have to get home quickly and close all the windows. If that noxious smoke got inside, the fumes would take hours to dissipate.

But when she maneuvered her SUV around the corner of her street, she saw the fire engines. The smoke was not from burning trash. The smoke was coming from the rubble that had once been her house.

She slammed on her brakes and jumped out of the SUV. She ran toward the black smoke billowing into the air. The sickening smell assailed her nostrils. Her lungs burned as she desperately tried to scramble over the debris.

Hands grabbed her, pulled her back. Hands that smelled of smoke. Hands of men she knew. Men who knew Paul.

Men who had played poker with him many times in the home that was now only charred remains.

One of the pairs of hands had a face—a familiar, smoke-smeared face with sad eyes. "He's gone, Susan," the fire chief said.

*Paul...gone?*

"I'm sorry. He must have fallen asleep on the couch. That's where we found him."

On the couch. Where she had left him. Paul. Gone. *Oh God.*

"That damn plastic vent hose on the dryer caught fire," Paul's best friend said. She saw him slam his helmet onto the pavement.

"I thought Paul was going to replace that piece of crap months ago," another one of his poker buddies said as he spit black soot out of his mouth. "But he didn't even put fresh batteries in the damn smoke alarms. Man, I don't believe this."

The words echoed in her mind. *I don't believe this. I don't believe this.*

"Guys, not now," the fire chief said, as the fire truck siren suddenly went off. "I'm going to take Susan to the station house. Susan, is there anyone I can call for you? Susan?"

She couldn't think. She couldn't hear. Not with that damn siren blasting away.

Susan awoke to the ringing of the alarm clock. She slammed down the switch, desperate to stop the annoying noise. Honey let out a sigh of relief beside her. But even after the ringing ceased, the jarring of her nerves continued.

Her head throbbed. Her stomach felt queasy. Damn. She did not want to be sick this morning. Not in David's home. Not after the miserable night she'd spent missing him and trying so hard not to.

She reached for the thermos on the nightstand, quickly poured herself some of the milk shake. She leaned against the backboard of the bed, and sipped the soothing liquid.

She wanted to think of nothing, desperately tried to think of nothing. But the dream she'd been having would not go away.

This was the first time she had dreamed about the day Paul died. She didn't realize she'd forgotten so much. She knew shock could wipe out what you didn't want to remember.

The shock of losing Paul had worn off long ago. Yet, it had taken the dream to bring back the details of that day, just like the other dreams she had of Paul had brought back the details of those times with him.

A soft knock came on the door. "Susan?" David's voice.

"I'm awake," she answered quickly. "The alarm worked."

"May I come in and talk to you?"

"Not necessary," she said quickly. "I'll be down in a couple of minutes."

There was a discernable pause. "Okay. Fine."

He didn't sound fine. She heard his footsteps moving away. Maybe *he* could casually talk to a woman he'd made love to, while she lay in bed, and still keep his emotional distance, but she wasn't made that way. If he wanted to have a conversation with her, he could damn well wait until they were in a more appropriate place and were both fully dressed.

She had given herself wholeheartedly to him. Now that she knew he didn't want what she had to offer, she wasn't going to be put into intimate situations with him where she had to fight to hide her feelings.

Susan sighed. She was so tired of hiding her feelings. She'd had enough of it to last a lifetime.

"WARREN STERNE, I'm David Knight."

Warren looked up from his computer. His chair squeaked as he swiveled in David's direction. He had a bush of black hair, thick horned-rim glasses and was at least six feet and probably close to two hundred and fifty pounds. He didn't get up.

"You're the one who called, right?"

David nodded.

"Pull up a chair," Warren said, gesturing to one in the corner. David had to step over an assortment of empty potato chip bags and candy wrappers to get to the chair. He rolled it toward Warren's desk and sat down.

Warren Sterne's office had turned out to be little more than a hole-in-the-wall in a small town on the northwest coast. David had learned that the man's Internet business was projected to gross more than three million dollars at the end of the fiscal year. And Warren wasn't yet thirty.

"You said over the phone you had some business to discuss," Warren said, unwrapping another candy bar. "I've got all the investors I can handle at the moment. But if you want to leave your card—"

"Todd Tishman was in a serious accident a couple of months ago."

Warren stopped unwrapping the candy bar and dropped it on his desk. "Damn, so that's why I haven't heard from him. I thought he was just pissed at me."

Warren grabbed a piece of paper and a pen off his desk. "Where is he?"

"He passed away a few days ago."

Warren stared at David a moment before throwing the pen across the desk. He turned toward the wall and cursed. David just sat back and waited. Crying was the way most women released grief. Anger was the way most men chose.

"When did you last talk with him?" David asked, after

Warren had finally stopped spitting his angry epitaphs at the wall.

Warren gestured to the computer. "We mostly e-mailed."

"He e-mailed you from home?"

"Had to," Warren said. "Ardmore had Tishman steal Todd's personal journal out of his desk. When Todd caught his grandfather reading it, Ardmore claimed he was just trying to get to know Todd better. Nosy bastard. Todd destroyed the journal. Never wrote in one again. He kept his computer hidden."

David didn't remember seeing a computer in Todd's condo. Could have been stowed away in a drawer. Might be worth asking the Ardmores about on Tuesday.

"Did he smash his car?" Warren asked.

"No, an accident at the lab."

"He hated that damn place," Warren said. "Couldn't wait to leave. Ardmore pushed him into working there. Set him up in a condo. Gave him his car. All just a way to control him. Even his mother tried to tell him that."

"Molly didn't want him to work at Ardmore Industries?" David asked.

"She knew what a controlling bastard her old man was. He'd screwed up her life making her marry Tishman. Just when she was finally going to break free from that bastard and get her chance with Todd's *real* dad, they get themselves killed. Man, life can really suck big-time."

"Todd's biological father was Steve Kemp?" David said, the news bringing him up straight in his chair.

Warren turned to face David, suddenly seeming to become aware that he'd been rattling on to someone he didn't know. "Why are you asking all these questions? Who are you, anyway?"

David had hoped to learn more from Warren's post-shock spewing before being asked to identify himself. But he was grateful for what he had learned.

"I'm a private investigator."

"Ardmore couldn't have sent you," Warren said. "Or Tishman. Neither of them would give a rat's rump if I ever found out about Todd having died."

"Why do they feel that way?"

"I broke away from my old man and made a living on my own. They were afraid Todd would break away from them and come to work with me."

"Why didn't he?"

"He thought he could change things for the better at his grandpa's company. Hell, I knew he'd never convince those corporate cockroaches to stop polluting the planet. Money is all they care about. Only one who ever really cared about Todd was his mother. Then she had to go and die on him."

"At least he had you."

Warren's huge shoulders hunched. "Yeah, he had me. His best friend. Who told him he was an ass."

"Why did you tell him that?" David asked gently.

"He'd called to say he'd fallen for this woman he'd spent *one* night with. Todd didn't know squat about women. I told him she was just after his grandpa's money. Told him he was an ass to think otherwise. He told me to go to hell and hung up. That's the last thing we said to each other. The last damn thing."

So Todd had fallen for Susan. David could understand that. What he couldn't understand was why Todd hadn't been there when she woke up the next morning.

"Look, I appreciate your coming by to tell me about Todd," Warren said. "But I really don't feel much like talking anymore."

David pulled a card from his pocket. "If you want to talk, I'll be at that number."

Warren took the card. He was still staring at it when David left.

SUSAN ENTERED the coffee room at work looking for both Barry and Ellie. She saw Ellie sitting at the back table, weeping softly. She hurried over to her.

"Ellie, what's wrong?"

"Skip's gone," Ellie sobbed. "He left the magazine, and he left me."

Susan sighed as she leaned over to give her friend a hug. "Want me to make you an espresso?"

Ellie shook her head. "I've already had three this morning. One more drop of caffeine, and you'll have to scrape me off the ceiling."

"So, tell me about the louse," Susan said as she took the chair next to her friend.

"Someone might come in."

"Not for a while. Everybody's in Greg's office waiting for him to return from a meeting. I was looking for you so you could join us in yelling, 'surprise.'"

"Surprise? Oh, right. It's Greg's birthday. I forgot."

"They won't miss us. Why did the scum leave?"

"His uncle offered him a job at his ranch. Skip told him he'd take it a week ago, but he waited until last night to tell me he was leaving for Montana today. Can you believe the bastard? After swearing he loved me, he just up and left me at the first chance to herd cattle!"

Susan laid her hand on Ellie's arm. "He deserves to be buried in cow manure. And on a Montana ranch, you can bet he will be."

Ellie let out a deep sigh. "We didn't even know each other that long. I don't know why I hurt so much."

"Sometimes our feelings just get tangled up so fast, we don't know what hit us," Susan said, aware she spoke from her own recent experience. She'd always felt a sense of superiority to Ellie when she listened to her romantic disasters, probably because she never thought one could happen to her. She didn't feel so superior today.

"I called you three times last night, Suz."

"I'm sorry. I was with…a distant cousin I met recently. Was Barry there for you?"

"Barry was no help at all. He told me I was an idiot for crying over Skip. Told me there were plenty of guys who'd treat me right, but I was too stupid to see them. Then he stalked out of the apartment, slammed the door behind him. You'd think someone had dumped *him!*"

"Maybe Barry's upset because he knows he's one of those guys who'd treat you right."

Ellie stared at her. "No way."

"El, just before I went out on my shoot last Friday, I got one of Barry's rerouted calls from his lawyer. Barry's ex never got to Washington. The psycho met some guy on the way here, and they got married in Vegas. She's his problem now, and Barry's known this for at least ten days."

"He never said a word," Ellie confided, shaking her head in disbelief.

"If he had, he wouldn't have had an excuse to stay at your place and interfere with your romance with Skip."

"No, I can't believe he'd do that. I know when a guy likes me."

"Could be Barry doesn't show you he likes you for fear you'll reject him."

"Well, he's hardly my type."

That was a damn shame. Susan just knew that Barry would appreciate Ellie and treat her right. Ellie deserved that and so much more. But saying all this to her wouldn't change a thing. It wasn't possible to talk someone into love.

"What *is* your type, El?"

"Walks upright. Opposable thumbs. Oh hell, I don't know. I'm thirty-three, and I've had at least that many love affairs. Not one of them turned out well. You're not out there, Suz. You have no idea of the pond scum that pass for men these days. I don't want to settle for less, but there just aren't any guys like Paul left."

"Paul was far from perfect."

"Yeah, right," Ellie said. "He was only handsome, smart, courageous, daring, loving—"

"And careless as hell," Susan said with sudden heat.

Ellie stared at her. "Susan?"

"Paul forced me on a roller-coaster ride that made me sick for a whole day. He embarrassed me by insisting we make love in a place where we'd be discovered. I got badly sunburned on our honeymoon because of him. He cracked one of my ribs rolling me around in a muddy trench he'd dug. He was careless of my safety, El. And his own."

"But, Susan, you always said—"

"That he was perfect. I know. But he wasn't. Paul was a fireman who knew firsthand about the dangers of plastic sheathing on a dryer exhaust hose, but he never replaced ours with a heat-resistant material. He didn't even bother to check that we had working batteries in our smoke detectors. *He* could have prevented his death, but he didn't because he was so damn careless!"

Susan suddenly realized she so angry that she was shaking and tears were streaming from her eyes. Ellie got up to put her arms around her shoulders. She held her for several minutes until Susan regained her composure.

"Susan, I'm so sorry. I never imagined...I never thought...why didn't you tell me?"

Susan grabbed a tissue out of her pocket and dabbed at her eyes. "I didn't know."

"Come again?" Ellie said, clearly confused.

"When Paul died, all I could think about was how wonderful he'd been. I mourned that perfect Paul. I had to. Anything else would have seemed heartless and unspeakably disloyal. I couldn't make myself acknowledge, much less express, my anger at him for the carelessness that had cost him his life.''

"He was gone and you wanted to remember him with love,'' Ellie said softly, with sudden and perfect understanding.

Susan nodded. ''But deep down I knew he was careless, because I kept dreaming about when he had been. I couldn't understand what those dreams were trying to get me to face until now.''

Ellie hugged her quietly. ''All this time I thought you'd had the perfect love. I guess there are no perfect loves.''

"Probably because there are no perfect people.''

"Ain't that the truth,'' Ellie said as she leaned back to look into Susan's face. ''Do you realize this is the first time I've ever seen you cry?''

"I guess I can't tough it out like I used to.''

"I'm glad, Suz. Everyone needs to get rid of the rubbish with a good cry now and then.''

Susan was astonished to realize that Ellie was absolutely right. Being able to cry and get her anger at Paul out in the open had been necessary. She felt a tremendous, glorious relief!

"You ready to get some of Greg's birthday cake?'' Ellie asked.

Susan looked down at her wedding band. ''Soon as I take off this ring.''

# CHAPTER THIRTEEN

DAVID HAD GIVEN SUSAN his cell number, but she had called his office number and left word with Harry that a meeting would keep her late. He was waiting in the lobby for her when she got off the elevator. She smiled at a co-worker and waved goodbye. But when she turned and saw him, her smile disappeared.

The wedding ring was gone from her finger. He wanted to know why, but their relationship had become so strained over the past couple of days that he didn't know how to even approach the subject.

They sprinted through the drizzle to his truck. She ignored the hand he offered to help her up on the seat. With every passing moment, she withdrew farther from him.

He had been trained to talk to people, both as a psychologist and as a private investigator. Yet, he no longer knew how to talk to her. Their time together had been filled with awkwardness ever since the moment she'd told him their night together was "no big deal."

He had brought fresh towels to her room the next morning in the hope they could discuss things, but she wouldn't let him in. She didn't ask him about the case anymore. She was sitting right beside him in the truck, but he couldn't reach her.

"We're going out to eat tonight," he announced, not even aware of what he was going to say until the words were out. But once they were, he knew exactly where they would eat and why he wanted to go there.

"I need to feed Honey."

"I put out extra kibble this morning for him as well as my dogs. He's probably been romping around with them all day having a great time. We'll bring him a steak in a doggie bag."

"I don't feel like eating out."

"I do."

He was determined she would not change his mind. She didn't try anymore. That made him feel worse, because he realized that she didn't even care enough to fight with him.

The restaurant he drove to had just three good points. A table was always available. The piano player favored slow music. And the dance floor was dark and secluded. As soon as they'd ordered, he took her hand and led her onto the dance floor, ignoring every one of her immediate and adamant objections.

David didn't like to dance. He just wanted an excuse to get close to Susan. Getting her to dance with him was the only thing he could think of. When emotional connections collapsed, the basic bridge of human touch was all that remained to reach someone.

But until he took her into his arms, he didn't realize how much he'd needed to hold her. Through several scattered pulse beats, her body remained stiff and unyielding. Then she sighed, wrapped her arms around his waist and leaned against him.

And that's when David knew that she had needed to hold him, as well.

"The service here is terrible," he whispered near her ear as they slowly swayed to the music.

"Okay."

"They'll take half an hour even to get the salads on the table."

"Okay."

"The food is even worse. They'll probably burn the steaks."

"Okay."

He brushed a kiss across the top of her hair. "You were wrong, Susan. The other night *was* a big deal. For both of us."

She was quiet for such a long time that he wasn't sure she was going to say anything. But she did, right after resting her cheek against his chest. "Okay."

He let out a long, relieved breath as his arms tightened around her. "Your safety has to come first. I can stay away from you because I must. But I can't stand your not talking to me. Please, Susan, talk to me."

Her sigh was sweet and shaky and went right through his heart. "Okay."

"LET ME TAKE YOUR assignment this afternoon," Barry said.

"You were on shoots all day yesterday and this morning," Susan said as she checked her latest prints. "What are you trying to do, work yourself to death?"

Barry paced around her cubicle, his normally cool demeanor completely gone. "I just don't want to be cooped up in the office today."

More likely, Barry didn't want to run into Ellie.

"Ellie told me she discovered you'd moved out when she got home last night," Susan said carefully. "Everything okay?"

"Just peachy. You should have heard her sob over that idiot Skip."

"Sometimes a woman needs a shoulder to cry on," Susan said. "Ever think of offering her yours?"

"Greg's picked one of your bear pictures for the cover of the next issue," Barry said, ignoring Susan's question. "You have two other full-page spreads. You don't need to stand out in the drizzle today, trying to get some doe to look cute for you. I'll handle the assignment. Go enjoy yourself for a change.''

''Susan will be happy to take you up on your offer.'' David's voice came from the entrance to her cubicle.

She swiveled in her chair toward him, her heart picking up an extra beat. ''Hi. This is a nice surprise. Barry Eckhouse, I'd like you to meet—''

''David Knight,'' he said, stepping inside the cubicle and extending his hand to Barry before she could finish. ''I'm the lucky man in Susan's life these days.''

Barry looked from David to Susan and back to David in surprise. He wasn't the only one surprised.

While David and Barry shook hands, she gave herself a mental shake. David had clearly instructed her to introduce him as a distant cousin to her friends and associates. Now he was introducing himself as her lover?

*The other night was a big deal. For both of us.*

Hardly a declaration of love. But her heart had swelled with relief when he'd said those words. She was free to smile and be herself with him again, and the past two miserable days were over.

''Where are we going?'' she asked a few moments later, as David whisked her down the hall toward the elevators.

He pressed the elevator button. ''Since Todd's biological father was Steve Kemp, I thought a talk with his relatives might be a good idea. Steve's mother, Irene, has agreed to see us.''

''She doesn't mind that I'll be with you?'' Susan asked as she stepped into the empty elevator that had arrived.

''She specifically requested I bring you,'' he said as he followed her.

''How does she know about me?''

''One of the first questions I intend to ask her.''

''Speaking of asking questions, cuz,'' she said, turning

toward him once the elevator doors had closed, "why did you introduce yourself that way to Barry just now?"

"Because being your lover is a better cover." He paused to smile at her. "And a much easier role for me to play."

He was still smiling at her when the elevator arrived at the lobby.

"Susan?" Ellie's voice called.

Susan turned a flushed face toward her friend. Ellie was standing at the elevator door, a sandwich from the deli down the street in her hand, a startled look on her face.

"Hi, this is David. David, Ellie. We've got to run now, El. Talk to you later."

She moved outside quickly because she knew her friend was going to be asking some pretty intense questions.

And, at the moment, Susan didn't quite know how to answer them.

"SUSAN, PLEASE MAKE yourself at home," Irene Kemp said. Since the moment Susan and David arrived at her modest home in Mason County, Irene had been smiling and fussing over Susan as if she were her long-lost grand-daughter.

"I'm so glad you're here," Irene said. "Ever since we heard about the baby—"

"What baby is that, Mrs. Kemp?" David asked.

Irene turned a surprised look in his direction. "My great-grandchild, of course."

"How do you know about the baby?" Susan asked.

"Vance Tishman had the decency to call and tell us," Irene said.

"And who have you told?" David asked.

"My grandson, Carl, and I are the only ones who know. Vance told us to be sure to keep the news to ourselves. He's not a bad man. I can see that now. None of what happened all those years ago was really his fault. He was just another puppet controlled by Robert Ardmore.''

''What exactly did happen all those years ago, Mrs. Kemp?'' Susan asked.

Irene sighed. ''Yes, you should be told. You're part of the family now. Can't believe nearly thirty years have passed. In a way, seems like yesterday.''

Irene got up to retrieve a picture off the mantel. She brought the framed photo to Susan. ''My son, Steve, was the star of his high school basketball team at the time. So tall, so handsome, so talented.''

''He was very handsome,'' Susan said, returning the picture to Irene.

Irene replaced the photo as she continued. ''Steve met Molly when he played against the boys from that fancy school she attended. They fell in love. But Molly knew her father wouldn't approve, so they had to meet secretly.''

''Did you know?'' Susan asked.

Irene shook her head as she retook her seat. ''Seventeen-year-old boys don't tell their parents these things. Of course, when Molly got pregnant, everything came out. She was only sixteen.''

Irene paused. ''They'd been so very foolish, but Steve did want to marry her. Only, Ardmore wouldn't let him. He said he wasn't having *his* daughter marrying the son of a garage mechanic. He threatened to take the baby away from Molly if she didn't marry his business associate. Vance Tishman was twelve years her senior. She hardly knew him. But there was nothing Molly could do. She wanted her baby.''

''What did Molly's mother think about this?'' Susan asked.

''Nancy Ardmore is one of those society women who are bred to be doormats,'' Irene said with obvious disdain. ''Everyone knows Robert Ardmore only married her for her money and social position. That's all that matters to him. He didn't care about the happiness of his daughter or his grandchild. He forbade Molly ever to see Steve again or to tell her child about his real father.''

''Fathers have legal rights,'' David said.

''Not when the grandfather of a child is Robert Ardmore,'' Irene said angrily. ''He threatened to ruin my husband's business and impoverish our entire family if Steve ever went near Molly again, or tried to see his child.''

''So your son stayed away for your sake,'' Susan said.

''He was a good boy, my Steve. Always trying to do the right thing, even when that brought him pain. Tishman married Molly before she gave birth, so the boy was legally his. Steve was kept away from his son all those years. My husband passed a few years ago. He never once saw his grandchild.''

''Did you ever meet Todd?'' Susan asked.

''Last year, Molly told Todd the truth about his dad,'' Irene said. ''She brought Todd here to meet Steve and me. Todd was so thrilled to be with his real dad. Molly and Steve never stopped loving each other, even after all that time apart. Susan, I wish you could have seen them. They made such a beautiful, loving family.''

''What a piece of crap.'' A male voice sounded from the doorway.

''Carl!'' Irene said with indignation. ''Why aren't you at work?''

David had been carefully watching the man who had stood at the entrance to the room for the past minute, staring at Susan as he rubbed his grease-stained hands on a dish towel.

Carl swaggered into the room and threw the dish towel on a table. He was at least six-two and wore dirty jeans and a soiled sweatshirt. He ignored David and his grandmother, as he headed directly for the couch where Susan sat and plopped down beside her.

"I let myself off early," Carl said. His eyes still hadn't left Susan's face. "I'm Todd's half brother, the one no one talks about 'cause my grandpa wasn't worth a baboon's butt, much less a few billion."

"Carl," his grandmother said, "some civility, please."

"I get on Grandma's nerves 'cause I'm too crass and blunt," Carl said, obviously happy to be both. "So you're the lucky lady carrying the sole heir to the Ardmore fortune. I never thought Todd had any taste, but you are changing my mind. Babe, what did you ever see in him?"

"Carl, Todd was your brother," Irene said, clearly upset.

"Half brother," Carl corrected. "Don't be misled by Grandma's heartwarming family stories, Susan. She wouldn't be nearly so interested in you if you weren't going to be giving birth to a billion-dollar baby. We Kemps can be mercenary bastards. Take my father. He sure as hell didn't latch onto Molly Ardmore for her looks."

"Carl, your behavior is inexcusable," his grandmother said in exasperation.

"Oh, right," Carl said sarcastically. "*My* behavior is inexcusable. The guy who's keeping the business going by working sixteen hours a day. My darling half brother had everything handed to him. All he turned out to be was a worthless piece of s—"

"*Carl!*" his grandmother yelled.

Carl smiled at Susan. It wasn't a nice smile. "Only thing that surprises me is he actually had the balls to kill himself."

"Please, Susan, don't listen to him," Irene said. "Carl doesn't know what he's saying. He's still upset over the death of his father."

"Like hell I am," Carl said. "He got what he deserved."

Irene gasped. "What a horrible thing to say!"

"Is it? Let me tell you about my mother, Susan. She's dying of cancer. She's lying in this big, old hospital bed with tubes stuck up her nose. And where is my dad? He's off with his high-society bitch for a weekend at a fancy B&B. He and his bitch got what they deserved, all right."

"I CAN STILL FEEL his anger," Susan said as they drove away from the Kemp household.

"Carl isn't exactly reticent about expressing his feelings," David agreed. "You realize he could have been the one who tried to abduct you in the wildlife refuge?"

"Why would he direct his anger at me?"

"His motive may not have been anger at you. Could be he planned to demand a ransom from Ardmore for your safe return."

"Even if Ardmore paid such a ransom, Carl would certainly have been caught. Doesn't sound like a very smart move."

"Smart may not be part of Carl's gene pool. But some of what he said raises a question or two."

She turned toward him. "If you mean that part about Irene Kemp being interested in me because she thinks I'm carrying the Ardmore heir, she's being foolish. I'm not an Ardmore."

"Whatever Irene Kemp's interest in you might be, Susan, your child *is* the only blood heir of the Ardmores. I feel certain that's the reason you're in danger."

"Aside from that kidnapping-for-ransom scenario we just discussed, I fail to see why."

"I believe whoever tried to abduct you either wanted possession of Ardmore's great-grandchild or wanted to eliminate that great-grandchild. That could be anyone who knew about the baby, including Ardmore himself.''

"The man who grabbed me was much bigger than Ardmore."

"Ardmore could have sent one of his bodyguards. A man with his money can buy just about whoever and whatever he wants.''

Her head was shaking. "But he seems satisfied that I'm going to have the baby. Why would he have me abducted?''

"Possibly to ensure you *did* have the baby. He didn't know at the time what your decision was, remember?''

"Do you believe he'd do that, David?''

"I'm not ruling anything out. Your life is at stake. Jared has used his connections to arrange a meeting for me with Lucy Norton's husband this afternoon. Want to come?''

"Very much.''

David looked up at the threatening sky. The forecast had only predicted drizzle, but in western Washington, a hearty rain could always be expected.

"Ready for some lunch?'' he asked.

"I left my sandwich back at work.''

"Good thing I packed a picnic basket,'' he said as he took a quick look in the rearview mirror before turning off onto a side road.

"*You* packed a picnic basket?''

"Okay, I had a restaurant pack one. Hungry?''

"Depends on what restaurant did the packing. If it was the one from last night—''

"No,'' he said. "This time the food will be edible, I promise. But I'd still trade a good meal for that dance floor.''

She sent him a smile of remembrance that had his heart revving.

He parked on a hill with an open view of the water

below and an even better view along the high bank of a single, enormous Douglas fir with a cratered top. He had seen the bald eagles courting in the skies a few weeks before, and had followed them with his binoculars to their nest in the tree.

He spread a blanket over the flatbed of the truck. They sat on the blanket and ate the assortment of sandwiches, salads and fresh fruit. Susan finished off a bottle of spring water as she observed the eagle's nest through his binoculars.

He sipped a soft drink as he watched the excitement on her face.

"Can't tell if there's an egg," she said. "I would love to get a shot of an eagle hatching."

She put down the binoculars and turned to him. Her smile made up for the missing sunshine. "This is a great spot to eat a picnic lunch."

"Like I told you, I only know the best places."

She sent him a grin as she set down the empty bottle and wrapped her arms around her knees. "Ardmore said he'd give me the letter Todd wrote tonight."

"Be interesting to see what that letter says. According to Warren Sterne, Todd considered his time with you very special."

"I'm glad he had Warren. His half brother sure didn't like him. I wonder how Vance Tishman felt about Todd?"

"Warren implied that he was as controlling of Todd as was his grandfather. People with money often use it as a way to exert their will over others. The records show Ardmore bought out Tishman's chemical company for a sizable amount over the market value at the time Tishman married Molly."

"Sounds more like a business merger than a marriage. Do you know why Tishman's in a wheelchair?"

David shook his head.

"Maybe Tishman is reaching out to the Kemps because he feels guilty about the part he played in keeping Todd from knowing his biological father for all those years."

"Maybe," he agreed.

The crisp breeze was filled with the promise of rain. When she shivered, he moved behind her and wrapped his arms around her. She leaned her back against his chest, laying her arms on top of his. He turned his palms upward and entwined their fingers, gently rubbing the pale skin where her wedding ring had been.

"You took it off," he said softly.

"Paul's gone."

"And the dreams?"

"Also gone."

The intensity of David's relief startled him.

"Why were you at the wildlife refuge the other day?" she asked.

He could have lied to her. A few days ago, he probably would have. But not now. "I was watching you take pictures of the bears."

"Have you been at any of my other shoots over the past few weeks?"

"Every one of them," he said, resting his cheek against her hair as a cold gust of air hit them.

She was smiling as she snuggled against him. He flexed his arms around her, his biceps inadvertently brushing the sides of her breasts.

"Warmer?" he asked.

"Nearly perfect," she sighed.

He had to know. "What would make it perfect?"

"A softer seat. The bed of this truck is quite hard."

"I'd offer you my lap," he whispered near her ear, "but at the moment I don't think you'd notice much of a difference."

He felt her start as the meaning in his words hit her.

Her burst of surprised laughter was better than music. The first drops of rain made a pinging sound on the roof of the truck. They scrambled to get inside the cab.

FRANK NORTON of Norton's Aviation Academy was a short hefty man in his early fifties whose eyes swept over Susan and then settled on David. He vigorously chewed on a piece of gum.

"The sheriff told me I had to cooperate with you," Norton said as he closed the door to his private office and yanked down the blind. "But you tell Ardmore I said a word, and I'll call you a liar."

"Are you afraid of Ardmore?" David asked.

"Hell, yes," Norton said, spitting his chewing gum into a wastebasket as he headed for the coffeemaker in the corner. He poured the black liquid into a ceramic cup. It smelled more like burnt rubber than coffee.

Norton faced him, took a sip and grimaced. "Ardmore could squash me like a bug. He would, too, if he could prove my Lucy was what that snot-nosed bastard claimed she was."

"A drinker," David said, as he gestured for Susan to take the guest chair in front of the man's desk. Frank obviously wasn't going to invite them to sit.

"Lucy never drank a day on the job," Frank said, anger flushing his face. "Never. Not even when she wasn't scheduled to fly."

"Who is the snot-nosed bastard?" David asked.

"Terry Nettles. He's the kid of a guy who owns a liquor store in the next town. And, no. Lucy never bought any liquor from Terry's old man."

"So why did this kid say she was a drinker?"

"Because my Lucy flunked him on his ground school test. He tried to bribe her to pass him. She got the word out to other flying schools in the area, so he wouldn't try to pull the same crap on them. Made Terry angry as hell.''

"So, the snot-nosed bastard wanted revenge," David said, knowing that each time he referred to Terry by that title, the tension in Frank eased a fraction more.

Frank nodded. "We teach flying and we do charters, but the real money is in our school. We want our students to pass. Hell, we'd be out of business pretty quick if they didn't. But Terry didn't want to do the work. When the NTSB investigator came by after the crash, Terry couldn't wait to lie about Lucy drinking."

"Surely you told the investigator that the snot-nosed bastard was just trying to smear her name," David said.

"Loud and clear. I showed him Terry's flunking scores, too."

"That should have put an end to the lie."

"Would have, if they had recovered enough of…her to rule it out."

That told David what he hadn't been able to find out from his other sources. The cause of the plane crash would not be determined from the autopsy on the pilot.

"What do you think really caused the crash, Frank?" he asked.

Frank shook his head. "Damn if I know. I checked that Skyhawk out from wingtip to tail before they took off that day. I was a commercial airplane mechanic for fifteen years before my Lucy and I opened up our business here."

"Why did Molly Ardmore Tishman select your charter service?"

"Wasn't Molly. Steve Kemp's been a friend of our family for years. He used to coach my kid in basketball. He booked the trip 'cause he knew we'd be discreet."

"And the need for that, Frank?" David asked, pretty sure he already knew but wanting Frank's confirmation.

"Steve and Molly were in love," Frank said. "Had been

since they were teenagers. But Steve's wife was dying of cancer. He couldn't bring himself to leave her, no matter what he felt for Molly.''

"So they asked Lucy to fly them elsewhere so they could have some private time together.''

Frank nodded. "Lucy had flown them to the coast several times before, over the previous months.''

"Was there anything unusual or different about this time?''

Frank shook his head.

"Did Lucy have any medical conditions?''

"She wouldn't have been a pilot if she had,'' Frank said, immediately back on the defensive. "Lucy was in great shape. Didn't smoke. Rarely drank. Her only addiction was those fancy coffees Molly brought along for her and Steve in a thermos. They were homemade mocha-latte-caramel-crème kind of things. Lucy said Molly's brews were better than Starbucks'. She always brought along enough for everyone. Molly was a nice lady, real thoughtful. No fancy airs at all. Just like my Lucy.''

Frank stared down at the coffee in his cup. "I still can't believe she's gone. I keep hearing the engine of that Skyhawk circling above, getting ready to come in for a landing with her at the controls.''

Frank's eyes grew red as he turned his face away. David nodded at the question on Susan's face. She rose quietly, and they let themselves out.

SUSAN STUDIED HERSELF critically in the mirror. Her hair was a circle of braids at the top of her head. Her deep-green dress had simple, straight lines, a high collar, long sleeves and a hem just below the knee. The shade brought out the color of her eyes, but the cut was rather plain. Ah, well. She'd never been one to make a fashion statement.

She turned to the side and was relieved to see that at

least her stomach looked flat. She wondered when she would begin to show.

She smiled as she rested her hand on her tummy. *Never mind, sweetie. You just keep growing. I don't care if you make me as big as a buffalo. Promise.*

A knock came on the door. ''We're due at the Ardmore estate in forty minutes,'' David said.

''I'm ready.'' She swung by the bed to pick up the small, black purse she'd packed with basic essentials, then opened the door.

David looked wonderful in his dark suit. When she saw the open appreciation on his face as he smiled down at her, she decided maybe she didn't look too bad, after all.

THE DINING ROOM WAS impressive—heavy crystal chandeliers, brocade wallpaper, gold velvet drapes, a twenty-foot-high carved ceiling, and a table that could probably seat a hundred. Susan thought such places only existed in the imagination of moviemakers, but Ardmore's estate was real enough.

''Dinner was excellent, thank you,'' she told Robert and Nancy Ardmore as they retired to the adjoining room, another elaborately appointed space with paneled walls, original oil paintings and thick soft carpeting the color of marshmallow.

A fire burned in the massive fireplace. The feel was cozy and comforting, but Susan knew the fire couldn't be real. The air temperature was too even and perfect.

Real things, like real people, were uneven.

She and David sat side by side on a couch adjacent to the hearth. Nancy was across from them on a matching love seat. Vance rolled his wheelchair beside her. Ardmore lounged back in a leather chair beside his wife. The servants were dismissed.

"Nancy, would you mind getting the letter?" Ardmore said.

Nancy went to the rosewood desk in the corner. She drew a single piece of writing paper from a drawer. She brought the letter to Susan.

Susan held the letter between herself and David so that he could read along. The date at the top was five days after the bereavement seminar.

Dear Susan,

Making love to you last Friday night was one of the most important things that has ever happened to me. I'm telling you this first because I don't want you to throw out this letter before you hear my explanation of why I wasn't there when you awakened.

I went to my car to make sure it hadn't been towed away during the night. When I returned, you were gone. I had seen your name on your camera tag but couldn't remember the name of the magazine. It wasn't until I was at the library today and found a copy of *True Nature* magazine that I remembered. I mention this so you understand my tardiness in getting in touch with you and why I have sent this letter to your business address.

Susan, my full name is Todd Tishman. My telephone numbers, address and e-mail are at the bottom of this letter. Please contact me. I've been thinking about you constantly since that night. I want very much to see you again.

Todd

Susan was touched by the sincerity in the letter. She looked up to see the Ardmores and Tishman watching her. Nancy smiled. "I found the letter in his desk drawer," she said. "He must not have had a chance to mail it. You see, the next day was when he…"

Susan understood what Nancy couldn't say: the next day Todd set the explosion in the lab.

"When your name came up as one of Mr. Knight's contacts," Ardmore said, "I realized you were *the* Susan who worked at *True Nature* magazine. From everything my investigator had learned about you, she was convinced you wanted to find Todd because he was the father of your baby. But then you stopped trying to find him. Why?"

She looked to David to see if he would approve of her telling Ardmore. He nodded. "Because Mr. Knight discovered that Todd had been badly injured in a suicide attempt and was not expected to survive," she said.

Ardmore looked at David in some surprise before returning his attention to her. "I would prefer the specifics surrounding my grandson's death do not become public knowledge."

"I have no intention of telling anyone," she said.

Ardmore nodded, seeming satisfied. "The sheriff tells me they still have no leads on the man who tried to abduct you. Mr. Knight is clearly a competent private investigator. But being a bodyguard is not his specialty. I own a security company that employs only the very best. Two of their top men will accompany you home tonight. Two more will arrive tomorrow morning. Four will be with you at all times."

"Thank you, but Mr. Knight is the only bodyguard I need."

Ardmore frowned at her as he tapped his fingers on the arm of his chair. "You're rejecting my offer?"

"I appreciate your offer very much. But I feel quite safe in Mr. Knight's hands."

Ardmore tapped some more. "I've seen your photographs in *True Nature*. You have exceptional talent. I'll arrange for you to have a full-time nanny from the moment the baby is born. You'll be able to pursue your career without interruption.''

''That's very generous of you, but I don't want the nanny.''

''You'll need a monthly stipend to cover essentials,'' Ardmore said. ''I'll start it at five thousand.''

*Five thousand a month?* ''Look, I know you only mean well by these offers, but I can support my child. What's more, I fully intend to. I neither want nor need your money.''

''You're carrying my great-grandchild,'' Ardmore said, his fingers drumming to an even faster beat on the arm of his chair.

''Which is why you and Mrs. Ardmore will always be welcome when you wish to see the baby. As will Mr. Tishman.''

He stared sternly at her. ''You must consider your child's welfare.''

''I have.''

''I intend to see that my great-grandchild is properly raised.''

''So do I.''

''Early mental stimulation and proper nutrition are essential,'' he said. ''You need to heed my advice on these matters. You do not have enough money to provide the basic necessities.''

''I'll be happy to listen to your advice,'' she said. ''But trust me. You don't have enough money to get me to heed that advice if I believe it to be wrong.''

''Ms. Carter—'' Ardmore began.

''Mr. Ardmore,'' she interrupted. ''I want my child to love you for who you are, not for the money you have. Don't you want that, as well?''

Ardmore's tapping fingers made dents in the chair's

leather. His expression was far less than pleased, but he sounded less gruff when he finally responded. "If you're going to insist on winning this argument, the least you can do is call me Robert."

"I'd be happy to, Robert. Call me Susan. And let's not label this an argument. I'd much prefer to think we've formed an alliance. We both have the baby's welfare at heart. As far as I'm concerned, that makes us both right."

Her smile was warm and engaging.

The slight curve to Robert Ardmore's lips was probably as close as he ever came to a smile. "If my grandson had met you sooner, you might have made a man out of him."

# *CHAPTER FOURTEEN*

WHILE NANCY TOOK SUSAN to the edge of the room to look at family pictures, David joined Ardmore at the portable bar. Ardmore poured two glasses of vintage cognac and handed one to David.

The cognac was rich and smooth and slid down David's throat. He nodded his approval at his host's selection. "Susan's in jeopardy because she's carrying your greatgrandchild."

"Whatever the reason someone tried to grab her," Ardmore said, "you should convince her she needs those extra bodyguards."

"Is there anyone you suspect would try to get at you through the child?" David asked, ignoring Ardmore's comment.

Ardmore shrugged. "I didn't rise to the top by making friends."

"This would have to be someone who knew she was carrying Todd's child. Who did you tell when McKinney gave you the news?"

"Just Nancy and Vance. If that's the reason, Susan must have told someone."

"Susan has told no one."

"Then, she must have been a random target."

David didn't believe that. He wondered what Ardmore would say if he knew Vance had told the Kemps about the baby. He decided to keep that piece of information to himself.

"Have the investigators closed the case on the explosion at the lab?" David asked.

Ardmore sipped his expensive cognac, but the expression on his face reflected no enjoyment. "Last week when Todd passed away. I'm surprised your brother didn't tell you."

"I didn't ask Jared. What were their findings?"

"They determined his death to be an accident," Ardmore said, then added quietly, "as a favor to me."

David understood the man was hurting. If what David suspected was right, he'd be able to take away some of that pain. "You read the letter that your grandson wrote to Susan. Would you say that was a love letter?"

"My grandson wasn't what you'd call sophisticated. Susan was probably the first woman he'd been with who wasn't after my money. I've no doubt he thought himself in love."

"That first rush of romantic love can be heady stuff."

"Is there some point to that comment?"

David ignored Ardmore's querulous tone. "A very important one. Romantic love puts a man in a euphoric state. A man in such a state is not a candidate for suicide."

"Good thing you gave up that psychological career, Knight. Todd's suicide note was anything but euphoric."

"I'd like to see what he wrote."

"He didn't write it to you."

"Then, let me see Todd's personal computer."

Ardmore glared at him through narrowed eyes. "What are you after?"

"What else he might have written."

"He didn't have a personal computer."

"Warren Sterne told me he did."

"Sterne was either mistaken or he lied. We found no computer in Todd's effects. If he communicated with Sterne via one, he must have used his office computer."

"May I have a look at it?"

"The computer was destroyed along with the rest of the lab."

Which meant David was going to have to get to the truth another way. "Mr. Ardmore, I believe there's more to your grandson's death than—"

"Look, Knight. I owe you for saving Susan and my great-grandchild. I also owe you for not blabbing about my grandson's suicide. I'm not an ungrateful man. But I don't intend to let you dredge up all this unhappiness again. Todd was laid to rest last week. Damn it, let him rest in peace."

"DON'T LET HIS GRUFF manner fool you, Susan," Nancy said as she showed her the picture albums of Molly as a child. "Robert loved Todd dearly, just as he loved our Molly. He only wanted the best for them both."

"Molly was tiny, wasn't she?" Susan said, staring at the picture of the slim, solemn-faced girl in her high school uniform.

"Barely five-three," Nancy said. "All us Todaros are petite."

"Did the nickname Todd come from your maiden name, Todaro?"

Nancy nodded. "Molly's choice. She was a very sweet and loving mother. But I missed her so much when she left home to marry. She was still so very young, just a baby herself."

Nancy paused. "Robert was too strict and demanding with her. He tried to be more lenient with Todd. He delayed work on several promising new insecticides at his chemical plant just to give Todd a chance to pursue his natural species predator approach."

"Shame the approach didn't work," Susan said.

"He realized some success, although not enough to recoup the several million dollars Robert lost from his investment. He never told Todd about the loss. More than anything he wanted to give him a chance to succeed.''

''Did Todd ever talk about going into business with his friend, Warren Sterne?''

''A couple of weeks before his...death he mentioned over dinner that he was leaving the research lab. He didn't say what he was going to do.''

''Todd's decision to leave the lab must have hurt his grandfather.''

Nancy nodded. ''Robert told Todd that a man was only a failure if he quit. He offered to back another research project on natural predators because he so wanted Todd to succeed. When Todd took his own life it...devastated Robert.''

''Because Todd had given up,'' Susan guessed.

''Exactly,'' Vance Tishman said as he rolled his wheelchair up to them. ''Robert's faced adversity, failures and many hardships. Not once did he ever think of giving up. Nancy, would you be a dear and get me another cognac? I can't seem to get this damn chair close enough to the bar.''

''Of course,'' Nancy said as she took his empty snifter and headed for the bar on the other side of the room.

When Susan saw Ardmore and David standing there, she wondered why Vance hadn't asked them for assistance.

''Forgive me, Susan,'' Vance said quickly, ''but that was just a ploy to have a moment to speak with you alone.''

''Yes?''

''Irene Kemp called me to say that you had met with her. She wanted me to extend her apologies again for Carl's behavior. He is in agony over his mother's illness, Susan. He is neither thinking nor behaving rationally, I'm afraid.''

"I believe I understand."

Vance squirmed in his wheelchair, suddenly looking physically uncomfortable or embarrassed, Susan couldn't determine which. "Robert doesn't know I'm in touch with the Kemps. Far as he's concerned, Steve was to blame for Molly's death. He firmly believes that Steve only went after his daughter a second time to make trouble for him."

"What do you believe?" Susan asked.

Vance let out a heavy breath as he straightened the thick glasses that had slid down his nose. "I believe I made a mistake marrying someone whose heart had already been given to someone else. But even if his mother could not return my love, Todd was my son in all the important ways. You won't mention my keeping in touch with the Kemps to Robert?"

"I see no reason to."

"Thank you, Susan. Please, call me Vance. If I can ever be of assistance to you, don't hesitate to call. Here, take my card."

Vance reached into the pocket of his dinner jacket and pulled out his business card. Susan glanced at it briefly. "You're president of the Ardmore Chemical Company?"

Vance nodded. "The company may have changed names, but a Tishman has been at the helm for more than eighty years. I always hoped Todd would follow in my footsteps. But I suppose all fathers want that of their sons."

Nancy was on their way back to them. Vance leaned closer as he lowered his voice. "Todd was as bright and good a son as any man could have. Don't let his grandfather convince you otherwise. Robert was always far too critical of the boy."

"YOU DON'T THINK TODD committed suicide?" Jared asked on the other end of the phone line.

272 BABY BY CHANCE

David had waited until they'd returned to his home and Susan was giving Honey her attention before calling his brother. He wasn't ready to disturb her with these suspicions.

"How was the explosion in the lab set?" David asked his brother.

"With a lethal combination of some common chemicals."

"Not chemicals specific to the lab?"

"They were certainly available in the lab," Jared said. "But they could also have been purchased elsewhere and brought in, if that's what you mean."

"So the investigators assumed suicide because of the note they found."

"Plus the fact that Todd was the only one in the lab at the time," Jared confirmed.

"What did the suicide note say?"

"That he was angry about his mother's death, angry at his grandfather and angry with a lab that produced and disseminated toxins."

"Anger at situations or people outside oneself doesn't lead to suicide," David said. "Anger turned inward that engenders hopelessness is what leads to an individual taking his own life."

"I bow to your expertise in that area," Jared said.

"How was the note delivered?"

"Through the shared computer system."

"I thought the computer he used was destroyed."

"Everything in the lab was blown up, but the suicide e-mail was sent to his grandfather before the explosion."

"Jared, this feels wrong."

"In light of the letter you mentioned he wrote to Susan Carter the day before, I agree the case could use another look."

"You do realize that if Todd's death wasn't suicide,

then whoever killed him could be tied in to the attempt on Susan?''

''None of the major players owns a black van, David, unless Carl Kemp borrowed one from a customer.''

''Where was Carl at the time of Susan's attempted abduction?''

''Supposedly working. Hard to verify since he runs the mechanic's shop he inherited from his dad. I'll see if I can pin down where he was when the lab exploded.''

''That could be helpful,'' David said. ''What have you discovered on the money trail?''

''Todd's assets were minimal. He owned his car and had a small bank account. Ardmore held title to the Falls Island condo. Since Todd died without a will, his assets will end up in the hands of Vance, his legal father and nearest next of kin.''

''There's no other family money that was his?''

''Smart, rich folks set up trusts in lieu of wills to avoid probate. That way they also avoid public disclosure when money and property get transferred to successor trustees. Ardmore told me about his trust, but I have no guarantee he told me the truth.''

''Your disclaimer is duly noted,'' David said. ''What did he tell you?''

''Ardmore's trust distributes his assets to his wife and charities. He never made a provision for either his daughter or Todd. He told me that a parent's job is to see that his children and their children have the best in care and education. But Ardmore said he's a firm believer that once a child reaches adulthood, he should be ready to care for himself—which doesn't exactly jibe with the fact that he gave Todd a job and a condo to live in.''

''The basic dilemma for parents,'' David said. ''Urging their children to stand on their own two feet, but unable to watch them fall on their faces. Still, if Ardmore told you the truth, I can't see anyone benefiting financially from Todd's death.''

"On the contrary. Warren Sterne may have been the one doing all the work over the past four years establishing his computer business, but Todd was a full partner.''

"Warren was sharing the profits with him?''

"The enterprise was in the red for the first two years,'' Jared said. "Profits from the third year were reinvested in the business. Warren would have had to share his substantial profits at the end of this fiscal year if Todd hadn't died. Their partnership was drawn up with a right of survivorship clause. Warren Sterne now owns everything.''

"So what you're saying is Warren had a motive to kill Todd,'' David said.

"And it's called pure greed.''


"OKAY, SUSAN CARTER,'' Ellie said, plopping down in a side chair the moment Susan entered her cubicle. "Out with it. Who is David?''

"The man in my life,'' Susan said simply, setting her thermos and shoulder bag down on her desk. That was their cover story—and the truth.

"When did all this happen?'' Ellie asked.

"A while back,'' she said, deliberately being vague. "El, I'm sorry I haven't mentioned him before, but our relationship didn't begin in a conventional way. I wasn't even sure where things were going.''

All of which was true.

"So, where are things going?'' Ellie asked.

Susan sighed. "Haven't a clue.''

"Does he love you?''

"Haven't a clue.''

"Do you love him?''

"I'm afraid so.''

Ellie shook her head. "Susan, this isn't like you. Can you trust him?"

*With my life? Definitely. With my heart? That's another matter entirely.*

"I know he wouldn't think of hurting me," Susan said.

"Men don't think about hurting us. They hurt us because they *don't* think."

Wasn't that the truth.

"So how are things with you and Barry?" Susan asked, hoping to get off the subject of her love life.

"Like he's the Middle Ages, and I'm the Black Plague," Ellie said. "If he sees me coming, he runs the other way. Did I tell you that he sent me a *check* for the time he spent at my place?"

"El, you know men look at this money thing differently than we do. Could be the check was just Barry's clumsy way of saying thank-you."

Ellie stabbed at a cuticle. "If clumsy is a euphemism for moronic. I sent the damn check back to him. He bought all the groceries the entire time he was there. Cooked every night. He doesn't owe me anything. Except an apology for being an ass."

The telephone rang. Susan picked up the receiver and answered.

"Susan, this is Nancy Ardmore."

"Oh, hello," she said. She gestured to the phone to tell Ellie that she needed to take the call. Ellie nodded and left the cubicle.

"Susan, I need to speak with you. Can you meet me for coffee?"

She hesitated.

"Please, Susan. It's very important. Anywhere you say."

Susan named a café a couple of blocks away. When

Nancy agreed with the time and place, Susan hung up and called David to let him know.

"Sounds odd she couldn't just tell you over the phone," David said.

Susan took a quick look over the top of her cubicle to be sure no one was in the immediate vicinity before whispering back into the phone. "I doubt she's going to pull a pistol on me in a café. I'd like to hear what she has to say."

"Are you wearing your cell phone?"

"Clipped to the waistband of my slacks beneath my blouse."

"Okay. Jack will meet you in the lobby of your building to walk you over and back. I'll be tied up on the coast."

"Anything important?"

"Tell you about it when I get back. Susan, don't use the ladies' room in the coffee shop. Don't go anywhere Jack can't. He needs to keep you in sight."

She agreed to follow David's instructions. As she hung up, she once again remembered what he'd said. *The other night was a big deal. For both of us.*

She kept telling herself not to read more into his words than he meant, and not to hope for too much. But hope was one of those emotions that didn't take conscious direction well.


"YOU CAN'T BE SERIOUS," Warren said.

"We're very serious," David said. "If you don't think so, Jared will be happy to take you to the Sheriff's Department to ask these questions."

Warren's look was uneasy as he stared at Jared, who wore his full deputy's uniform. Fortunately, he didn't know that Jared was out of his jurisdiction in this county.

"You told me Todd was in an accident," Warren said as he turned back to David.

"Now I'm telling you it probably wasn't an accident."

"I never would have hurt Todd," Warren said. "Besides, I've never even been to Ardmore Industries. Only time Todd and I got together, he came here."

"When was the last time?" David asked.

"Must've been six months ago."

"Odd that your partner and closest friend was so uninterested in the business."

"He had his mind on his job," Warren said. "Besides, he trusted me to run things here, and we kept in touch by e-mail. Just check his PC."

"Robert Ardmore told me Todd didn't have a personal computer."

"He's lying. I helped Todd pick out his laptop two years ago."

Warren swung his chair in front of his computer monitor and began clicking the keyboard. "I still have most of Todd's e-mails. When you see his return e-mail address, you'll know he sent them from his home."

"How will I know?"

"He used the local access provider for Falls Island. They only serve the island. Ardmore Industries is out of their jurisdiction."

"He could have used the lab's computer and called into the Falls Island Internet Access Company," David said.

"Most of our stuff was sent at odd hours," Warren said. "You think Todd drove all the way back to his job and made a toll call into the local company on Falls Island for access to the Internet?"

David had to admit Warren had a point.

Warren clicked on an e-mail folder named "Todd." A full page of listed messages appeared. He scooted his chair aside so David could see them more clearly.

"The times are all at night or weekends, and every one

of his e-mails came through his account at the Falls Island Internet provider,'' Warren said. ''Check it out.''

''Hand me a floppy disk and I will.''

''I didn't say you could copy them. There's a lot of personal stuff in there.''

''You don't want to catch the killer of your friend?'' Jared asked.

Warren exhaled heavily. ''Oh, what the hell. Copy the whole damn hard drive if it'll help.''


''THANK YOU FOR MEETING ME, Susan,'' Nancy said. She had led Susan to the corner booth at the back of the café. She had waited to speak until the waitress had served them and left. Susan understood that she didn't want anyone to overhear their conversation.

Even now she leaned forward and kept her voice low. ''What I have to say is confidential. I would prefer you tell no one.''

Susan gave the request a moment of thought. ''As long as I'm not harming someone by remaining quiet, I don't see a problem.''

''Fair enough,'' Nancy said. She squeezed a slice of fresh lemon into her cup of black tea and took a sip before she began. ''When I married Robert, my parents insisted that our money not be intermingled. Robert was already a wealthy man, but my parents weren't convinced that he was marrying me for love. According to the marriage contract that my father made him sign, everything I had before we wed, and what I inherited at my parents' death, remained mine.''

''Robert must have really loved you to agree to that,'' Susan said.

''We fell in love the moment we met,'' Nancy said, suddenly meeting Susan's eyes and smiling. ''He's been a loving and faithful husband all these years, even if he can also be a king-size, controlling pain in the butt.''

Susan held back her smile as she picked up her glass of water and sipped.

''I don't want you to tell him about our conversation today,'' Nancy said, ''because he'd be hurt to learn I went against his wishes.''

''What wishes?''

''Molly was a shy, unsure girl, easily intimidated. When she married Vance, I didn't want him to bully her like her father had. So, without Robert's knowledge, I quietly put a good part of my inheritance in trust for her. The trust went into effect the day before she married. That way the money remained her property alone. I hoped that the money would give her a sense of control over her life.''

Nancy paused to take a sip of her tea. ''I give in to Robert's need to be the decision maker in our family because I want to make him happy, not because I have to. Having money enables me to make that choice. Do you understand?''

''Yes,'' Susan said. She wouldn't have been happy in Nancy's kind of marriage, but she understood that the arrangement worked for her.

''The interest earned on the principal in Molly's trust came to her in a monthly allotment,'' Nancy said. ''At current interest rates, that's about a hundred thousand. Todd was her successor trustee. Any child born of him during his lifetime, or within nine months of his passing, is also a successor trustee. Your child will be Todd's heir.''

Susan gulped down the water in her mouth so fast she nearly choked.

''The executor of Todd's trust will require DNA proof, since you weren't married,'' Nancy continued. ''The moment I heard you were pregnant, I foresaw that contingency and instructed the doctor to preserve a sample of

Todd's DNA before he passed away. There'll be no question to your claim.''

Susan sat utterly still, frozen in shock.

Nancy leaned across the table and put her hand on Susan's. ''This money comes to you with no strings attached. You will spend the funds as you see fit, not as Robert will dictate. I have already told the executor of Todd's trust about you. The money will remain securely invested until the birth of your baby. Once the DNA results are confirmed, the fund will be totally in your hands.''

DAVID STUCK THE DISK on which he'd copied Todd's e-mails into his office computer. There were nearly a hundred messages. He started with the oldest.

Todd wrote a lot about his hopes for the success of his natural predator program at the research lab. The only women in his life he mentioned were his mother and grandmother. He clearly loved them both and was closest to his mother. When he wrote about his grandfather, Vance, and Carl Kemp, he expressed different emotions.

As David carefully read all of the e-mails, four in particular caught his attention. The first was dated a little over a year earlier.

I met my real father today. He was great to me. My half brother hates my guts. I feel that if I turned my back, he'd be happy to stick a knife in it.

The second was written eleven months ago.

Vance came to the lab today. He told the team my predator species had failed, and we were going to have to go with the pesticide. Then he looked at me and smiled. He wanted it to fail. Three weeks ago I overheard him on the telephone telling my grandfather he was throwing his money away backing my ideas. My mother's never loved the bastard. I think she'll leave him now that my real father is back in the picture.

The third e-mail was sent after the plane crash.

My grandfather is hushing the crash up, Warren. He said my mother's infidelity would bring censure on us all. He cares more about his reputation than her death. Now that I've got money, I'm getting away from him. I should have listened to my mother and left long ago.

The final e-mail was dated a week and a half before he died.

I gave Vance my two weeks' notice. He told me he was sorry I was leaving the company. As if I'd swallow that crap. He's been acting like the wounded, betrayed husband ever since the plane crash. I don't believe he ever loved my mom or me. I just know he and Carl are glad my mom and Steve are dead. I hate both the bastards.

David's private line rang, and he answered.

"Warren's alibi checks out," Jared's voice said on the other end of the line. "He couldn't have been in the lab at the time of the explosion. He's also right about Todd using a home computer to send those e-mails. Todd's calls to the Falls Island Internet access provider originated from his home number."

"So, Ardmore lied," David said.

"He probably didn't want to let you have the PC because of what he knew his grandson wrote about him."

"His grandfather wasn't exactly one of Todd's favorite people, but after having read Todd's e-mails, I have to say Vance and Carl had higher priority on his hate list. Jared, didn't you say that Todd's suicide note mentioned he was angry about his mother's death, his grandfather and the lab?"

"In that exact order, yes."

"But the note said nothing about his being mad at Vance or Carl," David said. "Interesting."

"Maybe whoever really wrote the note didn't know Todd well enough to be aware of his animosity toward the two men."

"The note writer knew about Todd's feelings about his mother's death, a death that was carefully hushed up. I believe the more logical explanation as to why Vance and Carl aren't mentioned in Todd's suicide note is that one of them wrote it."

"Carl was in and out of his mechanic's shop that day. He could have driven to the lab and killed his half-brother. But Vance is in a wheelchair. How could he incapacitate Todd, rig the explosion and get out in time to set the stage for suicide?"

"All good questions for which I have no answers. What's his financial status?"

"He got a wad of cash when Ardmore bought out his company. That plus the fat salary in the middle six-digit range he's been drawing all these years have managed to keep him off the streets. Hell, the guy's got an estate on Falls Island and a new Ferrari sitting in his four-car garage."

"Ferrari?" David repeated. "How does a guy in a wheelchair get into a Ferrari?"

"Maybe his chauffeur lifts him into the driver's seat."

"Maybe he has others running errands for him, as well.

Jared, can you see who he employs and where they were at the time of Susan's abduction attempt?"

"You're serious about this?"

"The suicide note points to him as well as Carl. Let's see what else might."

"Okay. I'll see what I can do."

"Call me on my cell. I'm going to see Ardmore. I have a few questions. I'm guessing he's the one who can answer them."

SUSAN WAS STILL REELING with the news when she returned to her office. *A hundred thousand dollars a month.* What would she do with that kind of money?

She was just about to reach for the phone to call David and tell him about the trust when she stopped herself. She'd promised Nancy she wouldn't say anything unless the secret would hurt someone. Would it?

Before she could decide, Barry barreled into her cubicle.

"Susan, I've been looking everywhere for you. Greg's chartered us a boat. He wants you, Ellie and me to head out to the San Juan Islands now. The Whale Watch Network has reported that the orcas are on their way."

"All three of us are supposed to go?"

Barry nodded. "In addition to the orcas, the islands are full of seals, sea lions, otters, birds—including your favorite, the tufted puffin—and even some bald eagles stealing food from the gulls. Greg's decided he wants an entire issue devoted to the wildlife of the Islands."

"I need to get on my computer and update my schedule."

"We don't have time," Barry said. "The taxi to take us to the boat is waiting downstairs. Ellie and our equipment are already inside. Besides, Greg knows where you'll be. He'll tell anyone else who needs to know."

"Just one quick call," she said, picking up the phone.

Barry took the receiver out of her hand. "You can use my cell phone to make your call when we're in the taxi. Come on. We cannot afford to miss this boat."

"ARE YOU CALLING ME A LIAR?" Ardmore asked David, his face getting more flushed by the second.

"I have proof that Todd had a PC in his condo and that he used it to e-mail Warren Sterne," David said. "Here are several copies of the e-mails that he sent. Take a look at them. You can see his return address is the Falls Island Internet access provider."

Ardmore grabbed the sheets out of David's hand. He walked over to his desk, snatched up a pair of glasses and put them on to scan the e-mails.

David had been careful to bring only those e-mails that had no disparaging comments about Ardmore. He even included an e-mail in which Todd had told Warren he appreciated Ardmore's offer to fund another research project using a natural predator to control pests. David wanted Ardmore's cooperation. He knew the man would be more helpful if he wasn't distracted by the unresolved issues between him and his deceased grandson.

Ardmore turned to David. "All right. You've proved Todd had a personal computer. Since we didn't find one in his condo after his death, that means he destroyed the PC before his suicide."

"Who had access to his condo?"

"Todd and I had the only keys. When the doctors told us his condition was terminal, I arranged to have his things brought here. Vance told Nancy to take what we wanted and dispose of the rest as we saw fit."

"You didn't go to the condo?"

"Vance and Nancy went."

"Then, Vance could have taken the computer, and you wouldn't have known."

Ardmore went over to the intercom on his desk and pressed the button. "Is my wife home yet?"

"She's just come in, sir," a maid answered.

"Would you ask her to come into my study?"

"Yes, sir."

A moment later, Nancy entered the room. She nodded a greeting at David and then turned toward her husband. "What is it, dear?" she asked.

"When you were with Vance at Todd's condo, what did he take away with him?" Robert asked.

"Just a couple of small photos he slipped into a black briefcase," Nancy said. "Why do you ask?"

"Mr. Knight is the one asking."

"Did he bring the briefcase with him, Mrs. Ardmore?" David asked, turning to her.

She shook her head. "He got the briefcase from Todd's desk drawer."

"Could the briefcase have been a laptop computer in a black carrying case?"

"I don't know," Nancy said. "I know nothing about computers."

"That black briefcase your wife saw could very well be the missing laptop computer," David said as he swung back to Ardmore.

"If Vance wanted the computer, he had no reason to hide the fact from me," Ardmore said. "Todd was his son. He had the right to take anything he wanted."

"If you knew Todd had left a computer, would you have wanted to see his personal files and correspondence?"

"Yes, of course," Ardmore admitted. "But there's no reason Vance wouldn't have been glad to show me."

"I doubt Vance would have wanted you to see what Todd had written about him. You do know that Todd hated Vance?"

"They may not always have agreed on how things

should go at the lab,'' Ardmore said, ''but Todd respected his father.''

David handed over the two e-mails Todd had written about Vance. As Ardmore read them, his frown deepened.

''You know about the Kemps,'' Ardmore said, dropping the e-mails on his desk.

David nodded. ''And the Kemps know about Susan and the baby. Vance told them.''

Ardmore shook his head. ''Vance wouldn't do that to me or himself.''

David didn't waste his time arguing. ''In one of his last e-mails, Todd mentioned that he'd come into money. Where did he get it?''

''For three years, he'd invested nearly all his salary in a business venture with Sterne,'' Ardmore said. ''I understand that business has turned profitable.''

''Those profits wouldn't have been realized until the end of June,'' David said. ''Todd implied he already had the money.''

''Well, he didn't get any money from me or Vance. We both believe the future generations should make their own money.'' Ardmore gestured awkwardly toward the last two e-mails. ''Todd was probably only angry at Vance because Vance supported my wishes as to how the boy should be raised.''

''How did Vance end up in a wheelchair?'' David asked.

''He slipped and fell a couple of weeks ago. Injured a disk in his back.''

Two weeks ago? Then, Vance wasn't in a wheelchair at the time of the lab explosion.

''The wheelchair is only temporary,'' Nancy added. ''His doctor says he'll be walking soon.''

David carefully digested that news as other suspicions began to take hold. ''Who is Vance's doctor?''

"How the hell should we know?" Ardmore said.

"So you didn't actually talk to a doctor," David said. "You just believed what Vance told you when he showed up in a wheelchair two weeks ago?"

"You trying to say he faked that injury?" Ardmore asked, his tone incredulous.

"I'm saying he could have. Mr. Ardmore, Susan's life and the life of your great-grandchild are at stake. Please think carefully before you answer. Could Vance benefit from both Todd and Susan being out of the way?"

"Absolutely not," Ardmore said. "The suggestion is ludicrous."

David blew out a frustrated breath. The suicide note. The likelihood that Vance had taken Todd's computer. The injury that probably was no injury at all. Everything was telling him that Vance was behind Todd's death and the abduction attempt on Susan.

There *had* to be a motive. What was it?

"Oh dear," Nancy said suddenly. "I can't believe… No, he wouldn't… Oh, dear!"


"I FEEL LIKE I'VE JUST photographed every sea lion, seal and sea otter in the Sound," Ellie said as she dragged her camera equipment up to Susan. "Try saying that three times fast. Did you get any good stuff?"

"I sure hope so, after firing off all that film," Susan said. "You're still pretty damp. Aren't you uncomfortable in those wet clothes?"

"Miserable," Ellie said. "If I ever find the orca that bumped the boat and dumped me waist-deep into the water, I'll punch its lights out. Where's Barry?"

"His cell phone kept cutting out when he tried to call for a taxi. He went around the block to see if there was a pay phone. He should be back soon. Here, take my jacket."

"Thanks for the thought, Suz, but your size small jacket is never going to fit over this large frame. Besides, I can't put anything on top of these wet clothes."

"Taxi will be here in a minute," Barry said as he jumped up on the curb beside them. "When I called into the office there was a message for you, Susan. David Knight wants you to wait here on the dock. He's coming by to pick you up."

"Thanks, Barry." She hadn't been able to reach David by cell phone all day because of poor reception. She was relieved to learn he'd checked with the office and found out about the impromptu shoot.

Barry turned his attention to Ellie. "You look like a drowned rat."

"You're not exactly my pick for the prom, either."

"Ellie needs to get out of her wet clothes," Susan said.

Barry gallantly pulled off his bulky sweater and held it out to Ellie.

"There's no place around here to change even if there was time," she said through chattering teeth. "The taxi will be here any minute, remember?"

"I'm going to stand in front of you and open my jacket," Susan said. "Barry, move in closer and block the view from behind her. Yes, just like that. El, no one can see now. Put on Barry's sweater."

Ellie shivered through a few more seconds of indecision. Then she pulled off her blouse and bra. Susan shielded Ellie until she had slipped Barry's sweater on.

"God, that feels good," Ellie said, hugging the warm sweater to her chilled body. She smiled as she turned around to face Barry. "Thanks. Guess I owe you a hug."

Barry stared at Ellie for several moments before replying. "Guess this is as good a time as any to collect."

Barry wrapped his arms around Ellie and drew her to

him, kissing her soundly. Ellie was right there with him. Susan grinned.

When the taxi pulled up, she helped the driver load the camera equipment into the trunk. Her friends were still clinched when Susan nudged them into the back seat of the taxi. She gave the driver the address of the magazine office.

Just as well David was going to pick her up here. Three in the back seat of that taxi would definitely be a crowd. As the taxi drove away from the curb, Susan let out a sigh of relief. Her two friends had finally found each other.

She had a good feeling about this. A very good feeling.

Susan was so lost in her thoughts that she didn't even realize there was a gun at her back until someone suddenly said from behind her, "If you move or say a word, I'll shoot you through the heart."

## CHAPTER FIFTEEN

DAVID WAS IN JARED'S office at the sheriff's station when he got the call from Jack.

"Susan didn't return from an unscheduled photo shoot at the San Juan Islands," Jack said. "A message was left at the magazine saying that you would pick her up at the dock."

Raw fear ripped David's stomach. "Vance sent that message."

"Vance's butler claims he's in bed with the flu," Jared said, cupping the mouthpiece of his phone as he relayed the information to David.

"What do you want me to do?" Jack asked in his ear.

"See if you can pick up their trail," David said. "Get back to us on Jared's cell. I need to keep this line open."

David closed the connection and turned to his other brother.

"When I told Vance's butler I was coming by," Jared said, "he said he'd refuse entry to anyone without a court order. I don't have enough for a court order."

"I don't need a court order to know Vance isn't there," David said. "He's gone after Susan. He may already have her."

David punched in Susan's cell number on his phone. With each unanswered ring, his fear ripped deeper.

SUSAN FELT THE CELL PHONE vibrating beneath her jacket. She struggled against her bonds as she lay on the floor behind the front seat of the black van. Her ankles were fettered, but when Vance had tied her hands behind her, she had tensed them.

She could feel some space now in the rough, knotted rope. If she could just push the cell phone at her side around to her back where her hands were, she might be able to get it open.

"You can't get loose," Vance said. She looked up to see him watching her in the rearview mirror as he drove.

One last wiggle landed her on her side. The cell phone was now at the small of her back, but she had taken too long. The vibrating had stopped. She worked her hands beneath her jacket, bending her elbows, trying to reach the phone. The taut rope sliced into her twisting wrists. She ignored the pain.

"You don't need a wheelchair or thick glasses," she said, hoping to distract him from what she was attempting to do.

"The glasses are quite necessary when I'm not wearing my contacts," Vance said. "But you're right about the wheelchair. A clever ruse, don't you think?"

She didn't comment because she wasn't in a position to tell Vance what she really thought. Her hands inched upward. Finally, she felt the soft case. She threaded her free fingers inside, feathering them over the keypad, trying to visualize where the number one digit was on the dial—the digit David had preprogrammed with his number. If she hit the wrong button, all her effort would be for nothing. She made her selection, said a silent prayer and pressed.

"I don't understand why you're doing this," she said. She had to get Vance talking. *If* she had hit the right button and *if* David answered, making noise was the only way she had to caution him not to say anything and alert Vance that she had an open line. "Vance, what do you hope to gain?"

''That should be obvious. The trust money.''

''But you have money.''

''*Had* money,'' he corrected. ''The Tishman Chemical Company was bankrupt when Ardmore bought it. My old man had milked the business dry to cover his gambling debts before he skipped out, leaving me with nothing but a worthless title. Ardmore's money paid off the debt. But the president's salary is only five-hundred thousand a year. Barely subsistence.''

Amazing what some people were forced to get by on.

''When my plain, amenable, little Molly offered me the substantial allotments from her trust fund to refrain from performing my husband's duties on our wedding night, I was delighted to accept.''

''She paid you *not* to sleep with her?'' Susan asked.

''A very satisfactory arrangement. I was discreet with my women. I gave her my name and total freedom. Then, out of the blue, she tells me she wants a divorce to be with Kemp! She was going to cut me off from all that money. I couldn't believe she'd be so ungrateful.''

*Susan* couldn't believe this man.

''She was so relieved when I told her she *should* be with the man she loved that she blabbed all about her plane trips to that B&B and how she shared her homemade coffee with the pilot. One of the perks of heading a chemical company is having access to the ones you need. I slipped into the kitchen before the last flight and loaded up her thermos with powerful knockout drops. Then I sent her off to the man she loved.''

Vance's smile chilled Susan.

''Only then, I discovered that Molly's trust was written with Todd as succeeding trustee, so, of course, I had to get rid of him.''

The man had just admitted to killing the boy he had raised as a son, as though it meant nothing to him at all.

"As Todd's legal next of kin, the principal in the trust would have come to me, if you weren't pregnant with his kid. I would have preferred getting you that day in the wildlife refuge, or that night at your home. Ardmore wasn't sure of the kid then. But, this will work out."

She swallowed the fear clogging her throat and called upon every ounce of her courage to keep herself calm. "They'll know you did it, Vance."

"A man in a wheelchair at home in bed with the flu? No, they'll think Carl Kemp is the culprit. I called him right after picking you up at the dock. We're on our way to his shop now. He thinks I'm just stopping by with a couple of cold beers. The one I'll give him is drugged. They'll find him passed out in here beside your dead body."

"You told the Kemps about me and the baby just to set up Carl."

Vance smiled, clearly pleased with his cleverness. "The drug in the beer will give Carl amnesia so that when he wakes up, he won't even remember my stopping by. Such a vulgar, angry young man. The jails are full of his type. He'll have plenty of company when they send him away for life."

Vance seemed to have thought of everything. As the minutes and the miles raced by, Susan tried to think of some flaw in his plan, some way of talking him out of this insanity.

But she knew there was none. He had told her what he had because he knew she wasn't going to be alive long enough to repeat it to anyone.

Vance turned off the paved road onto a bumpy one. She was suddenly buffeted back and forth. Desperately struggling to remain on her side, she tried to protect the cell phone, all the while praying the line was open.

"We'll be in the vacant lot behind Carl's shop in a few

more miles,'' Vance said. ''I'll make it quick. A sharp blow to the back of the head, just like I gave Todd. Neither he nor Molly suffered. All you have to do is cooperate, Susan, and you won't feel a thing. I'm a civilized man.''

*A civilized man.*

The van dipped into a deep pothole. She lost her balance, bounced hard onto her back. She felt the cell phone crunch beneath her weight.

Swallowing hard, she faced the fact that her chance for rescue was gone. She knew Vance hadn't gagged her because he was taking her where a scream couldn't be heard. But if there were any way she could fight back, she would. She had no intention of being cooperative and making her death easy for this *civilized* man.

Her death. Susan felt the tears stinging her eyes. She wished she could have held her baby just once before she died. She sent it a silent message. *Even the dream of you has been wonderfully exciting, sweetie. Please know that every moment you have been part of me, you have been loved.*

She had no doubt David would take care of Honey. *David.* She wished that she'd told David she loved him when she'd had the chance. Didn't seem nearly so important now that he might not be able to love her back.

The bumpy road seemed to go on forever. The van finally slowed and rolled to a rocking halt. Dust plumed past the windows. Vance remained in the driver's seat with the windows rolled up, patiently waiting for the dust to settle.

A moment later he picked up the greasy crowbar that lay on the passenger seat with one gloved hand and pushed open the driver's door with his other. She heard his boots crunch the gravel as he came toward the side of the van. He slid open the door and stared down at her. His expression was calm, completely detached. Killing her and her baby meant nothing to him.

Anger seethed inside Susan. She readied her leg muscles for action. When Vance bent over her, grasping her shoulder to turn her onto her stomach, she kicked out at his exposed groin with all her might. Her boots connected with a satisfying *thud. That's for you, sweetie.*

Vance's breath came out in a contorted wheeze as he doubled over and staggered back. She used the reprieve to wiggle like a snake, working her way to the other side of the van, as far from the open door as possible.

But her struggles were for naught. Vance recovered quickly, lunged inside the van and grabbed her. As he pulled her toward him, her spine hit the back of the front seat, knocking the breath out of her.

She stared into Vance's face—now full of white-hot rage—as he raised the crowbar.

Something that sounded like a sonic boom cracked the air. Once. Twice. Vance jerked each time. A look of astonishment flashed across his features. The crowbar fell out of his hand. He followed it out of sight.

Dizzy and disoriented, Susan closed her eyes and sucked in air. She thought she heard faint voices, then hands struggling with the ropes around her arms and legs. But everything seemed so unreal and far away that she couldn't be certain.

Then two warm strong arms wrapped around her, and a familiar voice whispered close to her ear. ''Susan, it's over. You're safe. I'm here.''

''David,'' she sighed as a comforting blackness claimed her.

''SHE HAS A BUNCH OF bruises and some wrist and ankle rope burns, but otherwise she and the baby are fine,'' the E.R. doctor said.

David felt light-headed with relief. ''May I see her?''

The doctor nodded. ''She's been asking for you steadily

since she came to, Mr. Knight. Go on in. As soon as I complete her chart, she'll be free to go.''

David entered the examination room to see Susan fully dressed, sitting on the edge of the white-sheeted table. She looked over at him and smiled.

He closed the distance between them, and took her in his arms. The doctor came back a moment later. She took one look at them, set the signed release down and left, closing the door behind her.

''You have this wonderful habit of saving my life, David Knight,'' Susan said.

''You saved yourself. If you hadn't dialed me on the cell phone and got Vance talking, we never would have known where he was taking you and arrived there in time.''

''Vance is dead, isn't he?'' she asked as she finally leaned back to look up at David.

He nodded, smoothing a strand of hair off her forehead. ''I shot him. We were too far away to stop him any other way.''

A shiver snaked through her. ''He killed them all for money.''

David gently hugged her to him. ''I know. Nancy Ardmore finally told us about the trust fund this afternoon. Jared taped Vance's entire conversation while the cell phone line was open. As difficult as that conversation was for Robert and Nancy Ardmore to listen to later, they were relieved to learn that Todd didn't commit suicide.''

''I share their feelings. David, I could never accept that trust money now. It's drenched in so much innocent blood.''

''Then, we'll find a way to donate the money to charity.''

''You don't think I'm stupid to turn it down?''

He caressed her cheek with his fingertips as he looked

into her eyes. "I think you're one of the smartest people I've ever met. You understand what's really important in life. I've never been prouder to be with anyone than I was the night I sat beside you in Ardmore's home and heard you refuse to accept all his offers of money. You see past the things that blind most of us because you see with your heart."

He carefully took both of her bandaged wrists in his hands, planting a soft kiss on each palm. "I lived through hell listening to that conversation, not knowing if I was going to reach you in time. And then when the line suddenly went dead…"

He stopped, swallowed hard, stared down at the small hands he held in his. He had almost lost her today. He wanted so much to tell her what was in his heart. But this wasn't the right time or place.

"I love you, David."

Her words caught him completely by surprise. When he looked up and saw the glowing smile on her face, his heart nearly stopped. "Susan, you don't know how much I want to…but you're so vulnerable, I—"

"I'm anything but vulnerable. I faced death today. I can face the truth. I'm telling you I love you because that's how I feel, and I'm not hiding my feelings anymore, even if you can't return them."

He pulled her close against the sudden wild beat of his heart. "Can't return them? I love you so much I ache with it. How could you have any doubt?"

Joy bubbled inside Susan as she hugged him back. "Oh, David. I have none now."

He smiled at her. "You want to know the truth? I started to fall in love with you the moment you surprised me in my office and made me spill coffee all over myself."

She chuckled with happiness. "I think I started to fall in love with you when I woke up at Camp Long and discovered you'd carried me a mile and a half after I'd fainted.''

"Ah, so my muscles impressed you," he said.

"Actually, what impressed me was the fact that you didn't forget my camera equipment.''

He gently kissed her forehead. "If I promise to always love, honor and cherish your camera equipment, will you marry me?''

Her heart gave an exultant leap. "Now, what serious photographer could possibly refuse such a proposal? Yes, David. I'd love to marry you.''

He bent down and molded his lips to hers in a deep, lingering kiss. When he leaned away a moment later, he put his hands on her waist and lifted her off the examination table to set her on her feet.

"Let's go home where we can discuss this fully and properly," he said, his voice husky.

"I don't have to give the Sheriff's Department a statement?''

"Jared will handle things until tomorrow. Your statement may not even be required then. Ardmore is already exerting his influence to hush everything up.''

"I hope Ardmore succeeds in keeping the facts surrounding Vance's death quiet. This is not a legacy I want my baby to inherit. Telling her the story someday will be difficult enough.''

"Her?''

"So the ultrasound insists," Susan said, smiling.

He brushed a kiss against her hair. "Don't worry. When the time comes to speak of what happened, I'll regale our daughter with the details of how damn smart and brave her remarkable mother was through it all.''

*Our* daughter, he'd said. She wondered if he had any idea how wonderful that sounded.

*Well, sweetie, looks like I'm going to make good on that promise of two loving, committed parents, after all.*

Susan placed her hand on David's chest where she could feel the strong beat of his heart. She looked up into his steady smile.

''And I'll tell her about the many times her amazing dad came to our rescue.''

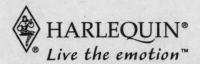

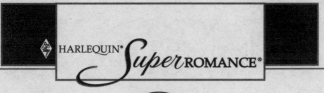

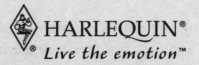

# eHARLEQUIN.com

Sit back, relax and enhance your romance
with our great magazine reading!

- **Sex and Romance!** Like your romance
  *hot?* Then you'll *love* the sensual reading
  in this area.

- **Quizzes!** Curious about your lovestyle?
  His commitment to you? Get the
  answers here!

- **Romantic Guides and Features!**
  Unravel the mysteries of love with
  informative articles and advice!

- **Fun Games!** Play to your heart's content....

**Plus...romantic recipes,
top ten lists,
Lovescopes...and more!**

**Enjoy our online magazine today—
visit www.eHarlequin.com!**

If you enjoyed what you just read,
then we've got an offer you can't resist!

# Take 2 bestselling love stories FREE!

# Plus get a FREE surprise gift!

**Clip this page and mail it to Harlequin Reader Service®**

| IN U.S.A. | IN CANADA |
|---|---|
| 3010 Walden Ave. | P.O. Box 609 |
| P.O. Box 1867 | Fort Erie, Ontario |
| Buffalo, N.Y. 14240-1867 | L2A 5X3 |

**YES!** Please send me 2 free Harlequin Superromance® novels and my free surprise gift. After receiving them, if I don't wish to receive anymore, I can return the shipping statement marked cancel. If I don't cancel, I will receive 6 brand-new novels every month, before they're available in stores. In the U.S.A., bill me at the bargain price of $4.47 plus 25¢ shipping and handling per book and applicable sales tax, if any*. In Canada, bill me at the bargain price of $4.99 plus 25¢ shipping and handling per book and applicable taxes**. That's the complete price, and a savings of at least 10% off the cover prices—what a great deal! I understand that accepting the 2 free books and gift places me under no obligation ever to buy any books. I can always return a shipment and cancel at any time. Even if I never buy another book from Harlequin, the 2 free books and gift are mine to keep forever.

135 HDN DNT3
336 HDN DNT4

| Name | (PLEASE PRINT) | |
|---|---|---|
| Address | Apt.# | |
| City | State/Prov. | Zip/Postal Code |

\* Terms and prices subject to change without notice. Sales tax applicable in N.Y.
\*\* Canadian residents will be charged applicable provincial taxes and GST.
All orders subject to approval. Offer limited to one per household and not valid to current Harlequin Superromance® subscribers.
® is a registered trademark of Harlequin Enterprises Limited.

SUP02                                          ©1998 Harlequin Enterprises Limited

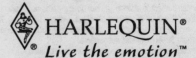